Bestselling author **Tina Ga**[...] and mechanical engineer w[...] for pleasure helped her get [through years of] academia. Tina also writes the bestselling Kebab Kitchen Mediterranean cozy mystery series as Tina Kashian. She grew up in the restaurant business, as her Armenian parents owned a restaurant for thirty years. English is her second language. Tina's books have been Barnes & Noble top picks, and her recent book, *How Not to Marry a Duke*, is a double winner of the prestigious NJ Romance Writers' Golden Leaf Award for Best Historical Romance and Best Book by a New Jersey Romance Author. Tina lives in South Jersey and is married to her own hero and is blessed with two daughters. Please visit her website at www.tinagabrielle.com to join her newsletter, receive delicious recipes, and learn about upcoming releases.

You can also find Tina at:

X: @TinaGabrielle
Facebook: Facebook.com/TinaGabrielle
Instagram: @TinaGabrielleAuthor

His Cinderella Duchess is **Tina Gabrielle**'s debut title for Mills & Boon Historical.

Look out for more books from Tina Gabrielle coming soon.

Discover more at millsandboon.co.uk.

HIS CINDERELLA DUCHESS

Tina Gabrielle

MILLS & BOON

First published in Great Britain 2025
by Mills & Boon, an imprint of HarperCollins*Publishers* Ltd,
1 London Bridge Street, London, SE1 9GF

www.harpercollins.co.uk

HarperCollins*Publishers*, Macken House, 39/40 Mayor Street Upper, Dublin 1, D01 C9W8, Ireland

His Cinderella Duchess © 2025 Tina Sickler

ISBN: 978-0-263-34532-2

08/25

MIX
Paper | Supporting
responsible forestry
FSC
www.fsc.org
FSC™ C007454

This book contains FSC™ certified paper
and other controlled sources to ensure responsible forest management.

For more information visit www.harpercollins.co.uk/green.

Printed and Bound in the UK using 100% Renewable Electricity
at CPI Group (UK) Ltd, Croydon, CR0 4YY

For Laura.

I'm proud of the young lady you have become.
Always follow your dreams and your future is bright!

Chapter One

London, May 1820

Rain slashed the windows of the coach. Lena Harper gripped the padded seat as the wheels hit a rut in the road, causing her conveyance to lurch wildly. The storm had started soon after her journey began, slowing their progress. Outside the coach the night was inky black. Clouds filtered the moonlight and cast the trees and bushes into shadowy spectres. Cold air seeped into the coach and gooseflesh rose on her arms.

The driver turned onto a long road where tall trees lined the gravel road like silent sentinels. A bolt of lightning streaked across the sky, illuminating a massive mansion. Lena gasped. Grey stone, two tall turrets, and a dozen gilt-framed windows appeared. The stone of the far west section was blackened from fire.

The clouds shifted across the crescent moon, revealing a man standing in one of the alcoves of a turret. He was shielded from the rain, but not the cold. What was he doing? A sinking feeling of dread settled in her stomach.

She blinked, and he was gone. Thunder crashed and she jolted in her seat. Her mind must have been playing tricks on her. That was all. She was tired and cold and anxious.

The coach rolled to a stop and moments later the door was opened. Water pooled from the driver's greatcoat. 'We've arrived, miss. I'll see to your trunk. Meanwhile, you hurry up to the door.'

She pulled up the hood of her cloak and stepped out of the coach. The Berkeley Square mansion seemed large and looming before her. Rain pelted her face as she rushed up the steps. She lifted the door knocker and rapped. After a good minute, the door blessedly opened.

A butler with the saggy-jowled expression of a bloodhound looked down at her.

'My name is Mrs Lena Harper,' she said. 'I'm the new governess.'

'You are late.'

She wiped rainwater from her cheek, peering beyond the man into the warm, dry vestibule. 'The weather is horrid.'

'His Grace abhors lateness.'

She was at a loss for words. 'Perhaps it's best if I go to my room first to change into dry clothes before meeting the duke. I will be quick.'

'No.' The butler shook his head. 'His Grace left specific instructions to see you immediately upon arrival. My name is Barnes and I'll escort you.'

This was unexpected. Would the duke decide if she stayed or left based on a tardy arrival? The agency had assured her of the position as governess to the duke's niece.

She'd always loved children and wanted one of her own and believed it was a good fit. Then the agency had advised her that she'd be the sixth governess in four months. Was the difficulty in retaining employees due to the niece or the duke? She was beginning to believe the latter. Either way, she needed the position and the salary that accompanied it. Dismissal before she began was not an option.

'Very well.' She nodded to the butler. 'Please lead the way.'

She was exhausted and drenched. Still, if she had no choice but to face her new employer in her state, then so be it. She raised her chin and stiffened her spine. She would do her best to be presentable.

Her mother's words were never far from her mind.

Dearest Lena, you are worthy. Do not let anyone tell you otherwise. You have half English blood, high and mighty as any other aristocrat. And your Arabic blood, your other side, is even more ancient and noble.

She'd never forgotten those words even though they'd been whispered over fifteen years ago when her mother was still alive. Now, more than ever, Lena needed the strength those words gave her.

She stepped inside, glad for the immediate warmth. A black and white marble floor shone and a spectacular crystal chandelier held at least a hundred candles. A grand staircase with polished bronze balustrade led to a second floor. As Lena followed the butler, drops of rainwater trailed in her wake. She suppressed a shiver.

Lena caught occasional glimpses inside rooms as they progressed down the hall. Some were lit with lamps, and servants dusted while the spaces were unoccupied. A blue drawing room, a gold drawing room, a music conservatory, and a dining room with the largest dining table she'd ever seen. It was a wealthy nobleman's home, yet something was missing.

No warm or personal touches greeted visitors. Paintings by masters hung on the walls, landscapes by Gainsborough and Hogarth. Gilt-framed mirrors and ornate mantel clocks graced the drawing rooms. She'd seen a Chinoiserie vase on display in the vestibule. The show of wealth was expected of a duke, yet told her nothing about the man.

No family portraits of ancestors, current family, or of the duke himself hung on the walls. Did he ride? Did he have a favourite hunting hound? Did he prefer books or shooting grouse? His furnishings gave no clue. She only knew what the agency had provided. Her new employer was a scarred war hero, they'd said. A man who avoided High Society and the frivolities of the *beau monde*, and rarely left his mansion. A former rake. She hoped to learn more about her employer and the kind of home she'd be occupying. Was he a complete recluse or did he leave for pleasure or business?

Halting in front of a closed door, the butler knocked once. A gruff voice sounded from inside. 'Enter.'

The door was opened for her. She clasped her reticule before her, stepped inside the study… And froze at the first sight of her new employer.

The door closed behind her.

The duke of Ravenwood rose from behind a large desk. 'Mrs Harper.'

Somehow, she managed a curtsy. Then, she found her voice. 'It is a pleasure to—'

'You're late.'

If not so absorbed by his appearance, she may have taken offence to his manners. The agency's description of the duke failed to do him justice. He was striking in an unexpected fashion. One side of his face was near perfection with a straight, aquiline nose and chiseled chin with a divot. He had thick, dark hair, and his eyes were a piercing blue—as dark and roiling as the Mediterranean Sea on a clear summer day. But the other side of his face was ravaged by a vicious scar that ran from his hairline, down his cheek, curving like a scimitar to mar part of his lower lip. It was as if God's hand had molded half of a perfect face, one that ladies would find irresistible, but the other half was forbidding and frightening.

If only Lena were like most women.

She wanted to reach out and trace a finger along the scar, come dangerously close to those sculpted lips. She saw strength behind the wound. A result of tragedy and war, which she knew a man had to be strong and determined to survive.

One wounded soul recognized another. It wasn't the scar that caused a shiver to course down her spine.

It was the iciness in those hard blue eyes.

'The weather slowed the coach, Your Grace,' she said quickly, realizing she'd been staring. 'The roads are almost impassable.' A half-truth.

'The storm came on later in the day.' He raised a brow. 'You were expected earlier.'

No sense arguing. He was right. She'd been delayed in town by her late husband's despicable business partner, but that was not something she cared to discuss. Her stomach churned and she forced herself to meet his gaze. 'Will I meet your niece, Miss Claire, tonight?'

'She's abed.'

It was only eight in the evening. The agency had told her the girl was sixteen years old. It seemed early for a young lady to retire. Was she ill? 'Are you certain she's not awake? I only require a moment to change into dry clothing. I would love to make her acquaintance and—'

'She's abed. It doesn't matter if she is sleeping. Her schedule requires it. You shall meet her in the breakfast room tomorrow at seven sharp.'

Seven sharp.

She was filled with a bewildering mix of emotions… annoyance, concern, and…interest. What had made him so curt? She cleared her throat. 'Is there anything I should know about Miss Claire?'

'She's a sixteen-year-old, who has lost her parents and now lives under my guardianship. Her schedule will be delivered to you in the morning,' he said matter-of-factly.

Again, no sense arguing. He was her employer and paying her salary. If he wanted to act like a general in his own home, then that was his right. 'If that's all, Your Grace. I'd like to retire for the evening.'

He nodded. 'Barnes will see that your trunks are delivered to you. Meanwhile, I shall show you to your room.'

'I don't mean to be trouble. Your housekeeper can escort me.'

'She's also abed with a cold. If you'd like to change out of those wet clothes, then I suggest you allow me to show you the way.'

His dismissive demeanour sparked her temper, but she forced herself to swallow any complaint as he moved past her to the door. She needed the job and if he insisted upon escorting her like a common servant, who was she to argue? Her wet gown lay heavy and cold on her skin. She trailed behind him from the room and down the hall, following him up the grand staircase. She was not short, but the duke dwarfed her. He was tall and broad-shouldered, his waist trim. They reached the landing, and when he stopped and turned suddenly, she ran into his solid chest.

'Oh!' Her cheeks grew warm.

Strong hands grasped her forearms to steady her.

'Easy, Mrs Harper.'

Standing this close, blessed warmth radiated from his body. Under different circumstances she would seek his heat. His eyes flashed with a curious look, the first emotion she'd witnessed other than the iciness, and her pulse skittered with awareness. Before she could act, he took a step back.

'Avoid the west wing, which is under construction.' His voice was gruff. 'Your chamber is this way.'

Her cheeks grew hotter as she hurried to follow. She knew about the fire in the west wing. His father, the old duke, and his brother and sister-in-law had perished in the blaze. Fortunately, his niece had been staying with family friends and hadn't been harmed.

Lena risked a sidelong glance up at Ravenwood's face,

his scar faint in the light of a sputtering wall sconce. At last, he halted by a closed door, then opened it, motioning for her to step inside.

It was a much larger bedchamber than she was accustomed to. In the nine months since her late husband Oliver's death, she'd resided in rented rooms in a less desirable section of London. Her heart quickened as she took in her new accommodations. A four-poster bed with a sheer white canopy and cream coverlet dominated the center of the room. A small table was by the bed, an escritoire in the corner. The walls had been freshly painted a pale cream. Across from the bed was a malachite fireplace with a gilt mantel clock nestled between two porcelain doves. A servant had already lit the coal brazier. Lena wanted to weep with relief. She walked right up to the hearth and extended her hands, not caring what the duke thought.

'Is it suitable?' Ravenwood inquired from where he stood in the doorway.

If he'd seen her current lodgings, he would never have asked. The chamber was comfortable and warm. Still, aside from the fireplace, the room was pale, almost colourless, like a blank canvas. She hoped his niece's chambers were more distinctive.

He was waiting for her answer. 'Yes, the chamber is perfectly acceptable, Your Grace.'

Whatever warmth Lena had glimpsed in his expression a moment ago vanished in an instant. 'Don't get too comfortable, Mrs Harper. You must gain not only my niece's approval but mine. Breakfast is at seven sharp.'

* * *

Brent Ainsley, the Duke of Ravenwood, reached for the whisky decanter on the sideboard in his study the next morning. He splashed several fingers' worth into a crystal glass. It was too early to drink, but he'd spent another restless night awake, and the new governess was due any moment to discuss her first day before breakfast.

The scar on his face pulled taut as he sipped the whisky, a familiar ache and reminder of a war he'd never forget. The nightmares had started after his return from the Continent. Even more unnerving, unexpected noises brought panic. Other than a coffee shop or Manton's with his one long-time friend—and his required duty to cast a vote in the House of Lords—he dreaded leaving the house in fear he'd make a fool of himself from a sound as simple as the crack of a hackney driver's whip, the first toll of a church bell, or the slamming of a shop door. And there was another sound from his past that haunted him, one even more distinct and relentless in his nightmares…

He pushed the thought away, settling behind the massive pearwood desk, but the ledgers on the blotter failed to distract him. They were another reminder of loss. He'd survived hell on earth only to return home and learn of his father's and brother's deaths from a fire eighteen months prior. He'd inherited a dukedom, a large mansion with a burnt wing in need of repair, and his brother's sixteen-year-old daughter.

He'd resented the roles ever since.

What did he know about being a proper duke and managing the estates and responsibilities that came with the title? Even more damning, what did he know about being a father to a grieving girl, one who hated him and rebelled at every opportunity? He wasn't cruel; he realized the girl suffered. But his attempts to help her had failed. Saying he was sorry—speaking it out loud—seemed trivial to him in comparison with her devastating loss.

Christ. It was as if he were being punished forever. He deserved it—every ache and every nightmare. He'd crawled off the battlefield at Waterloo alive when so many others had not. Claire did not deserve her suffering. Now it was his duty to care for her, and yet he found he could not do so adequately.

There hadn't always been this strange distance between them. She'd been a fun-loving, easy-going child. When she was very young, he'd play tea party with her and her favourite dolls. She'd hold his hand when he'd take her shopping to purchase a piece of candy from the confectioners. He'd even taken her for her first ride on her new pony to Hyde Park, and she'd hugged and kissed him before he'd been shipped off to the Continent. Now, years later, after life had been cruel to them both, he'd returned home to a sullen, grieving young lady who he couldn't connect with, couldn't help.

Perhaps the new governess could help Claire.

His thoughts turned to her. She was unlike the others… Midnight hair and dark brown eyes. High cheekbones and full lips. She had an olive complexion, unlike the porcelain white of most English ladies. Last night, she'd worn her hair back in a tight knot at her nape. Her dress was uncomely—a heavy wool gown that covered her every inch from its high neck to the long fitted sleeves. She attempted to hide her appearance, but nonetheless, he'd been struck by her beauty. The prior governesses had dressed modestly, but Mrs Harper had chosen an ugly gown. The fact she'd tried to hide behind the hideous dress and uncomely hairstyle intrigued him more.

She had gumption, a spine, and she hadn't flinched at the first glimpse of his face. Nor had she cowered from his demeanour or demands. Rather, she'd squarely faced him.

It had been a refreshing change from the others. The five previous governesses had been a nameless, faceless string of women. Mrs Harper's gaze brought forth unbidden memories of a time when women had looked at him without seeing a twisted, scarred man. When females openly eyed him with interest and lust. A lifetime ago.

A soft knock sounded on the study door. Mrs Harper entered. 'You asked to see me this morning, Your Grace?' Her voice was soft and smooth.

Best if he got business out of the way on her first day. He'd decided it was important enough to summon her to his study this early, even before breakfast.

He leveled her with a gaze. 'I want to know how you will proceed with my niece. We did not have time to discuss those details yesterday.' The woman had arrived with a gust of wind and rain. He'd sensed her unease while drops of rainwater pooled on the plush Wilton carpet of his study.

Today, Mrs Harper had changed from a damp blue wool gown into another of the same colour and unflattering cut. As before, it covered every inch of flesh. Not a scrap of lace or adornment decorated it. If she had curves, they were hardly discernible beneath the heavy fabric. Her ebony hair was brushed and pulled back in another severe bun.

She was hiding. Like him.

It was an unlikely disguise. He knew her hair was curly. He'd seen a few unruly curls escape the pins from the storm's humidity the prior evening. The curls had framed her oval-shaped face, and he wanted to know how she managed to tame all that thick hair. He also wondered how long it might be. Would the mass of curls reach past her shoulders and to her waist?

He shoved the thoughts aside. She was here for one purpose: to assume his niece's care. He owed his brother and sister-in-law. His relationship with his father had been strained at best, but they had been tolerant of him during his youthful, carefree years and had always invited him for weekly dinners and holidays. And… He cared for Claire, always had, and if he wasn't able to be a fit guardian or 'father figure,' then he would ensure she had a capable governess.

'You are asking how I am to begin with your niece?' she asked.

'Yes.'

She looked at him directly again. No veiled disgust flashed in her eyes. 'Pardon, Your Grace, but I haven't yet met Miss Claire. How am I to properly inform you before meeting the girl?'

'You must be aware you are not her first governess.'

'The agency told me I'm the sixth.'

'Precisely. You should know that my niece can be quite spirited.'

He still had trouble accepting the tragic turn of events. If only the staff had caught the fire before it had consumed the entire west wing. If only the flames hadn't taken *both* of Claire's parents. He, more than most, knew how tragedies of the past affected one's present.

He'd go through the entire agency until he found a suitable governess. He eyed the woman before him, and his gaze dropped to Mrs Harper's mouth before he held up a hand. 'She also has a schedule. I expect you to follow it.' He reached into his desk drawer and handed her a piece paper.

Routine and strict military protocol had been a comfort to him in his own life. After he'd returned home from war and struggled to sleep, a schedule had been a strong sense of balance and much-needed respite, and he hoped it would help his niece with her mourning.

She scanned the foolscap, her eyes widening. She looked up at him. In the light of the day, he could see her more clearly. Her large eyes were as dark as his morning coffee without cream. They were slightly slanted at the corners with thick dark lashes. Her lips were full and pink. Lips that a man would fantasize beneath his. Her face was striking.

He cleared his throat. Lusting after the new governess was not his intent. He needed Mrs Harper to take charge of his niece.

She lowered the paper and a crease formed between

her eyes. 'This is a rigid schedule. Your niece is sixteen, correct?'

'Correct.'

'This schedule is for a young child.'

'She is a child.'

Her lips pursed. 'No, she is not. She is a young lady.'

'Let me make myself clear. You are here at my bidding. I alone pay your salary to watch over my niece. Structure will help the girl. Rules.' Routine would help Claire cope. Like it had helped him. He wouldn't argue with Mrs Harper on this.

'Structure, yes. But this may go too far.'

'How so?'

'She is not in the King's army.' She scanned the foolscap again. 'For one, a sixteen-year-old girl does not retire at eight in the evening.'

'Would you rather she be up all night?'

'Of course not.'

'Good. It's settled then. Consider yourself on a probationary period. I shall watch you.'

Chapter Two

The duke was impossible!

How on earth was she to impose such a ridiculous list of rules on a young lady? She gripped the schedule tightly as she walked briskly towards her new charge's bedchamber. The first three rules were too strict in her opinion.

Arrive in the breakfast room at seven sharp each morning.

Your bedchamber shall be kept neat and orderly. Inspection can occur at any time.

Practise the pianoforte one hour each day.

Other than the pianoforte, had he taken this straight from military protocols? It was as if he were still living in the army, abiding by army rules.

She folded the horrid list into a tiny rectangle, shoved it into her skirt pocket, then rapped on the door. She'd always had a gift with children, and, although her ward was not a child, she hoped she could establish a good rapport. 'Miss Claire? My name is Mrs Harper. Lena Harper. I'm excited to meet you.'

No response.

'May I come inside?'

Again hearing nothing, Lena pressed her ear to the door. It was before seven in the morning. Was the girl still sleeping. Or more likely ignoring her? Lena imagined Claire lying in bed, pulling a pillow over her head.

Lena placed her hand on the door handle and turned. To her surprise, it was unlocked. Lena cautiously inched open the door until she stood in the doorway. She gasped in delight as she scanned her charge's bedchamber. The room was decorated with splashes of colour—a pink bedspread with flowers, a four-poster with a sheer pink canopy, and a fireplace mantel with figurines of dancers. But it was the colourful paintings on the walls that caught her attention. These were not paintings of masters that she'd seen in the duke's vestibule, but the work of a budding artist. A vase of flowers and a still life of a bowl of fruit hung on one wall. A simple landscape with fields of colourful wildflowers hung above a dainty writing desk. Another of a night sky with a full moon like a celestial pearl. The girl was an artist.

She was also in bed. Lena had better wake her if she were to be on time for breakfast in the dining room. Lena approached, swept the sheer drape of the canopy aside and reached for the bedspread. The girl was gone. A mound of pillows had been stuffed beneath the bedspread to give the appearance of a sleeping figure.

A cool breeze blew in from the window. The casement was open, the curtains fluttering. It had stopped raining but was still cool outside.

A trickle of unease raced down Lena's spine. She went to the window and pushed the white curtains aside.

And gaped.

The girl was sitting in a tree.

There was only one logical conclusion. She'd climbed out the window to slip out of the house last night and was returning this morning. It was brilliant, really. Claire could escape her room whenever she wanted each evening, and no one—including her uncle—would know.

'Hello, there,' Lena called out the window.

Claire looked up. She was pretty, with brown hair and blue eyes. Her features shared a noticeable resemblance to the duke.

'You're number six,' the girl called out.

'Number six?'

'The sixth governess or chaperone or whatever he's decided to call you.' Claire's face held more than a tinge of annoyance.

'Yes, I suppose I am number six. You can call me Mrs Harper. Or better yet, please call me Lena.'

'You are a widow?'

'I am.' At twenty-seven years old, she would never have been able to obtain this position and live unchaperoned in a duke's home had she been unmarried. As a widow, her circumstances offered her such a freedom. Perhaps one of the only good things to come out of her miserable marriage to Oliver Harper. Thirty years her senior and a stockbroker in the London Stock Exchange, he'd served her father, the Marquess of Grisham, for years. Despite their age difference, she'd tried her best and trusted Oliver with her heart. But he was a cold man, who'd looked down on her for her mixed race, and his jealous nature kept her nearly imprisoned at home. Her marriage had taught her an important lesson—never trust a man with her heart.

'Do you have children?' Claire asked.

'No.' It was another deep regret. She always wanted babies of her own. It wasn't *she* who had failed in that regard.

From her perch, Claire watched her. 'You're young. Did you kill your husband?'

The question was inappropriate and forthright. The fact that the girl was questioning her from outside the window would have been comical if it weren't serious. 'No.' Lena did not want to discuss her past or her unhappy marriage with her new charge. Oliver's death had freed her. Or so she'd thought. His business partner had fleeced her and left her penniless and in need of this position.

She may be number six, but she *must* be the last.

Lena leaned on the windowsill. 'Are you coming up?'

Defiance flashed in the girl's eyes. 'I was. Now I think I'll go back down.'

This was not going well. Lena couldn't afford to lose sight of her now, within moments of meeting her. She needed to at least gain the girl's interest if not her trust. Claire shifted, about to step onto a lower branch.

'Wait!' Lena called. 'I'm coming to join you.'

Instantly gone was the annoyance in Claire's expression, and in its place was a hint of shock. 'Up here? In a tree?'

'Why not?' Lena shrugged, her eyes never leaving the girl's.

Lena knew this was a test. Her first one. It was also a

benefit versus risk assessment. After studying the tree, she made her choice. She tucked the front hem of her gown into her waistband—no easy task since the wool was cheap, it's draping stiff. The bench seat beneath the window must have aided Claire's escape. Stepping onto it, she reached out the window for the nearest branch. It was a thick branch, and she tested its strength.

The room was just one story off the ground, but still, it would be a fall sufficient to break a limb. The branches were close to the casement, even brushing the side of the mansion. Lena swung one leg out the window, then the second.

She scooted farther out until she faced Claire. Now a different thought occurred to her. How on earth were they going to get back inside? Or down?

'You actually did it,' Claire said, her voice tinged with surprise.

Should she tell the girl that this was not her first tree? That she'd climbed the fig trees in her grandfather's orchard in Lebanon as a girl. She used to reach for the tastiest, ripened figs and eat them while resting on one of the branches. Big and purple and with sweet flesh, figs had been her favourite treat as a child and one of the things she missed from her life in the Middle East.

An ache centered in her chest. She shoved it aside and focused on the tree. That time was long ago.

She chose a thick limb across from Claire and, grasping a higher one, swung her legs over it. A riding skirt or even trousers would have been much preferable to her heavy skirts. 'Where were you going?'

Claire wrinkled her nose. 'What makes you think I was going somewhere?'

'You are not afraid to be out here, which suggests to me that you have done this before.'

'You are not afraid either.' Claire studied her. 'This is not the first time you've climbed a tree, is it?'

'Do not change the subject. Does the duke know you have left your room this way?' Lena asked, keeping her tone kind but firm.

'Will you tell him?'

'No. Not if you tell me the truth.'

'Fine. I often leave my room this way.'

'Where do you go?'

'That's not your concern.'

'As you pointed out, I'm number six. It's my concern now.'

Claire scowled, then turned away. Clearly she did not intend to answer. Fine. For now, Lena would be patient. The agency had told her that Claire had lost both of her parents in a fire a year and a half ago. Her world had been tragically torn from her in an instant.

Lena understood loss. Her own mother had died when she was only ten. Lena had lovely memories of living in Lebanon with her mother and her grandfather. They'd owned acres of fig orchards and grapevines and had vacationed on the Mediterranean Sea. First her grandfather had died, then her mother, and Lena had been sent to live in her father's country.

England had been bone-chilling and rainy, like the weather when she'd arrived at the duke's pile of stone.

She'd spent the first year shivering, no matter how many layers of clothing she wore. She'd learned her father was a titled man, the Marquess of Grisham, and that he had his own wife. Lena had also learned the words 'illegitimate' and 'bastard'—from her own stepmother no less. Her father was not a cruel man, but his marchioness was unkind, and rather than allow Lena to live with them, she was sent away to live at a school for girls with wealthy fathers.

Thereafter, the only time her father had invited her to the Picadilly mansion was a year later for her eleventh birthday. She'd been filled with excitement. She'd dressed in her best, a pale pink muslin with a bit of lace on the wrists. She'd arrived rosy-cheeked and smiling, and the butler had escorted her to the loveliest parlor she'd even seen. It was decorated in shades of blue, and she'd sat on a blue-and-gold-striped sofa as she'd waited. But rather than seeing her father and receiving a gift, she saw the marchioness sweep in. 'There has been a bit of confusion, my dear. You are not welcome here. *Ever.* The marquess will visit at the school.' Lena's smile had faded beneath the lady's withering stare, and she'd rigidly held her tears in check. It wasn't until she was back in her room at school that the hot tears slipped down her cheeks.

Years went by, and she'd been taught at the school to act like a lady, albeit without the title. While she had never been brought out to society, her manners were proper and her English perfect. She could dine with a King, dance with a duke, play the pianoforte, and drink tea with any of the patronesses of Almack's. The marquess had visited twice a year, until, on her nineteenth birthday, he had arranged her marriage to his broker, Oliver Harper, at the London Stock Exchange. To his mind, he'd done his duty.

Her wedding was the second time she'd seen her father's wife. Lena had been nervous, almost panicking as she'd waited for her father to escort her down the aisle. She'd overheard an argument between the marquess and her stepmother. She was concerned that if the marquess escorted her, then it would cause unwanted gossip. So it was decided that Oliver's business partner, Stanley Peterson—a man she'd also grown to distrust—would walk her down the aisle instead of her own father.

Claire shifted on the tree branch, drawing Lena's attention back to the girl. 'Since you braved the tree, I will give you fair warning, one that I've never given to the others.'

Lena tilted her head and regarded her. 'I'm flattered. Such as?'

'I won't make your time here easy or pleasant.'

Before Lena could respond, the girl swung her legs over the side of the branch and leapt down to a lower branch, scurrying down the tree with the agility of a monkey until she reached the lawn. With a jaunty wave, she walked around the side of the mansion and disappeared from sight.

Lena let forth an unladylike curse. So much for bonding with the girl on her first day. She'd never catch Claire now and learn where she was headed.

Lena glanced up at the casement, then down to the ground. Her fingers tightened on the branch and her heart missed a beat. Her earlier assessment now seemed more risky than beneficial. A paralysing fear spread through her. As a girl, she'd never been afraid of heights, but looking down from her high perch changed her perspective. The lower branch Claire had easily reached seemed too far away.

'What the hell are you doing up there?'

Oh, no. The angry masculine voice was unmistakable. A tremor travelled down Lena's spine that had nothing to do with her precarious situation.

Instinct told her not to confess that she'd followed his niece out the window. Whatever fragile trust she had established with Claire would go up in a puff of smoke if she blurted out the girl's secret on her first day. Lena needed this job. Returning home and asking for help from Oliver's former business partner would be disastrous. Heavens knew, she'd tried before and failed.

She swallowed and looked down into the Duke's scarred and angry face. Her mind tripped with excuses. 'I… I… The view is lovely from up here.'

As soon as the words left her lips, she knew this sounded absurd. Stuck with her lie, she continued, 'You can see London for miles. It is an unusually pleasant day and the constant factory smog which normally clouds the view is gone,' she blurted out in a nervous rush.

The duke's mouth formed a grim line. 'Get down this instant, Mrs Harper.'

Clearly, he'd thought her explanation just as ludicrous.

She was faced with another pressing problem. She wasn't sure *how* to get down. It had been years since she'd climbed a tree, and the fig trees had offered many lower branches one could use to descend. This oak tree had sturdy branches, but few of them. Her legs could barely reach the next one.

'Do you need me to come up and fetch you?' Ravenwood demanded.

Good God, no. That would be even more humiliating. 'I can do it.'

'Lower your right leg. There is a thick branch three feet down.'

With her skirts tucked into her waistband, he could see her legs encased in wool stockings. Her cheeks flamed hot with embarrassment. There was nothing she could do about it now. She had no choice but to obey. She lowered her leg, and the tip of her slipper brushed the branch. Taking a deep breath, she stretched until she stood on the lower limb.

She could do this. With his guidance, she could climb down.

'Now jump,' he ordered. 'I'll catch you.'

Her gaze snapped to his. She was nearer to the ground now, but jumping required a level of trust. Could she do it?

She glanced down. His eyes never left hers for an instant. 'Unless you are comfortable climbing down the rest of the way, I suggest you follow my instructions.' His voice held no warmth. He issued the order like a commanding officer.

'But—'

'Jump.' The command was brusque.

She released her hold, and her breath let out in a great whoosh as she fell. In a flash she was safe in strong, sure arms. Her hand latched on to his chest, hard and muscular.

His heart beat strong beneath it. The feel of that strength was as shocking as the fall. Startled, she looked up at him and found him watching her, his blue eyes shaded by thick, dark lashes. His face appeared almost savage in intensity. Her lips parted on a silent gasp and his eyes dropped to her mouth, an intrigued look flashing across his features. An unexpected ripple of excitement heated her body.

He slowly lowered her to her feet. His scar was an angry red slash across his cheek, and a bead of perspiration formed on his brow.

For the first time, she wondered if the visible wounds were not the only ones the duke had suffered in war.

'Your Grace, I'm—'

'Where is my niece?'

Blast! Her stomach clenched at his harsh tone. Without a clue, she grabbed at the first thought to come into her head. 'I believe Claire went inside.' She hoped it was so.

'I suppose I should thank you,' he said.

She gaped. 'Thanks?'

'Now that I know how my niece has been escaping the house at night, I will instruct the gardeners to cut down this tree.'

'Oh.' Her stomach sank. Cutting down the tree wasn't the answer. He should begin by speaking to his niece. And of course, Claire would blame *her* if the tree was removed. This wasn't what she wanted on her first day. Not at all.

'Perhaps you should not act rashly, Your Grace,' she began. 'The girl is in mourning.'

His expression became guarded. 'It's not your place

to advise me, Mrs Harper. I'm not paying you for your advice.'

Her nerves tightened. The way he set forth his demands put her on edge. 'I see. Will you send me back to the agency, then?'

His eyes pierced the distance between them. 'I haven't yet decided. Your behaviour warrants it. Take the rest of the day off, Mrs Harper, while I decide if your employment should continue, and I shall see you tomorrow morning. However, if I do choose to dismiss you, then you should be congratulated.'

She blinked. 'Whatever for?'

'You will hold the record. The prior five governesses lasted more than a day.'

Chapter Three

Lena was waiting for Claire in her bedchamber. She'd chosen a book in the duke's library and sat in an armchair in the corner of the room. Her thoughts were a tangle of confusion and worry. Ravenwood had ample reason to send her packing. Would he, or wouldn't he? She stared at the page, not reading more than a paragraph as she thought of returning to her dismal lodgings. Once more, she'd be alone and in need of money. After a solid hour, the bedchamber door opened, and Claire tiptoed inside.

'Leaving me in that tree wasn't very nice of you,' Lena said.

Claire let out a squeak when she spotted Lena in the corner.

'I wasn't worried.' Claire straightened her spine. 'You seemed familiar with climbing trees.'

In hindsight, following the girl out the window had not been the bonding experience she'd desired. 'You should know that the duke found me in that tree.'

Claire froze in the center of the room. 'You're jesting.'

'Sadly, no.'

'How long did you dally?'

'I didn't *dally*. The truth is that I remembered how to climb up, not down. If it wasn't for His Grace's help, I might still be stranded.' Lena had missed breakfast that morning. Her stomach growled.

'My God! You told him everything, didn't you?' Claire said.

Lena resisted the urge to roll her eyes. 'The man is no fool. He surmised the truth, and he now knows how you have been sneaking out of the house.'

The girl clasped her hands in front of her. 'What will he do?'

Lena inwardly cringed. After the duke had set her two feet down on solid ground, his fury had taken hold. 'He plans to cut down the tree.' *Among other things.*

Claire collapsed on the edge of the bed, rubbing her temples. 'This is a disaster. My only bit of freedom will be taken away.'

'Perhaps you are overreacting.'

The girl's eyes sparked in outrage. 'Overreacting? You know nothing about my life here. It's intolerable.'

Something twisted inside Lena. Claire had experienced tragedy, and yet she knew nothing about hard living. 'You have a comfortable house and plentiful food. There are others who have it much worse.' Lena heard the frustration in her own voice. She'd struggled since Oliver's death. She'd had to move from their house into rented lodgings and it had been difficult to keep the place warm during the colder months. Coal was expensive and food was a necessity.

'You are no different than numbers one through five.' Claire stood, and her hands fisted by her sides. 'Wait! I take that back you are worse!'

Lena's heart squeezed at the girl's anguish. She threw hurtful words like stones out of loss, not anger. Regardless, Lena's first day was a disaster. The duke didn't trust her. Claire hated her *and* didn't trust her.

She could be sent packing at any moment. She sighed deeply.

'You never said where you went,' Lena pointed out.

Claire eyed her incredulously. 'You believe I would tell you now? The tree was my means of freedom from my uncle's ridiculous rule.'

Lena let out another slow breath. 'I agree his rules are… strict and some unreasonable.'

There was a pause, and the girl's eyes widened. 'You do?'

'I also think sneaking out of the house is dangerous and not the way to change your uncle's mind.'

Claire snorted. 'His mind cannot be changed. He is a stubborn man.'

'Anyone's mind can be changed.' If the circumstances were right, then Lena believed it possible. She'd been very young, only three years older than Claire when she'd married Oliver, and ignorant when the marquess had arranged her marriage to his stockbroker. She hadn't protested the match, even when she'd first met her husband-to-be and was aghast at his grey hair and wrinkles. Her husband had been older, much older, and set in his ways. Lena had tried to be a good wife, even though he wasn't kind or yielding, and yet it hadn't been beyond Lena to convince him to change a dictate or two when it came to his wife.

'You are wrong when it comes to Ravenwood,' Claire huffed. 'He is unbending and entirely inflexible.'

A knot settled low in Lena's stomach. Instinct told her the girl spoke the truth. Which meant Lena was at serious risk of dismissal without a reference.

Ravenwood greeted his long-time friend, Mark Averell, the Earl of Kent, when the man arrived in his study later that afternoon. Ravenwood poured two whiskies from the sideboard, handed Kent one, and joined him in the opposite chair by the fireplace. Tall and fit with curly brown hair and hazel eyes, his friend had always easily attracted women.

Brent sipped from the crystal glass. 'The new governess arrived.'

'How long do you think she'll last?' Kent asked.

Lena had surprised him, but not in a way he'd ever have guessed. The sight of her in that tree had made his heart pound. Worried she'd fall and break her neck on her first day in his home, he'd panicked and rushed forward, demanding she come down. She'd clutched the tree as one leg sought purchase while he'd stood helplessly below. As he'd looked up, her wool stockings did little to hide surprisingly shapely legs. His imagination had run wild for a moment, picturing the rest of her.

Then she'd jumped.

When he'd caught her in his arms, she was soft and curvaceous. Curls had escaped her iron pins and brushed her cheeks. Relief, then anxiety had flashed in her doe-like dark eyes, and she'd clung to him. Her lush mouth was inches from his and his heart had galloped in his chest. It had been so long since he'd held a woman, even longer since he'd kissed one. He inwardly scowled. Maybe that was the problem.

Lust. Pure and simple.

'You look tense, my friend.'

Ravenwood looked at Kent. 'You may be right. Maybe what I need is a round or two with you in the boxing ring at Gentleman Jackson's.'

Kent's lips curved upward. 'I wasn't thinking of boxing but another way.' A twinkle gleamed in his friend's eye.

'Such as?'

Kent set down his glass. 'You need a woman.'

Ravenwood grimaced. 'What?'

'There are plenty of ladies. You never had a problem in the past.'

He had been thinking similarly, but hearing it from his friend caused his temper to rise. 'Christ, have you taken a good look at me?' Ravenwood's voice was laced with bitterness. He'd never been bitter in his youth. He'd been carefree. A rogue. Women had flocked to him, and he'd bedded his fair share. He'd prided himself on never disappointing a woman. His reckless antics had been the reason his disciplinarian father had purchased him the army commission. The former duke had threatened to stop his allowance if he didn't enter either the clergy or the military.

And he was *not* cut out for the clergy.

So, off he'd gone with a regiment. It was to be a safe

commission. England wasn't at war. Then that power-hungry French bastard had taken hold of the continent and Waterloo had resulted in death and destruction.

'Do you mean a mistress?' Ravenwood asked. He had never looked down on men who'd kept mistresses. Hell, he'd always thought he would be one of those men.

Kent shook his head. 'I'm not speaking of a mistress, although I wouldn't blame you for seeking one.' His eyes sharpened. 'I do not need to remind you that you are now a duke. You need a duchess and to produce the requisite heir and spare.'

'You're right. You needn't remind me.' He took a long drink of the fine whisky. Not long ago, he *was* the spare without worry for dukedoms or children. It didn't matter whether he wanted the title or not. He'd inherited it and it came with unavoidable responsibilities.

'Your niece will be presented to Court in the near future,' Kent said. 'You have to face it sooner than later. She needs a proper chaperone to help her enter society. As her guardian, you must escort her to balls and parties and everything else the *beau monde* devises as frivolous entertainment.'

'Good God, are you trying to ruin my afternoon?' Ravenwood said.

Kent sipped his own drink. 'I'm going through hell now with my twin sisters' debuts. The marriage market isn't for the faint of heart. I have to stand by and watch both Amelia and Audrey dance with eligible bachelors while navigating overeager and oftentimes aggressive mamas chasing me down in overly warm ballrooms. Soon, you'll be in my position. You need a suitable wife to help. I'm counting on my mother to find me one.'

Tension enveloped Ravenwood's shoulders. 'I take it back. You're ruining the entire day.'

Kent shrugged. 'I'm your only good friend left. You are not a very likeable man.' He set down his glass on an end table.

Ravenwood scowled. 'Since you are so set on determining my future, who do you suggest?'

'Francesca, Lady Powell, is a widow now that her second old husband, the Earl of Powell, has passed. She was quite enamored of you in our youth.'

Ravenwood's brow furrowed. 'She was a notorious flirt and became betrothed to her first rich lord during our affair. She wanted a title, and I didn't have one then. I doubt she would have interest in me now.' He'd enjoyed his dalliance with the lady when they were young, but Francesca had always been cunning—best to keep his distance. 'What other woman would want a scarred man who is frightening to look at?'

'Do not fool yourself,' Kent said. 'There are females who will look past your pretty face for the chance to be a duchess. You are a rich man.'

Ravenwood's eyes narrowed. 'And that's what I am to look forward to? A wife who wants my title and wealth and nothing else? It sounds just like my mother.'

If he took Francesca as his wife, he would have a marriage similar to his own parents'. He did not want that.

'Then we are back to the beginning.' Mark rubbed his

chin with his thumb and forefinger. 'Do you have anyone in mind?'

Once more, an image of the governess stuck in the tree flashed before him. The governess was as night from day to Francesca, who was a viscount's daughter and a blue-eyed blonde who'd always dressed in the height of fashion to flatter her willowy figure. Mrs Harper, on the other hand, with her beautiful dark features and the dresses she hid behind, was far more intriguing.

His inappropriate attraction to her, the way he'd relished the feel of her in his arms earlier, had had him abruptly setting her down on her feet.

He was no longer a womanizer. He may have been a famous lover, a rogue in his youth, the type of man protective mamas would fear. He'd mocked the poets who spewed nonsense about love. Sex, pure and simple, had consumed his nights, even many of his days.

Then everything had changed on a blood-soaked battlefield in France.

A simple liaison could suit his sexual needs until he found a wife. Yet the truth was he didn't want to go back in time…he could never go back. In a twisted way, his vivid nightmares reminded him of that fact.

'Perhaps you are right,' Ravenwood said. 'Claire needs a mother figure. I sure as hell do not know how to help or manage my niece and have little interest in escorting her to society events when she comes of age. My requirements are simple. A wife to take charge of my niece. Produce an heir. Then leave me in peace. Love is not required. A marriage of the mind suits my needs.'

Kent's eyes searched his face. 'What do you mean "of the mind"?'

Ravenwood sat back in his chair as his thoughts unfolded. 'I mean a union without affection. I can offer a wife security, wealth, and the title. In exchange, she takes charge of Claire. After my niece is married, then she can go about living her life as she wishes, attending whatever society events she chooses as a duchess of the realm. I do not want a demanding spouse prodding into my past.'

'And what of the required heir?'

Ravenwood let out a rough laugh. 'She must agree to that as well.'

Kent raised a brow. 'Don't you think some sort of attraction is required for that to happen?' he asked.

'She can extinguish the candles if she wishes.'

'You're worried about how she will look at you?'

Ravenwood fingered the scar down the side of his face. 'Don't be an idiot. If you looked like me, you would never ask.'

'I see,' Kent said, his brow creasing. 'Until then, what about the new governess? Will you retain her services or let her go?'

'Mrs Harper is different.' She *was* different. In so many ways. He was still surprised that she'd slipped out an open casement to follow his niece. What woman would be so bold, so brave?

'Different how?'

'I caught her up a tree.'

Kent burst out laughing. 'Up a tree? I suppose that's different than all the prior governesses.'

He shrugged. 'She followed Claire out the window. When I caught Mrs Harper in a precarious position, her excuses were preposterous. I told her to take the rest of the day off while I consider her continued employment.'

'That's rich!' Kent said. 'I hope you keep her so that I can meet her.'

There was no reason to keep her. He should have dismissed her already. Yet, a strange part of himself was torn about Mrs Harper. She was different and refreshing. But he didn't need the distraction. He had little peace as it was.

'Do not get your hopes up about the governess,' Ravenwood said. 'I will likely send her back to the agency when I see her tomorrow morning.'

Chapter Four

Lena entered her room and closed the door behind her, her heart pounding. She couldn't believe what she had just stumbled upon. She had left Claire's chambers and was heading to her own room when she'd overheard a conversation in the duke's study.

My requirements are simple. A wife to take charge of my niece. Produce an heir. Then leave me in peace. Ravenwood's voice.

Her pulse had quickened as she scanned the hall. Stepping forward, she'd pressed her ear to the wood. No servants were about and the temptation to eavesdrop was hard to resist. She'd heard their entire conversation, including the part at the end about her future.

I will send her back to the agency when I see her tomorrow morning.

For a heartbeat, the shock of defeat held her immobile, and she was assailed by a terrible sense of bitterness as she'd walked back to her rooms. Now alone, she laid her head against the closed door.

Once again, she would no longer have financial stability. The agency would be hard-pressed to take her on again after losing her position after a single day. Her rent would be due soon, and she'd have bills to pay.

Her thoughts turned to her prior husband's business partner. Stanley Peterson had taken what was rightfully hers after Oliver's death, her share of the marital property…along with her mother's jewels. Oliver had never included his wife in his will. Her father, for all his wisdom, had not drawn up a betrothal contract. Most likely, he did not consider an illegitimate child a priority. In the marquess's mind, he'd done his duty by paying for her tuition at the girls' school, then marrying her off. If the marquess and Oliver had reached any type of gentleman's agreement, it was completely useless to her now that she had to deal with Stanley Peterson. Both of the men in her life who should have protected her had failed. It was all terribly unfair. Years of a miserable marriage and she had nothing to show for it.

She'd visited Peterson before to get back what was owed to her, but once more she would try again. Her survival depended upon it.

With renewed purpose, she grabbed her reticule, then hurried down the grand staircase and walked out the door. She hailed a hackney at the nearest corner and arrived at Stanley Peterson's place of business fifteen minutes later.

Stanley had shared offices with her late husband. The offices were a stone's throw from the London Stock Exchange and, when Oliver was alive, both stockbrokers would run across the street early each morning to conduct business with other brokers and jobbers. Lena knew it to be hectic work but also financially rewarding.

She announced her arrival to a secretary and sat in one of two chairs in an outer chamber to wait. Yet she sat for over half an hour in vain, her fingers twisting the strings of her reticule in frustration. Stanley refused to see her—as he often did. Other times, the portly, balding man would make her wait only to come out and leer at her with his beady eyes, telling her he didn't have the time that day.

When the secretary called her over, she knew Stanley would once again dodge her today. Her face grew hot with humiliation and she debated demanding that the man come out right now, but she wouldn't cause a scene. So, she left the office.

Rather than return to the ducal mansion, she returned to her rented room. Lena's already deflated mood had turned sour. How things had swiftly changed from the morning.

It was dim in her room and she felt for the flint, struck it, and lit a lamp. A low glow illuminated the small room. There was space for one bed, a chest of drawers, and a kitchen table and pair of chairs. A hearth served for heating and cooking. She sat on the edge of a sagging straw mattress, then opened her reticule. A handful of coins remained. Not enough to pay the next month's rent.

Worse than her failure to retrieve the monies Stanley owed her was his continued refusal to return her mother's jewels. Her mother had always worn two pieces of jewellery—a necklace with a cross and a turquoise amulet with a white circle and black center that resembled an eye; and a bracelet bearing a similar amulet. In her culture, she believed in the 'evil eye.' Jealousy, one of the core evils, was never to be overlooked. Dynasties rose and fell due to it, and one could cast an 'evil eye' or jealousy or bad intentions upon a person and their entire family. Then there was the good eye, the *acht*, that warded off evil directed towards the wearer. The *acht* dated back to pagan times, well before Christianity, and many, including her own mother, wore necklaces with amulets—pendants of the protective *acht* and the cross.

Her mother's voice was never far from her mind. *Soon you will go to England and your father's people, Lena. It is what your father and I both agreed upon. You will encounter those who dislike you for your mixed blood, those who fear you, and those who will embrace you. Never overlook those who are envious. Protect yourself.*

Her mother had removed her necklace and placed it around Lena's neck. 'The *acht* will protect you and those you care for,' her mother had said. 'Wear it and think of me.' She'd placed a kiss upon her daughter's forehead.

She'd died an hour later.

The pain of being parted from her mother's keepsake was overwhelming, especially on days like this one.

She jumped when a knock sounded on the door, and she rose to open it.

Then wished she hadn't. 'Yer rent is due.' Her landlady, Mrs Porter, was short and plump with a full head of grey hair, her grey eyes reminding her of a metal fence post on a cold winter day.

'I know, Mrs Porter. If I could just have another two weeks or so.'

'I'm not a charity house. You have until the end of this week.'

The door closed in her face.

Until the end of the week! She'd only worked a day for the Duke of Ravenwood and hadn't earned any of her salary.

Still, she couldn't blame the duke for deciding to dismiss her. The conversation she'd overheard in the duke's study returned in a rush. How could he trust a new governess with his niece if he found her in such a compromising position on the first day?

No matter her dismay at the day's unfortunate events, her thoughts kept returning to the duke. She recalled what it felt like to be held in his arms. Her pulse quickened and she'd wanted to touch more of his chest. Oliver had been soft, with a sagging middle, and she'd avoided physical contact. But Ravenwood…goodness…when he'd caught her in his arms, her senses had reeled, and she'd been aware of the harsh, uneven rhythm of her breathing.

Another knock sounded on the door. She set the lamp aside and went to open it. Had her landlady changed her mind? Would she have just a day to produce the rent instead of a week?

Ivan stood in the doorway.

'Thank goodness, it's you!' Lena said. The horrible day seemed better already at the sight of her dearest friend.

'What a warm welcome,' Ivan said.

The son of a Middle Eastern merchant, Ivan had met Lena years ago when he and his father had delivered Oriental and Turkish rugs to the headmistress of the girls' school Lena had attended. The pair had immediately bonded, and their friendship had grown over the years. Of average height with dark hair and brown eyes, Ivan never stood out in a crowd. Yet he was like a brother to her. Ivan had helped her find a room after Oliver had passed and she'd had to leave their rented townhouse.

'I saw lamplight from the window and hoped you were home. Why are you here?' His eyes shone with concern. 'Please know I'm happy you are, but why are you not at the Duke of Ravenwood's home, looking after his niece?'

Lena thought of how best to explain. 'Please come inside. I haven't lit the brazier and it's not warm, but our landlady has keen hearing.'

Ivan followed her in where they sat across from one another at her small kitchen table.

'Things did not work out as expected at the duke's residence,' Lena confided.

'How so? Was the girl difficult?'

'Yes, Claire was unwelcoming at first, but she is not the reason for my departure.'

Two hot spots appeared on Ivan's cheeks. 'The duke disrespected you?'

'No! It's not what you think. Ravenwood made no unwanted advances.'

'Then what happened?'

She paused, not sure how she could explain, then she decided to just blurt out the facts. 'Ravenwood found me up a tree, then caught me on the way down.'

'What!'

She waved a nervous hand. 'I was chasing after Claire.

You see she climbed out the casement to escape. I spotted her and followed.'

Long seconds passed before Ivan spoke. 'I knew something like this was bound to happen.'

Now it was Lena's turn to be surprised. 'You knew I'd climb a tree after his niece?'

'No, silly. I knew it was a bad idea for you to take the position in the first place. The man is scarred from war. They say he lost his soul on that battlefield and came back a beast.'

She was still trying to figure out the duke. She could see how outsiders saw him as a beast, yet she was not convinced. Not yet. 'I counted on the position. I know it sounds silly since I was only in the duke's household for such a short time, but I *liked* Claire. She has suffered the loss of not one, but both parents and now must stay with her uncle.'

'I know how you feel about children.'

A familiar knot tightened in her chest. 'Claire is not a child. But yes, I want a child of my own. It doesn't matter if it's a boy or girl. I've always wanted one. Is that so wrong?' She used to play and read to the younger children at the girls' school. She'd hold them when they cried from homesickness or when they ached for a deceased parent. She'd sing lullabies in Armenian and Arabic and soothe away their tears. Children never judged or showed prejudice. They just wanted love. And Lena had endless love to give. Just not for a man.

She'd learned her lesson the hard way.

Ivan shook his head. 'No. But not being married poses a problem.'

She sighed, and an all too familiar despair settled in her gut. 'I'm aware of the struggles of the unwed mothers on the street. Even those from families with means. The woman is ostracized, and the babe is labelled a bastard all his life.' She herself was illegitimate. The marquess may have loved her mother, but he'd never married her. When Lena had arrived in England as a young girl, she'd soon learned how different things were for the wealthy and privileged. The marquess had never married her mother and Lena would not be accepted by Society. However, it was not uncommon for the upper class to take in an illegitimate child as a 'country cousin.'

It was not to be for Lena.

Ivan pursed his lips. 'It's cruelty.'

'Then there is my age. At twenty-seven, I'm considered long upon the shelf. A widow without a child. Some might believe me barren. It's untrue. Oliver was old and never able to…never could…' Her face turned hot, and her hands fisted at her sides to prevent them from pressing against her face. Ivan was her friend, but he was still a man, and she couldn't discuss such an intimate part of her life. In the beginning of her marriage, she'd tried to please her husband. It wasn't long before she'd soon grown to dread the nights Oliver had visited her bedchamber. He'd lift her bedgown, crawl on top of her, and attempt to perform in the marriage bed. She'd grit her teeth until he rolled off, panting, frustrated, and oftentimes angry at her. As if his inability were her fault. She'd tried hard to please him both in and out of the bedroom, at first…but over time, she came to accept that she never would.

Aware of Ivan watching her, she shoved the awful memories aside.

Ivan edged his chair closer. His eyes met hers. 'You are my friend, and you know I love you, Lena. If only I could—'

Her heart clenched and she reached for his hand. 'No, Ivan. We are dear friends. We cannot change how we feel for each other, nor would I ever ask it of you.' She loved Ivan as a brother. And Ivan longed for another—a young man who worked as a jobber in the London Stock Exchange. His family would never approve.

As for Oliver, it wasn't just his cruelty in the bedroom. He'd also rejected her culture. Oliver never wanted to acknowledge her Middle Eastern heritage. Whenever she'd tried to cook the savory dishes she'd craved—hummus, tabouleh, and shish kebab—he'd grown angry. On one instance, he'd tossed the hummus out the back door. She'd even had to hide her sacred Armenian Bible, written with its distinctive thirty-six-letter alphabet. She'd learned to hide other things as well, including her mother's jewellery. She'd worn the necklace and tucked the pendant and cross beneath her bodice and hidden the bracelet beneath her sleeve.

As for everything else, including the food she'd craved, Ivan had once again come to her aid. He lived with a large family and his two aunties would prepare food for her and he would deliver it in secret. She'd join him at the park, and they'd enjoy baba ganoush and fresh pita bread.

Her life lessons had made her the woman she was today. When it came to her future, especially marriage, she'd never risk her heart again. Never expose herself to vulnerability. She'd protect herself at all costs. The duke had said the same in his study to his friend, hadn't he? What was it he'd said again?

My requirements are simple. A wife to take charge of my niece. Produce an heir. Then leave me in peace.

Something about Ravenwood's statement left a pang in her chest. Like her, he was in a difficult position.

She grew aware of Ivan watching her. 'What did your landlord say?'

She bit her lower lip. 'My rent is due. And Mrs Porter is not known for her generosity.'

'Then allow me to help you with the rent.'

'I cannot.' Ivan was family rich, not money rich, and she could not in good conscience take from him.

His brow creased. 'If you will not let me aid you, then what will you do?'

'The duke gave me the rest of the day off, and when I return tomorrow morning, he is going to dismiss me. He has sufficient cause. I also thought I could stay silent over the way he runs his household, but holding my tongue has never been my strength.'

'That's what I admire about you. If only I could speak my mind.'

She knew he meant to his family. Middle Eastern culture was harsh with men like Ivan. Englishmen did not treat men like him any better. Like her, Ivan had known prejudice.

She sighed, thinking of where her dismissal would leave the duke's niece. 'I liked Claire because she has spirit. She's also clearly suffering from the loss of her parents. Why can't His Grace see it?'

'Perhaps he does see it and he's suffering himself.'

The words were delivered without inflection, but they struck a chord in her chest. She'd understood His Grace to be a survivor as soon as she'd seen his scarred face. Were his brooding demeanour and rigid military rules a way of coping, hiding his own pain?

Whatever the truth, she was in financial trouble. The thought of spending one more night in this dreary room made bile rise in her throat. After Oliver died, she'd been determined to take her life back and make her own decisions. Then Oliver's business partner had taken everything. Not only had she been left in a precarious position to pay rent, the scoundrel had also stolen much of the gumption she'd clung to through seven years of a miserable marriage.

No! She would not fall into self-pity. She was Lena, daughter of an Arabian lady and the Marquess of Grisham. She was strong, decisive, proud of her mixed race. If she wanted to create a life where she could make her own decisions, then she must take matters into her own hands. Once again, she thought of the conversation she'd overhead between Ravenwood and his friend.

The kernel of an idea formed in her mind. Both she and the duke found themselves thrown into life-changing situations that they must navigate. Perhaps they could help each other. He required a family. She'd always wanted a family. He needed someone to help Claire, and she wanted to help the girl. He could offer her financial stability, and she could offer him all the space he needed, the kind a traditional marriage couldn't provide. She was as far from a demanding Society lady as night from day. Anyone would think her mad. Anyone but Ivan.

'I'm going to ask Ravenwood,' she blurted out.

Ivan's brow furrowed. 'Ask him what?'

'To marry me. I overheard the duke tell a friend that he seeks an unobtrusive wife after an heir is provided. He needs an heir and a wife to look after his wayward niece. I will care for Claire, and I want a child of my own as well.'

Ivan's jaw slackened. 'Are you jesting?'

It wasn't precisely the reaction she wanted. 'Why not? I have nothing to lose.' She raised her chin. 'He's surely decided to fire me anyway, so there is no risk. And after seven years of an unhappy marriage, I swore to take matters into my own hands. To make my own decisions.' *To never love.*

'You also swore never again to fall beneath the thumb of a controlling husband.'

She'd pondered the same thought. But it was a risk that she was willing to take. 'I won't. We will be wed in name only and can live separate lives.'

It was what Ravenwood wanted as well. She just needed to logically outline her proposal. To somehow convince him.

'You do realize that you have to bed him to get with child?'

Her cheeks grew hot. 'I do.' Her heart skipped a beat

at the thought of sharing a bed with the brooding duke. She'd wanted to touch his scar the first moment she'd seen him. Then there was the moment he'd caught her as she'd leapt from the tree. He'd held her as easily as if she were thistledown, and a tingling had suffused her veins. Oliver had been old, his arms thin, his chest sagging, his belly round. The duke's physique was muscular, hard. It would be different. It had to be.

She'd deal with that later. The more she talked through her idea, the more she liked it. What more could she lose? She'd lost so much already. If he turned her down, she'd be back at the agency requesting another job—as she no doubt would have to do by week's end anyway. And if the duke actually agreed, well… 'I will put together a list of my requirements. Nothing unreasonable, but important to me.'

'You think he'll agree to your proposal and this list?'

The duke had his own ideas and requirements. Why not listen to her proposal? She was sure she could convince him of the merits of the arrangement if he gave her the time. 'I will convince him of my plan.'

'And you believe Ravenwood would agree?' Ivan asked.

'I do. It's what he said he wanted. It will be a mutually satisfying business arrangement.' The situation seemed perfect. For them both.

'He has a fierce reputation. You do not fear him?'

'No.' A little. *Yes.*

'Or that he will have the upper hand?'

'No.' Of this, she was certain. 'I will be the one taking advantage of *him.*'

Chapter Five

Lena took several deep breaths as she stood on the porch of the Duke of Ravenwood's home the following morning. She lifted the brass knocker. After requesting an audience with the duke, she waited in the vestibule until the butler escorted her to the study. After her first meeting in the masculine room, she found it difficult to be at ease. She sat in the same armchair. Only this time, Ravenwood chose to sit behind his desk rather than across from her. She contemplated the shadowed planes of his undamaged side, his angular jaw, and aquiline nose.

He rested his hands on the blotter of his desk and regarded her. 'Good morning, Mrs Harper. After a day to think of your employment here, I have decided to—'

'You are dismissing me.' She bristled, still put out from overhearing him admit his intention yesterday.

'Is that what you think?' he asked.

She straightened her spine. 'Yes.'

'I had decided to send you back to the agency. But now that you are here, I assume you will want to convince me why I should retain your services as governess.' He steepled his fingers beneath his chin. 'I'm willing to listen.'

She swallowed and struggled to level her breathing. She did want a position, but not as a governess. Goodness! Her nerves were wound tight, and she attempted to depict an ease she didn't feel. 'How is Claire faring?' she asked.

His eyes appeared to soften at her inquiry. 'I daresay, she actually inquired about your whereabouts last evening. I believe you made quite an impression.'

Her cheeks flushed. It took all her effort to meet his eyes. 'I'm happy to hear that.'

He lowered his hands to his desk and leaned forward. 'So, you *are* here for the position.'

She shook her head. 'I have a different proposal for Your Grace.'

'Oh? You wish to renegotiate your salary?'

'No. I wish to marry,' she blurted out.

His eyes blazed down into hers, and his lips flattened. 'Pardon?'

It was coming out all wrong. 'I'd like to set forth an arrangement…one that will benefit us both.' *One that was already on your mind.*

A muscle twitched by his unscarred eye, and it became impossible to steady her erratic pulse. The springs of his chair creaked as he leaned forward. Finally, he said, 'Go on.'

'I offer you a different union, one you can obtain if we marry. I propose a marriage of convenience. I promise to look after Claire. She requires a mother-figure. A lady to

ease her into society. And after I give you a son and heir,
I promise not to interfere in your affairs.'

His whole body stilled. 'You are offering to give me
a son?'

She couldn't tell if he wanted to hear more or toss her
out of his study. 'You are a duke and progression of the
line is of utmost importance, is it not?'

'It is a duty.'

Her confidence grew. 'I adore children. Have always
wanted them. As for Claire, I understand what she is going
through. I lost my own mother when I was young.' She
thought she saw something flicker in his gaze, but she
ventured on. 'Once we marry, you no longer need a string
of governesses disrupting Claire's life. She needs stability
and care, and I'll promise to provide both. You would be
hard-pressed to find a Society lady to love her as I would.'
She thought of her own experience with Lady Powell and
how the rejection had stung.

'I also understand Your Grace avoids society functions,'
she added. 'After I help Claire find a suitable husband, I
wish the same as you.'

'Which is?'

'To live separate lives. I take it you do not wish to be
burdened with a demanding wife?'

He angled his head towards hers, his eyes flashing with
amusement and…interest. 'But we must share time in the
bedchamber in order to bear this heir.'

Her nervousness returned, a different type of tingling
in her chest at the thought of intimacy with him. 'I'm a
widow, Your Grace. I'm not a wallflower or simpering

miss. I'm perfectly aware of what transpires between a husband and wife.' *Somewhat.* Her experiences were unpleasant, and she'd wished them to be brief. With Ravenwood, she would have no idea what to expect. He was the most masculine and virile male she'd ever encountered.

He was quiet for a long heartbeat. When he finally said her name, there was a glimpse of admiration in his eyes. It made her even more anxious and she shifted in her seat. 'What else, Mrs Harper?'

'There is something else.'

'I was sure of it.'

Her fingers tightened in her lap. Now was the time to set forth what else mattered to her. 'I will put together a list of my requirements. Nothing unexpected. A clothing allowance and a certain sum of pin money.'

He cocked his head with curiosity. 'Did your husband not provide for you upon his death?'

No, he did not. He made it easy for his avaricious business partner to take everything. Her discomfort rose.

Did he believe she was after his money?

'I'm a wealthy man, and my wife will be well provided for,' he said, 'including a generous clothing allowance, jewels, and accounts with all the London merchants she favors. She will have the freedom to attend events where she wishes. And most importantly, she will have the influence and coveted title of duchess.'

'You believe I am a fortune-and title-seeking woman then?' She was prepared for this argument, had expected it.

One dark eyebrow rose. 'It crossed my mind.'

'I will be honest. I *have* considered your wealth. I require a certain level of financial stability, but I do not require much. I am not a frivolous spender. Nor do I need trinkets, carriages, or to dress in the latest fashion. I'd rather see it go to the children's education and future. Including Claire.'

He sat back, watching her. 'You should have been a politician, Mrs Harper. There are few with a more silver tongue in the House of Lords.'

'Is that a yes?' She heard the hope in her voice.

'I am surprising myself…but *yes*.'

Excitement—and disbelief—leapt in her chest, but she shoved the thrill of success aside. He needed to know the truth, the full truth about her heritage before consenting. 'There is one thing that you must know about me. My father was the Marquess of Grisham and—'

He held up a hand. 'I know all about your background, Mrs Harper. The agency provided basic information. My man of affairs provided much more.' At her surprised silence, he continued, 'You don't think I'd have an unknown governess for my niece live in my house without a thorough knowledge of her background, do you?'

So. He knew of her mixed blood. Her illegitimacy. Her childhood upbringing in the Middle East. Would it make a difference?

'I know your history and it does not matter to me,' he continued smoothly.

"And the fact that I'm just shy of a full mourning period?"

'It does not concern me either. In the past, I had believed I wanted a wife with an impeccable background.'

A knot in her chest slightly eased. 'Why change your mind?'

He paused. 'You did not look away the first time you saw me. Nor did you look at me with pity or disgust.'

The breath stalled in her lungs. She recalled the first time she'd seen Ravenwood. She'd thought him fascinating. Even now, she wanted to stare at his beautiful face, trace the scimitar-shaped scar with her finger. How had it happened?

She shook her head, shifting focus and still trying to understand. 'I am not a lady by birth. Other women would give their right arm to be called a duchess.'

'Not as many as you think, without seeing me as a monster.'

A scar did not make a man a monster. His traits, on the other hand, did.

He nodded. 'I accept your proposal. Now send me your list of requirements.'

That evening, the butler advised Lena that she was to stay for the night. She arrived early in the dining room for the evening meal. The housekeeper, Mrs Hollins, entered soon after. A short middle-aged woman with steel-grey hair, she wore a black dress with a white collar and apron. A ring of keys hung at her waist.

'Miss Claire is spending time with a family friend. The duke sent his regards and said he will not be able to dine with you tonight,' Mrs Hollins said.

Lena had met the housekeeper when she'd first appeared as a governess and knew the woman was efficient.

'Is His Grace unwell?' Lena asked.

'You will learn not to ask,' the housekeeper said.

What on earth did that mean? If she became his wife, she should know if he was ill. But then again, their arrangement would be businesslike. If he wanted to send a servant to inform her of his absence, then that was his right.

'Cook has prepared a fine meal,' Mrs Hollins said before leaving Lena alone once more.

Lena opened her napkin and spread it on her lap. The long dining room table looked even more massive. A footman appeared and she feasted on turtle soup, roasted lamb, and asparagus. The food was delicious, seasoned to perfection, a much finer meal than any that Lena had eaten recently. The mansion was more luxurious than any home she'd occupied.

After dinner, the butler fetched her cloak, and she stepped outside, intending to enjoy the fresh air before going to bed. The ground was still wet from the storm. A breeze cooled her cheeks, and she pulled her cloak tightly around her as she walked the well-maintained grounds. Turning a corner, she halted and gasped in wonder.

The sunset over the estate grounds was lovely, a brilliant orange ball on the horizon, the sky streaked in shades of pinks and purples like an artist's palette. The Berkeley Square mansion was a distance away from the factories, far enough to escape the ever-present coal smoke. She'd seen as much when she'd clung to the tree earlier.

She came upon the impressive mews that housed the duke's horses. The smell of fresh hay and horse permeated the space. She glimpsed inside. Tack hung on the walls and thoroughbreds and matching bays filled the stalls. The duke's stables were superior.

Not for the first time, Lena wondered if Claire took one of the horses when she escaped the house.

Did she have a friend nearby? Was it a boy?

She hoped to ease Claire's relationship with her uncle. As far as she was concerned, both duke and niece would have to compromise if they were to live amicably beneath the same roof.

On the way back to the house, a flash of black streaked across her path. She jumped and cried out before realizing it was a cat. Not a cat, a kitten. It wiggled through a broken lattice beneath the house.

Lena crouched down to search the hiding place. The kitten's bright green eyes watched her from behind the lattice. 'Oh, my. You poor thing. What happened to your mother?' The mother had either abandoned the kitten or died.

The kit looked old enough to be weaned, but too small to be on its own. 'You are alone here just like me, aren't you?' A meow followed, and the kitten stuck out its head, then crawled out farther. Lena scooped the kitten into her arms. It immediately nuzzled its face into the crook of her elbow. It was all black with white paws.

Lena's heart melted. She couldn't leave the kitten in the cold, could she? What were the chances it would survive on its own? Once more, she looked around for its mother and did not find one. Making a quick decision, she clutched the cat in the folds of her cloak and headed back into the house.

She found the kitchens and the lingering scent of roasted lamb from the evening meal wafted to her. Glancing around to be sure no one was about, she found cream in the larder and poured a good amount in a bowl, then put the kitten on the floor. The feline curiously licked the cream, then stuck its face in the bowl and ate with eagerness.

'Good girl,' Lena said.

'What's that doing in my house?'

Lena started at the familiar masculine voice. The duke stood in the entranceway, tall and imposing.

First the tree, now the kitchens. Did the man have eyes and ears everywhere? And what was a duke doing in the kitchens at this time? He hadn't shown for dinner and the housekeeper hadn't given any reason.

Gathering her courage, she found her voice. 'The kitten was abandoned by her mother.'

He walked inside and halted across from her at the worktable. A look of strange amusement crossed his features. 'And that is my concern?'

'I will look after her and clean her sawdust box. You won't even know she's here.'

'I already know.'

He watched her with a keenly observant eye, and her mind whirled. He wore no coat, cravat, or waistcoat. His shirtsleeves had been rolled up to reveal muscled forearms with a sprinkling of dark hair. Had he been reading in his study and heard her open the front door?

He leaned casually against the worktable. There didn't appear to be an ounce of extra fat on Ravenwood, even his forearms. He had strong hands and long lean fingers.

Good God. Why was she thinking about this?

'Cats are clean.' She lifted her face to his.

'I've never had an animal in my house.'

'As your soon-to-be wife, it will be my house as well.' If he could be difficult, then she would just have to set forth her own arguments. He was a military man used to being in charge of his men. He must come to realize she wasn't one of his soldiers. And she couldn't start giving in so easily before they'd even wed.

Raising her chin, she faced him. 'Did you ever have a mouse? I cannot imagine a house this size without having a mouse at one time.'

A corner of his lip tilted upward. 'Are you suggesting that I have mice?'

'All big homes do. That's why most have house cats.' Lena held up the kitten for his perusal. 'She eats little and will work for you.'

They'd always had cats in their home in Lebanon. Her mother had adored the two spotted orange siblings and had named them Pasha and Princess. On occasion, the pair left dead mice in the vestibule for her mother as 'gifts.'

Ravenwood tapped his fingers on the kitchen worktable. His gaze flickered to the kitten, then back to her. She was keenly aware of his size and strength. She'd never been this close to a man like him, certainly had never touched one. Her face grew warm at the notion that he would be her husband. Soon, they would be intimate.

Her heart raced.

As she waited for his response, the anticipation was almost unbearable.

'What will you name it?' he asked.

She let out a slow breath. 'I haven't thought that far.'

'Think of a name for the cat,' he said, turning to leave. 'Then I don't want to see it.'

Why had he agreed to the kitten? Ravenwood left the kitchens, wondering what had just happened. Frustrated with himself, he grabbed a glass and bottle of whisky from the sideboard in his room and headed straight for the west wing. He often came here when he was restless or couldn't sleep.

Every time he shut his eyes, memories returned to haunt him. Battle cries. The deafening sound of a cannon blast. The sickening thud of bullets tearing flesh and smashing bone. Even that disturbing chinking sound that reverberated in his head during fitful bouts of sleep. If the wind slammed a door closed, he'd jump and break out in a sweat. He'd find himself walking through the mansion closing open casements. His servants looked at him as if he was crazed. *Christ.*

He reached the west wing. Much of the damage from the fire had been cleaned by the servants. The burnt furniture had been removed. The charred flocked paper on the walls peeled off, the walls washed and restored with a coat of fresh paint. The carpets had been tossed and new ones delivered. Still, the blackened stone, no matter how many times it was scrubbed, showed evidence of fire.

He entered the master chambers, which had been occupied by his brother and sister-in-law. His father, the old duke, had occupied a different chamber. After the battle Ravenwood had spent time recovering from his injuries in Brussels, then had stayed there to live a quiet life until he'd learned of his father's and brother's deaths. When Ravenwood had returned home, the first thing he'd asked was whether they'd suffered.

He'd seen death. Too much of it. A soldier had died from fire when the French had tossed burning oil on a group of men. The scent of singed flesh had permeated his nostrils.

He took a long drink from his glass. The fine whisky did little to ease his torment.

He had fond memories of his brother. Ralph was the heir, and Brent was the spare. His brother never made him feel inadequate though. Rather, he'd once told Brent that he was jealous of him. Their father had been a strict disciplinarian and hard on Ralph from the beginning. In their youth, the brothers would escape from the house and kick a ball in the country estate. Or ride and fish together. As they grew older, Ralph had to take on more and more responsibilities. He married a society lady who enjoyed balls and parties, and soon after, Claire was born. Brent was her godfather, and he recalled cradling the baby at the christening. He loved his niece, he still did.

As for his father, the old duke, Brent clashed with the man, and he'd eventually moved from the ducal mansion to bachelor's quarters on St. James's Street. He became a rogue, a womanizer, and deep inside, it was partly to irritate his father. It didn't last long before the old duke purchased him an army commission.

Carrying the bottle and glass, he took the stairs to the turret. It was a cool May evening, and a full moon illuminated part of the gardens and the drive. It had been a similar sleepless night when he'd spotted Lena's coach making its way to the mansion. He'd wondered then what the next governess would be like.

He'd never expected Lena.

She'd set forth her reasons to marry as smoothly as an experienced barrister in court. It was a logical offer, and more, much more. His gaze had traveled over her face and searched her eyes and he'd seen the sincerity there when she'd mentioned Claire. And there was another reason, one which was just as compelling. She challenged him, wasn't afraid to look at him, and the spark he felt when she was near made him feel more alive than he had in years...so he'd found himself accepting.

Which made him think about his behaviour tonight once more. Earlier that evening, he'd planned to meet her for a private dinner to go over her list of requirements. He'd arranged for Claire to spend the evening with a family friend. But before the meal, he'd sought a ten-minute respite to doze on the sofa in his study.

Ten damned minutes.

He woke sweaty and shivering.

He'd skipped dinner and sent the housekeeper to advise Lena of his absence.

Hours later, he'd headed to the kitchens for an apple when he'd found Lena standing by the worktable, a kitten lapping a bowl of cream by her feet.

His heart had thundered and all thoughts of hunger for food disappeared. A different type of hunger had surfaced.

And when she'd bravely faced him, swallowing her fear, the spark of challenge had made him forget his nightmare.

As for the cat, he really didn't mind the animal. What unnerved him was the way he'd reacted to her request. When he'd seen Lena cradling the kitten, something had shifted within him, a tiny fissure, a crack in his chest. Lena's eyes had softened towards the creature, and, for a brief moment, he'd wanted her to look at him the same way.

Madness.

He let out a deep breath, set down his glass, and scrubbed his hand down his face. Just thinking of her conjured images of mahogany hair, deep brown eyes, and hidden curves. She was a formidable force. A dangerous one. And if he wasn't guarded, he wondered what else he'd find himself agreeing to.

Chapter Six

Lena met Ravenwood in his study early the following morning. He was dressed in a coat of navy kerseymere, a snowy cravat, breeches, and polished Hessians. Unlike his informal attire the prior evening, today he looked every inch the duke.

She placed the foolscap on the table. 'I updated my list and thought it best if I gave it to you as soon as possible.'

His gaze travelled from her head to her toes, and she was conscious of her wool gown, the same one she'd worn on her first day. It had dried, and the stiff wool itched her throat and wrists.

'Please sit.' He motioned to one of the two wooden chairs before his desk. He waited for her to be seated before settling in his leather chair.

'Did you add the kitten to your list?' he asked.

'I saw no reason to do so, since we have already agreed to keep her.'

The only reaction was the arching of his unscarred eyebrow. She was getting used to this subtle but daunting response. She folded her hands in her lap, knowing any fidgeting or other display of nervousness could be used against her in their negotiations.

'If you prefer your solicitor to review it first,' she said as casually as she could manage, 'then I shall await your answer.' She started to rise.

He motioned for her to stay. 'That will not be necessary.' He opened the folded foolscap.

As he read, Lena had the opportunity to scan the room. A forest-green sofa occupied one corner, and a globe rested on a side table next to it. With the room's Wilton carpet, large desk, and side table holding crystal decanters, it was a masculine domain. She eyed the gold mantel clock, her stomach tightening with each second as she waited for him to finish.

'Two dresses a month,' he said. 'Permission to ride or walk in the park. A small allowance of five pounds a month.' He lowered the list and looked at her across the desk. 'These trivial requests do not concern me.'

Trivial? She'd had to fight for them during her first marriage. She hadn't received an allowance or many dresses. As for walks in the park, they were limited. Oliver had a jealous nature and feared she'd attract unwanted male attention.

'I'd still require it in writing, Your Grace,' she said.

'Fine. I'll make a note of it for my solicitor.'

'And the rest of my conditions?' she asked.

He continued to read. Dark hair curled at his collar. Nothing about the man was soft, but his hair…she wondered what it would feel like entwined in her fingers. A shiver trembled down her spine.

Seemingly oblivious, he continued reading. 'Permission to redecorate the ducal home since we will be hosting a ball for Claire's coming-out.' His dark eyebrows slanted in a frown. 'As long as you avoid the west wing, you can hire the *ton*'s most extravagant decorator for all I care.'

Her curiosity was piqued regarding the west wing. Did he not want her to enter there because it was not liveable from the fire or was there another reason? She took a deep breath and tried to relax. He'd agreed regarding the rest of the house and gave her permission to hire whomever she saw fit. Perhaps he was more reasonable than she'd anticipated.

Then his voice hardened as he said, 'You expect to attend society functions as husband and wife to prepare for Claire's debut?' His brow furrowed as he lifted his eyes.

Her ease dissipated and her nerves fluttered all over again.

'Yes.'

'No.'

'I don't understand. I thought a part of our arrangement was for Claire's benefit, including her coming-out ball,' she said.

'It is. A single ball for my niece is one thing. You never said anything about me attending other balls or silly parties.'

She couldn't understand his hesitancy. How else were they to launch a young girl into Society? 'As husband and wife, I expect you to attend functions to prepare for Claire's coming out.'

'Why? Guiding her will be your duty.'

'Yes, but to smooth her path, we must present a unified front as husband and wife beforehand. It will matter to the families of her suitors. When she comes of age, you must escort her to events for her first Season. Once Claire's made a suitable match, there will be no need to attend society functions any longer.'

He shook his head. 'This must be negotiable.'

'What is there to negotiate? This is only for Claire. Otherwise, we need not attend any functions.'

'I do not like large crowds.'

She'd heard he rarely left home. She'd also heard rumours that he hadn't always been that way. 'I was told you frequented events in the past. You attended dozens—'

'That was then,' he said harshly, cutting her off with a curt wave of his hand. 'I have not waltzed or danced or mingled at a ball or any other society event since I left for the army five years ago.'

Five years? 'I see.' She bit her lower lip. This posed a problem. It could also be overcome. He was just rusty, not unable. He needed a lesson or two. 'It still doesn't change my list.'

'I suppose you enjoy dancing,' he said.

'I do, but I rarely had an opportunity. Mr Harper did not find it agreeable.'

'Your late husband does not sound agreeable at all.'

'I do not wish to talk about him.' Her past wasn't something she would share. It had made her who she was and had taught her valuable lessons when it came to the heart.

'I'm willing to attend necessary soirées for Claire,' he said. 'But no waltzing.'

Then he was willing to meet her halfway. 'That is acceptable.'

He flipped the page of her list. And froze. Likely because he'd reached the last paragraph. 'No bedchamber visits until a proper time period passes for us to grow comfortable with each other.' His eyes snapped to hers once more. 'Are you serious?'

She sat up a bit straighter. 'We barely know each other. I'm not asking for romance but require a reasonable amount of time to become accustomed to our marriage before...before intimacy.' She felt her cheeks burn hot.

He raised both eyebrows. 'I see.'

Her fingers twisted in her lap. His eyes pierced the distance between them and all thoughts of appearing confident fled.

He leaned forward in his chair and folded his hands. 'You do recall the arrangement *you* proposed? You want a child. I need an heir for the dukedom. For either to happen, we have to share a bed.'

Her stomach tightened. She was by no means blind to his attractiveness. Still, mention of bedchamber visits made her heart thump hard in her chest. 'I understand but I still require time.'

'Set forth your proposed duration of time.'

'Three months after the wedding.' She knew this was long but meant it to be a point of negotiation.

His brow furrowed and he shook his head. 'A week.'

'A month.' She countered.

He lowered his voice, his gaze never leaving hers. 'A week.'

She pushed back her chair and stood. Did he not realize they were to compromise? 'You are being inflexible. However, since the banns of marriage must be read aloud in church for three Sundays prior to the wedding and you are suggesting a week after the wedding, then that will give us four weeks, or one month, to get to know one another. I'll agree to this.'

He rose and walked around his desk to stop before her. She stood her ground and raised her chin, trying to assess his unreadable features. To her surprise, an unwelcome surge of excitement at his nearness made her pulse leap. She also had the unnerving intuition that he was enjoying their heated negotiations.

He leaned casually against the desk. 'Banns are not required if a special license is obtained.' His voice was level.

She gaped. 'A special license? But...but...that requires the Archbishop's consent himself.'

'I know.' An unmistakable hint of arrogance tinged his voice.

She was too shocked to be angry. Special licenses were rare. She'd never heard of anyone, other than the royal family, securing one. 'You obtained one?' They'd just agreed to marry. No one could work that fast.

'Not yet, but soon.'

She eyed him with suspicion. 'How?'

'A relative of the Archbishop was in my regiment.'

Of course, he would have a connection. A different type of nervousness trickled down her spine. Just thinking of intimacy with him caused a swooping feeling in her stomach. As if reading her wayward thoughts, his gaze lowered to linger at her nape. Could he see her increased breaths? Did he believe it nervousness instead of aware-ness? She swallowed.

'During this week, what do you require?' he asked. He'd mentioned a week, assuming she'd agreed to it. If he ac-commodated her on what she needed from him, then she would consent to this timeframe.

Her eyes met his and she held up a hand. 'If I agree to this week, then I'd like to spend time together.' Hopefully, they would both get to know one another, and she would be less nervous in the bedchamber.

'It sounds like a courtship *after* marriage. Do you re-quire flowers? Chocolates? Or, heaven forbid, poetry?' He listed the items like they were bullet points in a mili-tary order.

He was missing the point. 'They are nice, but not what I had in mind.'

'Then you must be more specific.'

He asked as if he'd never spent time with a woman out of the bedchamber. 'Walks. I like walking in the park. It will give us a chance to grow comfortable with our union.'

He nodded. 'And riding in the park as well?'

'I'm not an experienced rider, but I'm not opposed to it. As long as you do not grow frustrated with me.' She thought of other things she would enjoy. 'I noticed a lake in the park as well...'

'You can swim?'

'No, silly. It's a perfect spot for a picnic.'

His lips curled in a smile. Awareness thundered through her veins along with embarrassment. 'You're teasing me.'

'It isn't difficult.' He hesitated for a moment before lowering his voice. 'What I don't understand are your true concerns. When you propositioned me, you pointed out you are a widow.'

He studied her with a curiosity causing her to shift in her seat. It was true she wasn't a virgin, but she may have exaggerated her experience.

'Was your husband lacking in the bedroom?'

Goodness! He couldn't be asking her *that*. 'My first marriage was not…was not…'

'Was not what?'

'Mr Harper called me frigid.' She slapped her hand across her mouth. The words had slipped out before she could stop herself.

He arched one dark eyebrow. 'Frigid, you say?' He reached out and gently removed her hand from her lips and held it in his larger one. 'I do not believe it to be true.'

'How can you say that?' she whispered.

'Because your heart is racing now. I can see the rise and fall of your chest. There is one sure way to know. An experiment of sorts. A simple kiss.'

Her lips parted. 'A kiss?' A strange fluttering grew in her stomach. 'Is a kiss wise?'

'Very.' His gaze lowered to her lips. 'Wouldn't you like to know yourself?'

She'd fallen right into his trap. Only she didn't feel entirely helpless or threatened in any way. He was giving her a choice. Her heart skipped a beat in her chest. Thoughts of kissing him had swirled in her mind the first time she'd seen him. Oh, he was intimidating, but he was also wildly attractive. Her fingers had itched to touch his scar, to kiss the corner of his perfect lips, then lick the damaged part, too.

His eyes were compelling and magnetic as he waited for her answer. 'Yes,' she said, her voice a faint whisper. 'I'd like to know.'

Then she stepped close, rose on tiptoe, and pressed her lips to his.

At the tentative brush of her lips against his, his heart hammered against his ribs and he grew hot.

She was far from frigid.

Ravenwood had kissed dozens of ladies in the past. Widows, unhappy wives, even misses (some who claimed to be virgins but weren't). Lena Harper was a widow.

Yet it was clearly her first real kiss.

Once again, she'd surprised him by kissing him first. It was thrilling to have her take the initiative. He remained absolutely still, letting her set the pace as her lips moved hesitantly over his. He wanted to take command of the kiss, but he feared frightening her. Her hands rose to his biceps then higher to his shoulders before he pulled her close. He kissed her back, and when she opened her mouth in a gasp, he took advantage to slip his tongue inside. She tentatively stroked her tongue against his, then grew more urgent. When her nails scraped his scalp, it was like a lit match to hay. It took all his restraint not to crush her to him.

He had to be patient. Her enthusiasm would kill him.

Her palms on his chest felt like burning brands and he

welcomed her touch. It had been so long since a woman had touched him, had wanted to. So long since he'd allowed it.

When her tongue came dangerously close to his scarred lip, he broke the kiss. She seemed unsteady, her eyes filled with burgeoning passion.

Good God. She was the one who wanted time away from his bed after the marriage vows? In his aroused state, he couldn't even recall how long they'd negotiated. He wouldn't last. She'd kill him first.

He was surprised by how badly he ached for the contact.

She'd challenged him at every turn and made him feel alive. Then she'd kissed him and made him feel too damned much.

What had he gotten himself into?

He should give her words of praise. A compliment. A sweet murmur that they were well-suited. Instead, his voice was gruff. 'I was right. You are far from frigid. What if you decide to visit my bedchamber first?'

She opened her mouth, then shut it. 'I do not think that will occur.'

It took all his restraint to step away from her and head to the door. 'I shall have my solicitor deliver your signed documents tomorrow.'

There were kisses and then there were *kisses*.

In a daze, Lena had returned to her bedchamber and sat on the bench seat by the window. The kitten cuddled beside her and Lena stroked her soft fur. She still hadn't come up with a name and thought of asking Claire. The smart kitten had settled in her room and had already begun using the sawdust box in the corner. She was liked by Cook, who left treats and allowed her to come and go through the servants' entrance.

Lena let out a long sigh. Now that she was no longer employed as a governess, she planned to pack up her remaining things and return to her rented rooms until after the wedding. Even as a widow, living beneath a bachelor's roof as a fiancée was much different than as his employee, and improper. A small trunk had already been set aside for her belongings.

She was in no rush to pack as memories of the kiss she'd just shared with her betrothed were fresh in her mind. The duke's lips were not hard as Lena had expected. They were soft and gentle as a caress. She'd boldly touched his chest just as she'd longed to do since the brief moment he'd caught her beneath the tree. Both times, his heartbeat had been strong beneath her palm.

The scarred corner of his mouth had brushed the edge of her lip. It didn't repulse her in any way. She wanted to explore it, lick it, reach up and trace it. When her mouth parted and his tongue slipped inside… Heavens.

Her past experience was woefully inadequate. Her prior husband had never bothered to kiss her, other than a chaste brush of his lips on their wedding day. Kissing was not required for his painful probing in bed.

But when she'd kissed Ravenwood, her heart pounded and she responded with a need that had been curled up and hidden inside her.

Her face grew warm with embarrassment, remembering she had shared her husband's accusation that she was frigid. Foolish, Lena! She'd sworn never to open her heart after her first disastrous marriage. Nothing had changed, not from a kiss. She was determined to keep her heart locked away in a chamber deep in her chest.

A knock on the door drew her attention, and she opened it to find the housekeeper outside.

'Hello, Mrs Hollins. I will leave an address for the footman to deliver my trunk until the wedding,' Lena said. The duke had assured her that everyone on staff had been made aware of their upcoming nuptials. Whether it appeared strange to them that she'd come a couple days ago as governess and was soon to be his wife… Well, she would not let it concern her. As long as they respected her as the mistress of the house, they would get on just fine.

'Very well,' Mrs Hollins said. 'When you return, you will not sleep here, but in the duchess's chambers. The rooms are much more spacious.'

More spacious? She couldn't imagine. She also had a strong suspicion that the duchess's chambers would be closer to Ravenwood's. Even adjoining. Which meant the duke could come and go from hers as he pleased.

Heavens. 'Thank you, Mrs Hollins. I understand things will be different for me after the wedding and I assume my duties as a duchess. I know I shall require your help with the household, and I'd like to be on good terms, even allies.' She smiled at the older woman. 'My mother was not English, and her ways were different than most Englishwomen. She would often say a good housekeeper is worth her weight in gold.'

The housekeeper's lips parted, and her eyes shone before she bobbed her head. 'I'd like that, miss.'

'I realize you and the staff know much about His Grace. Is there is anything I should know?'

The housekeeper hesitated before speaking. 'The household has learned His Grace has his moments.'

'His moments?'

'Time he is best left by himself,' Mrs Hollins said.

'I see.' Only she didn't.

Mrs Hollins bobbed another curtsy. 'Good day, miss.' The housekeeper departed, leaving Lena to wonder just what she could possibly mean.

Chapter Seven

Later that day, when Lena returned to her rented room, her landlady was on the porch.

'Good day, Mrs Porter.' Lena made to move by her.

'Not so fast, Mrs Harper. I've found another tenant for your room.'

Lena looked at her aghast. 'You cannot. You told me I had more time.'

'I changed me mind. Besides, ye found employment in a fancy duke's house.'

Lena saw no need to tell her she was no longer employed. She needed her rented room until after the wedding. 'I must stay.'

'No. Mr Morton is willn' to pay more.'

'Who's Mr Morton?'

'None of yer business, he is. All ye need to know is ye need to be out. I'll be generous and give you two days' time.'

That fast! Where would she go? She couldn't just move back into the duke's house. She wasn't an employed governess. And she wasn't yet his wife. It was entirely improper.

Ivan. He would help find her new lodgings until the wedding. Thankfully, she'd already had a note delivered to his home asking for him to stop by. 'Let me pass,' she told the older woman. 'As you said, I have two days to pack my things.'

Mrs Porter stepped away from the porch. Lena hurried inside the vestibule and to the door of her room. Using her key, she entered, then turned the lock. With one small window, which was dirty outside, it was dim inside. Striking flint, she lit a lantern. An orange glow lit the small one-room space. She began gathering her items and folding clothing.

She'd been in a state of packing and unpacking since accepting the governess position.

Now her future was set. A marriage to Ravenwood might give her stability along with the family she always wanted…but she couldn't hope for too much. Life had taught her that circumstances could change in an instant and dreams could be dashed.

A low knock sounded, and she hurried to open the door.

'Ivan!' She hugged her friend, and he returned the affection. His black hair was curled at the collar, and he wore a corduroy coat and trousers. While Ivan worked with his father selling rare Middle Eastern carpets and imported items for wealthy merchants and aristocrats, he dressed in corduroy one day a week to receive items at the docks.

'Did Ravenwood accept your proposal?' Ivan asked.

'He did.'

A shocked then troubled expression clouded his dark features and he reached for her hand. 'Lena, are you certain about this? Have you forgotten your marriage to Mr Harper?'

'I was young when I married Oliver Harper. I'm older, wiser.' *And smarter about protecting my heart.* 'I know what I'm doing.'

'Do you?'

'Yes.' Of this, she was certain. She would no longer allow others to make her choices.

Ivan's brow furrowed and his jet eyes watched her. 'I thought you wanted more.'

How could she explain? 'Ivan, I did. I still do. But I have to be practical. I will gain security. And, most importantly, children. You know I want both.'

'And love?'

She'd believed her father had loved her mother. But then he'd left her to do his own father's bidding and marry a titled English lady. Her mother had pined after the marquess for as long as Lena could remember. Then her father had married Lena off to his stockbroker. She'd opened her heart to both men and had learned a cruel but valuable lesson. Men, those who were supposed to protect and love a woman, were inherently selfish. Ivan was the only exception.

How could she ever believe in love?

Another knock sounded. This one louder. A sickening sensation settled in her stomach. Had Mrs Porter come to tell her the new tenant was here? She hadn't even had a chance to ask Ivan if he knew of available lodgings.

She held her breath as she opened the door. Ravenwood stood in the doorway.

Her anxiety turned into surprise, and her heart fluttered in her chest. 'Your Grace! I was not expecting you.'

'May I come inside?'

She realized she stood staring at him, one hand holding the door. She stepped to the side. 'Of course.' The duke entered, scanning the small space and old furnishings. Then he spotted Ivan. One dark eyebrow rose.

Lena made the introductions. 'This is my friend, Mr Ivan Abadi. This is His Grace, the Duke of Ravenwood.'

Ivan bowed. 'Your Grace.'

The two men faced each other, each taking the measure of the other, the tension palpable between them.

Lena cleared her throat. 'Ivan is my oldest friend. I met him when I was at finishing school and he and his father delivered a rare Turkish carpet to the headmistress.'

The men continued to stare at each other.

She turned to Ravenwood. 'How did you learn of my address?'

'Mrs Hollins.'

'Of course.' Lena had given the housekeeper the address so that her trunks could be delivered. 'Why are you here?'

He reached for a sheaf of papers that he held beneath his arm. In her nervousness, she hadn't noticed it. 'I decided to deliver your signed documents myself. I'm glad I did.'

What on earth did that mean? Was he talking about Ivan? 'I was expecting your solicitor or your man of affairs,' she said.

Ivan took that moment to speak up. 'As you two have business to discuss, I shall leave. Good day, Lena.'

The casual use of her Christian name was not lost on

the duke. Ravenwood's eyes narrowed a fraction until Ivan departed and shut the door behind him.

Once they were alone, she crossed her arms. If Ravenwood thought she would allow him to be unfriendly to Ivan, then she would have to stand up to him right away. 'You were rude.'

'Oh? I did not expect a man, a bachelor, to visit my future bride.'

'As I explained, Ivan is my oldest friend. He will most likely visit often.'

'You mean at my home.'

'*Our* home. Once we are married, I will live there, too.'

For once, he didn't argue. 'I see. And this man, this Ivan… Who is he to you?'

'I already explained. Besides, you have no reason for concern.' Ivan was not a threat, at least not in the way to worry any future husband.

'I didn't say I was concerned. I asked who he is to you.'

'He is my longest friend, as I said. Like a brother, really. As for Ivan himself—' she swallowed, not sure how to discuss her good friend '—he is not interested in—'

'You. I understand.'

He did? How? 'Good. Then I expect you to be civil to him when he visits *our* home.'

He sighed. 'I said I understand. But I find it difficult to have someone who dislikes and distrusts me in *our* home.'

'Ivan doesn't dislike or distrust you.'

He cocked his head to the side. 'Really?'

'Well, maybe a little. He is protective and just needs to get to know you. Which is why he must come visit.'

"Perhaps in time—"

'Goodness, no. Apparently I must amend my list of requirements to make an exception for Ivan.' She attempted to snatch the sheaf of papers from his hand, but he held them away from her. From his height, she could never reach them.

He laughed at her boldness. 'You truly are a good negotiator.'

'Is that a yes?'

He lowered the papers. 'There's no need to amend anything,' he said softly. 'Ivan can visit. But do not expect me to be suitable company. Part of our agreement is that I needn't entertain.'

'Agreed. For now.'

He chuckled. 'Amazing. You do not relent, do you?'

'Would you if something meant so much to you?'

'I suppose not.'

She smiled and held her tongue. Because she *did* expect him to greet Ivan in a drawing room or even share a meal with him in their enormous dining room in the future. As her closest friend, she wanted Ivan to feel welcome in her new home. And she secretly hoped the duke could form a friendship with him as well.

One step at a time, Lena.

The duke was a force. He could even be fearsome at times, but she was just as willful. And as much a survivor. For their marriage to work they needed to both give and take. Even without loving each other, they should—at a minimum—respect each other. And each other's loved ones. He might not agree. She just needed to show him…

'I have one more item for you before I leave.' He slowly stepped close, as if he feared she would bolt. Her heart rate skyrocketed when he looked at her as if he might kiss her. Delicate wings unfurled in her chest. Memories of their shared kiss returned in a rush.

His eyes bored into her as if he could read her thoughts. 'He reached into his coat pocket and removed a velvet box. He opened it to reveal a ring—not just any ring— a stunning sapphire surrounded by half a dozen brilliant diamonds.

Eyes wide, her heart pounded an erratic rhythm. He hadn't been thinking of kissing, but this…

'It was my grandmother's ring. My mother wore it on occasion. As my bride, you should have it.' His voice was low.

She opened her mouth. Words wouldn't come out.

'Do you like it? If not, I can have Rundell & Bridge make another.'

'No!' she rushed to say. 'It's lovely. I've never been gifted such a beautiful piece of jewellery.'

'It's not a gift. Not exactly. It's a promise to fulfill a contract.'

'A contract?' Her eyes left the ring to look up at him. Did he have to ruin the moment reminding her of business?

'You came to me like a bartering barrister. Would you call it anything else?' His eyes were a dark blue, like the roiling Mediterranean Sea during a storm. But his tone was not unkind. A faint stubble shaded his firm jaw and the divot in his chin. His lips were firm and she thought of the pleasure she felt at the touch of his mouth.

Taking her hand, he slipped the ring on her finger. The weight of the gold and gems felt unfamiliar. The man standing before her even more so.

'There is one more item to discuss,' he said, his eyes holding a sheen of purpose.

One more? She couldn't fathom what else he intended other than the officially signed list of requirements and the heavy ring on her hand.

'Your landlady. Mrs Porter, is it?'

Her mind whirled at the change of topic. 'Yes.'

'She told me you are to leave these premises.'

Her cheeks turned hot with embarrassment. 'She told you?'

He ignored the question and looked at her with a strange undisguised heat. 'There is more than ample room in my home.'

Her pulse quickened. 'We are not yet married, and I'm no longer employed as governess. It's improper.'

'Do you frequent society events?'

She almost laughed at the thought. 'No.'

'Then no one will know you are no longer employed as a governess. Meanwhile, I will have that special license in a week's time.'

She startled. 'Next week!' She knew it would be swift, just not that fast.

'You needn't worry. I will see to all the preparations, reserve St George's Church, and arrange the breakfast.' His gaze roved her garb. 'And the dress.'

She was conscious of her gown. Goodness. She could never walk down the aisle wearing practical wool.

'Your trunks are still at my home. Gather whatever you have here and I shall send a footman to come fetch the items later today. Meanwhile, make a list of who you'd like to attend the church. My list is small and includes the Earl of Kent and his sisters.'

The last request was even more disturbing for the simple fact that, other than Ivan, she had no one.

Lena wasn't the only one to return to the Berkeley Square mansion. Claire had returned from her stay with family friends. The efficient housekeeper, Mr Hollins, and the butler, Mr Barnes, had been prepared for her arrival.

Lena met Claire in the breakfast room at seven sharp the following morning, finding Ravenwood seated at the head of the table reading the *Times* and drinking coffee.

'Good morning, Your Grace.' Lena opened her napkin and placed it on her lap.

Claire snapped open her own napkin and reached for her water glass. Dressed in a yellow gown adorned with flowers, she looked young and innocent.

The door opened and household staff entered. A plate of eggs, bacon, toast, and fresh berries was set before Lena. A footman poured hot chocolate in her cup. The staff left as quietly as they'd entered.

Meanwhile, Lena was highly conscious of the silence between niece and uncle. She nudged Claire's elbow and lowered her voice. 'Aren't you going to greet your uncle this morning?'

Claire scrunched her nose, then looked at the duke. 'Good morning, Your Eminence.'

'Claire!' Lena eyed the girl. 'That's no way to address your uncle.'

Ravenwood lifted a hand. 'It's fine. At least she's up and dressed this morning. It isn't always so.'

Lena wasn't sure what to make of their icy relationship. 'I'd like to take Claire shopping to the milliners this morning,' she said. 'She can pick out a bonnet for a stroll in the park.'

'Truly?' Claire looked directly at Lena for the first time since she had entered the dining room.

Ravenwood set down his fork. 'She has pianoforte lessons scheduled for this afternoon.'

Claire stirred in her chair. Lena placed a hand on her sleeve before the girl could open her mouth. 'We shall return well before—'

Claire's fork rattled against the side of her plate, and she glowered at her uncle. 'I hate the pianoforte. I've told you this numerous times, yet you fail to listen.'

Ravenwood's voice was low and laced with steel. 'Music is part of a lady's well-rounded education. In less than two years, you will make your debut.'

Claire raised her chin. 'Mr Tillsdale is an arse. I refuse to come out of my room for his lessons.'

'Claire!' Lena shot the girl another warning glance. Riling the duke's temper would not help her cause.

Claire folded her arms across her chest.

Ravenwood clenched his jaw, making the bones of his face tighten. 'Then there will be no trip to the milliner's this afternoon. You can wait in your room until Mr Tillsdale's arrival.'

'You're a beast!' Claire shoved her chair back and fled the dining room.

A heaviness centered in Lena's chest as she watched the girl flee. As for the duke, they needed to discuss his niece. If Lena was brave enough, that was. She sneaked a peek at his scarred profile and her fingers twisted the napkin in her lap. It was her first day in his home, not as a governess but as a fiancée.

She cleared her throat. 'May we have a word?'

Stormy eyes met hers. Ravenwood tossed his napkin onto his plate. 'If you insist on speaking, then go ahead. I've already lost my appetite.'

Heavens, he could be intimidating. But Lena was never one to back down when she believed she could help.

He arched a dark eyebrow. 'Well?'

Lena's anxiety rose, and she resisted the urge to smooth any wayward curls that may have escaped from her bun. 'I'm sorry for the way Claire spoke to you.' It was best if she started out sympathizing with the man before offering any criticism.

'Startling, isn't it?'

Startling was one way to put it. Terribly rude was another. Ravenwood had every right to punish the girl and not allow her to leave the house. He also had a right to insist she continue with pianoforte lessons. But having a right and forcing Claire to go through with all the items on his 'checklist' did not make it the wise thing to do.

'How do you plan to correct my niece's behaviour?' he asked.

He thought she was the one to fix it? From what she'd

seen, they both needed to work on their behaviour. As well as heal their bruised relationship.

She'd been sixteen once and she'd desperately wanted attention from her father. The marquess had not ignored her, but he hadn't quite acknowledged her either. True, he'd provided for her and paid for the expensive boarding school, which took in many illegitimate daughters of the aristocracy. Yet the marquess had never truly involved himself in her life, never taken the time to learn her interests. To spend an entire day with her. To love her as a father should have—the way she'd desperately longed for.

Lena reached up to push a steel pin in place. 'Claire likes to paint.'

'Pardon?' The duke's gaze followed her movements, and she worried more curls were out of place.

'Have you seen the paintings on the walls in Claire's bedchamber?' she asked.

His brow furrowed. 'What does that have to do with her behaviour?'

'I think you should pay a visit to her room and ask her about her paintings.'

'Why?'

'She must have made them before her parents were killed and—'

'I'm aware of her loss.'

Exasperation made her sit forward in her chair. Her voice rose an octave. 'She wants attention. From you.'

He stilled, and a rare vulnerability flashed in his eyes. 'Don't you think I've tried? I've attempted with Claire, without success, and I believe she would rather not see me. After everything she has gone though, I do not want to cause her more distress.'

Surprised at his reaction, she shifted. 'You're wrong. She needs you.'

He frowned. 'How do you know?'

'Intuition.'

'Intuition?'

'And observation,' she was quick to add.

'I see. Forgive me if I'm a bit skeptical.' His eyes never left her face. 'And what of my rules, Mrs Harper? Do you believe structure will help Claire?'

Her voice was low but level when she replied, 'Rules and structure may have helped you, Your Grace, but they may not be the best way to help Claire.'

Ravenwood tapped long fingers on the arms of his chair. 'I'll make a note of your disapproval.'

Whatever vulnerability she'd seen was gone. His brusque tone told her he had no intention of heeding her. He asked for her advice, then dismissed her suggestions. Her discomfort veered into annoyance, and she straightened in her chair. 'Maybe you can find time this afternoon, Your Grace, *after* Claire and I return from the milliners.'

His eyes flashed at her defiance, and the unscarred corner of his lips twisted upwards. 'I already forbade Claire to leave the house today.'

In her experience, aristocratic men were arrogant, believed their word was law, and did not consider the emotional needs of those they considered beneath them. Her father was cut from the same cloth. The Duke of Ravenwood was worse. He had no idea how to parent. Worse, he didn't want to learn.

She pushed back her chair and stood. 'Banishing Claire to her room will not aid your cause. And your unbending rules will only make things worse.' She was surprised at her own audacity to challenge him. He rose, a massive muscular man almost an entire foot taller than her. She didn't fear him, not before and not now. Maybe she was the foolish one.

'How do you suggest I deal with her disobedience then?' he asked.

'First, it's not healthy to keep a sixteen-year-old girl isolated in this house. Second, like I said, Lady Claire enjoys art. She does not enjoy music. I suggest exchanging the pianoforte lessons for art lessons. Both are perfectly acceptable for young ladies of the *ton*.'

The sudden glimpse of grief in his gaze caused her heart to flutter in her chest. 'You should know her mother was a pianist and had arranged for pianoforte lessons. I am merely following through with her wishes.'

Lena felt as if she were walking on eggshells after he brought up Claire's mother. 'You are her guardian now,' she said softly. 'You must make the best decisions for your niece.'

'How? I never wanted to be a guardian, for Christ's sake.' He scrubbed a hand down his face. He may not have wanted to admit his concerns out loud, but it was the truth. She could not fault him for that, and her anger dissipated. Claire was hurting over the loss of her parents;

the duke had lost his father, brother, and sister-in-law and was wounded just as deeply.

Lena had to handle this argument tactfully. She took a deep breath. 'Claire's mother is no longer here. If she were, she would see her daughter has different interests. Children may start out seeking to please their parents, then find other talents. However difficult, parents must allow their children to pursue what is in their hearts and flourish. Otherwise, you may never know how great Claire could become.'

'How do you know this? You are not a mother.'

His tone was not cruel but simply curious. 'Not yet,' she agreed. 'But I was once Claire's age. My mother was a soprano. A talented singer. There was a group in a neighbouring village in Lebanon who would gather each week and practise. Their performances were local, and townsfolk and family would attend. I started singing, then realized I disliked it. I was not a soprano, nor an alto. I preferred to gather the neighbourhood children and play and read to them. Caring for children is my talent. Finally, and grudgingly, my mother accepted it.' She tilted her head to the side and watched him. 'Haven't you ever disagreed with your father?'

He let out a coarse laugh. 'My father was a strict disciplinarian. I made a career of pursuing ladies and pleasure.'

Her eyes narrowed. 'Then how did you end up in the army?'

'My father purchased my commission and put me there.'

'Then you should understand how children's interests

can differ from their parents. As for Claire, she clearly prefers art over piano.'

'And you think I should allow Claire to follow her heart, as you say?'

'I think you should see her room.' At his silence, she sensed she was finally making her case. Reaching out, she placed a hand on his arm and offered him an encouraging smile. 'Like I said, ask her about her artwork, Your Grace. But do so *after* we return from our shopping trip.'

Chapter Eight

Ravenwood met the Earl of Kent at Jonathan's Coffee House in the Strand. Coffee had quickly become a popular beverage, and Jonathan's was busy with merchants, jobbers, stockbrokers, and aristocrats all mingling to discuss trades in the London Stock Exchange or to read the latest newspaper editions. Every table was occupied this morning and several servers wove among the tables carrying trays of the steaming drink.

Kent took his coffee black and Ravenwood preferred it with sugar and cream.

'You are the only reason I'm up this blasted early,' Kent said. 'So what is so important?'

Ravenwood added a second lump of sugar to his cup. 'I'm getting married. I'd like you to stand by my side.'

Kent eyed him like he had two heads. 'Pardon?'

'I said—'

'I heard what you said. I'm digesting it.' Kent sipped his coffee.

Ravenwood assessed his friend. 'You sound like you had a bad meal.'

'You don't leave your house to attend Society functions. Where the bloody hell did you find a bride so fast?'

Ravenwood decided on the truth. 'She proposed to me. She is…*was*…the sixth governess.'

Kent choked on his coffee, then set it down. 'Go on.'

'Mrs Harper set forth a logical argument to marry. She wants a child. I need an heir. Like me, she seeks a marriage of convenience. She also promises to care for Claire like her own. After a son is born, we both live our own lives. So, you see, her offer is unique.'

'And you accepted this proposal?' Kent asked.

'Yes.'

'I would think you'd seek a titled lady with a noble bloodline as your duchess.'

'I know all about Mrs Harper's lineage. She is the illegitimate daughter of a marquess and a Middle Eastern lady. I had my man of affairs investigate her background before the employment agent sent her to me as a governess for Claire.'

Kent watched him. 'And it doesn't concern you?'

'No. I understand the aristocracy is consumed with pedigrees and memorizes *Debrett's* for fun. After my time abroad fighting beside commoners—some of the best men I've ever known—I do not care about her bloodline. Or what the ridiculous *ton* thinks. War has a way of changing one's perspective.'

'I know you and I know you would never agree to anything that you didn't want to,' Kent pointed out.

'So?'

'So I must meet your bride to be.'

'You will. At the wedding.'

Kent pinched his nose with a thumb and forefinger 'No. Beforehand.'

'Why is it important to you?' He *wanted* to marry Lena, had made up his mind. He'd initially surprised himself by accepting her offer. Now, after more consideration, he wanted to speed up the date and had inquired about the special license.

'I told you. I'd like to meet the woman who convinced my impossible friend to marry.' Kent said. 'What about Claire?'

'Lena will guide her through her first Season. I will do what is required of me and attend any functions to help the girl find a match.'

'That's it? Claire's debut and an heir? Then you will be free of her and she of you?'

'Precisely.'

Kent rested his elbow on the table and shook his head. 'Not particularly romantic, are you?'

'Romance is for foolish poets. I have no room in my life for such nonsense.' He grew agitated. He was determined to keep it a businesslike relationship and not let his bride into his heart. He was damaged, broken, and the last thing he wanted was an emotional obstacle. Happiness was not in his future. 'Why are you still looking at me as if I'm in need of advice?'

'Because,' Kent said, 'I cannot fathom how a man who used to attract women like bees to honey turned into a beast. You must woo your fiancée.'

'Funny you should say that. She insists upon spending

time together in her list of requirements.' He didn't mention that she wanted to wait to be intimate a full week *after* the wedding.

'She has a list?'

'She is quite the negotiator.' He admired her grit and determination. The way she had negotiated regarding his niece spoke volumes as well. She believed in herself, and he saw how she wanted to help Claire.

Kent sat forward in his chair. 'I'm adamant about meeting her. Is tomorrow too soon?'

'You know it is. I haven't even begun this wooing. I'm not even sure where to begin.'

'You used to be quite the lady's man. How did you do it then?'

Ravenwood scrubbed a hand down his face. 'Christ, it was a lifetime ago. And Lena is different.' He couldn't imagine sneaking her into the gardens during a party to kiss her.

Memories of their kiss returned in a rush. He'd kissed her to prove a point, yet it had turned out to be much, much more. It had taken every ounce of willpower to pull away from her.

'First,' Kent said, 'I would point out the favourable qualities in the lady. Her eyes. Her manners. How she gets along with your niece, Claire, when so many other governesses have failed. And most importantly, how she makes you *feel* when you are with her.'

'She doesn't look at me with disgust.' Ravenwood touched his scar. Kent didn't look away. It hadn't always been that way. After his return from abroad, it had taken a while before his friend could fully face him without pity. Only one other had regarded him directly without a bit of revulsion.

As for how he felt when he was with her…

Different. Not repulsive. From the first day, she'd looked him in the eye and had challenged him. The kitten, the excursion to the milliners' shop, and the protest of Claire's piano lessons were just a few ways Lena had fiercely expressed her opinions, and looking back, he'd welcomed them. He'd thought it refreshing. She hadn't cowered from his fierce frown or run from the room in feminine hysterics.

In truth, it had been a long time since he'd felt *alive.*

How would she challenge him next?

He was more attracted to his fiancée than he should be. He may have accepted her proposal and welcomed her into his home, but he would keep his emotional distance, no matter the cost.

Lena knocked once on Claire's door. 'Claire, darling, we're going to the milliners.'

The door cracked open. Claire stood there, her eyes puffy and red-rimmed. 'You plan to defy my uncle?'

Lena shook her head. 'I convinced him to agree.'

Claire opened the door wide for Lena to enter. The girl crossed the room and sat on the side of the bed, then pushed a lock of dark hair from her tear-stained cheek. 'Why on earth would you agree to marry my uncle?'

Lena leaned against the chest of drawers. 'It's more like he agreed to marry me.'

Claire pursed her lips. 'Is he that desperate?'

The insult was as loud as a trumpet blast. Rather than rise to the bait and say something she'd regret, Lena arranged a silver-handled hairbrush and comb on the chest of drawers before facing the girl. 'Claire, I truly hope we can get along.'

'You need money, don't you? My papa used to say everything is about money. He married my mother for her dowry.'

Those that had money never understood what it was like to live without it. But it wasn't just about financial security. She also wanted children, longed for them, and the duke needed one. So how could she explain everything to a young lady?

'Claire, I—'

Claire's chin turned up a notch. 'I won't make your time here easier. I will still call you Number Six.'

'That's horribly disrespectful.'

'I won't call you aunt, either,' Claire said.

'I would not ask that of you.'

'Then what am I to call you? Your Grace? Duchess? Or heaven forbid, stepmama?' The last name was delivered with more disdain than the titles.

Lena clasped her hands before her and inwardly prayed for patience. 'How about Lena. At least when we are alone together.'

Claire pursed her lips. 'How did you get my uncle to agree to anything, let alone shopping?'

'With logic.' *And bravery.*

'Simple logic? I don't believe you.'

'It's true. I've succeeded twice now.'

'Twice!'

It was time to use all the weapons in her arsenal. 'First, the milliners. Second…' She hesitated, then offered a small smile. 'I found an abandoned kitten outside the house, and he let me keep it.'

Claire's eyes grew wide. 'A kitten! How? He disapproves of pets.'

'I convinced him of the benefits. The kitten will earn its keep by catching mice.'

Claire slid off the bed to her feet, her eyes tearless now. 'Where is it? I want to see the kitten.'

Lena went to the door and held it open. 'She's in my room.'

Claire was on Lena's heels as they entered her bedchamber. The girl cried out in delight at the sight of the kitten curled atop the coverlet on the bed. She scooped the animal into her arms, stroked her under her chin, then kissed the top of her head. The feline opened sleepy green eyes and released a satisfied purr.

Claire's eyes were bright as she smiled at Lena. All signs that she had spent the last hour crying were gone. 'I love her! What's her name?'

Ravenwood had asked Lena the same question last night. She wasn't any closer to naming the cat. 'Would you like to name her?'

'Me?' A hint of wonder tinged her voice.

'Why not?'

Claire smiled down at the kitten in her arms. 'I'll name

her Bella! She is shiny and black with white socks and beautiful. Her green eyes are lovely, too.'

'Perfect. Bella it is.'

Clearly reluctant to release the kitten, Claire sat on the bed and held it. 'I want to know how to change my uncle's mind. I told the truth about the pianoforte lessons. I hate practising just as much as I despise Mr Tillsdale, my instructor.'

'I agree the pianoforte is not for everyone, but a lady does need some artistic pursuit. I noticed the lovely paintings on your bedchamber walls. I particularly like the vase of pink and yellow flowers. It reminds me of springtime.'

'I was happy when I painted it.' The girl's eyes glazed over, and Lena knew she was thinking of earlier days. Lena knew she herself looked the same whenever she thought of her mother and their home in Lebanon. There, the sun always seemed to be shining and the smells and sights of market day were like a colourful blanket. England was a world away.

'Will you teach me how to get around the duke, Mrs Harper?'

'Lena,' she corrected. As for Claire's question, she wasn't exactly certain. All she did know was that Ravenwood had accepted her proposal. And he'd allowed her to keep the cat.

'Lena,' Claire said slowly as if practising the name. 'You shall no longer be known as just Number Six.'

The significance of Claire using her name was not lost on her. 'When the duke visits, talk about your paintings. Let him see your artwork through *your* eyes.'

'You think he'll visit?'

'I hope so. Now, would you like to go shopping?'

Claire's smile was bright. 'I'd like to go *anywhere.*'

Chapter Nine

The Bond Street milliners were busy with ladies trying on an array of bonnets, turbans, and hats. Claire removed a straw bonnet adorned with silk daisies from a stand and wound the silk ribbon around her fingers.

Claire set down the daisy-adorned bonnet and reached for another, this one trimmed with blue ribbons the exact shade of her eyes. She slipped on the bonnet and looked at her reflection in a small looking glass on the counter. 'How do I look?' she asked Lena.

'Lovely.' The girl was pretty, especially when she smiled. Lena wanted to learn more about her. 'Do you go shopping often?'

'No.'

She didn't seem to do much at all. Lena wanted to know more about her relationship with her uncle. 'Does the duke prohibit you from leaving home?'

Claire took off the bonnet. 'He never said specifically that I wasn't to leave. But he also has never offered to escort me anywhere. The other governesses never bothered.'

Claire looked a bit sheepish before adding, 'They never stayed long.'

'Well, that changes now,' Lena said. 'A young lady needs to have friends and enjoy a bit of what London has to offer.'

Claire's voice was a whisper. 'I had two good friends before…a while ago.'

Lena's heart squeezed. The girl meant before the fire and when her parents were alive. 'We will have to invite your friends over one day for tea and girl talk.'

Claire shook her head and wrapped the ribbons around her fingers. The ribbons would soon be wrinkled from the way she worked them. 'I don't know if that is a good idea. I don't want them to look at me differently.'

'How so?'

Claire lowered her voice. 'With pity.'

Lena's stomach tightened. Life was terribly unfair. No one knew this more than she. But the notion that Claire had friends—good friends that cared for her enough to worry—was a wonderful gift. 'If they show sympathy, it is only because they love you and miss you. Loyal friends are hard to come by.'

She thought of Ivan. He was her best friend and very loyal. Oh, she'd had friends at the girls' school. But once she'd married, they'd lost touch. Oliver had isolated her and wanted her to focus her attention on him and entertaining the businessmen he'd occasionally invited to their home. Ivan refused to give up on her and would rap on the servants' door and ask to see Lena. She'd gotten into a routine of spending time with him each week. He would talk about the jobber he secretly adored, and Lena would share about helping run their household. Lena thought it ironic that Ivan fell in love with a man who worked at the Exchange, since Oliver had worked at the Exchange as well.

Another part of Lena, a secret part, didn't want to keep in touch with her school friends after marrying Oliver. She'd been unhappy with her marriage and, over time, had grown depressed.

She didn't want that for Claire. Lena knew from experience that isolation led to melancholy.

'What are your friends' names?' Lena asked.

'Harriet and Abigail.'

'Then we must be sure to invite both to visit. They will likely express their sympathies, but soon they will want just to spend time with you and go on as you all had in the past.'

Claire's eyes widened. 'You think so?'

'I do.'

Claire made her selections of bonnets—the clerk was delighted to serve the Duke of Ravenwood's niece—and all purchases were charged to his account. Packages in hand, they returned to the mansion. Just as Mr Barnes took their cloaks, the duke walked into the vestibule.

Lena's heart beat faster as his tall figure approached. With his vivid blue eyes, aquiline nose, and skin taut over the elegant ridge of his cheekbones, she could easily see how women had been drawn to him. Unscarred, his arresting good looks must have drawn the eye. Scarred and stern, his darkness drew Lena even more. Soon they would marry, and he'd have the right to visit her bedchamber. The right to take off her gown, touch her…make love to her.

Goodness. She resisted the urge to press a hand to her cheeks.

The corner of Ravenwood's unscarred lip curled upwards as he halted before them. 'Good afternoon, ladies. Did you enjoy your shopping trip?'

Lena's already heightened emotions soared at his unexpected smile, and she swallowed. 'As promised, we are back in time for the pianoforte lessons.'

'Yes, Mr Tillsdale is expected any moment,' Ravenwood said.

Claire's eyes flashed and her lips parted, but Lena grasped the girl's hand and shook her head. She lowered her head to whisper in the girl's ear. 'One cannot win a war in one battle.'

If Ravenwood heard her, he didn't speak of it. 'Go on ahead upstairs Claire,' he said. 'I need a word alone with Mrs Harper.'

Claire halted at the first step, her fingers tight on the balustrade. A second passed, then she turned to face Lena. 'I'll feed Bella,' she said, then stomped up the stairs.

Ravenwood's lips twitched as turned his attention to Lena. 'I can only assume you decided upon a name for the cat.'

'Claire named her, Your Grace. Right before we went shopping.'

'I see.'

That was it? No additional protests about the cat? He simply watched Lena with unwavering eyes. A shiver of anxiety travelled down her spine at his attention. 'You wanted a word?'

She followed him into his study. Meeting him in his domain was becoming too common. Again, she sat in the armchair across from his desk. The springs of his leather chair creaked as he settled.

Her fingers twisted the strings of her reticule on her lap as her nervousness grew. 'Claire selected two lovely bonnets and a turban. I believe she may be too young for the turban, but she had great fun trying it on and will use it when she comes of age.' She knew the Duke would have little concern for the hats Claire had chosen; she was rambling.

He steepled his fingers on the blotter of his desk as he watched her. 'You did not purchase a bonnet for yourself?'

She shifted, taken aback at the question. 'Today was for Claire… Do you feel we spent too much?'

'You misunderstand. I don't care about expenses. I want you to spend more. You should have purchased yourself several hats, shoes, fripperies, and anything else a lady might require.' His attention lowered to her dress. 'And please feel free to do something about those gowns.'

Her prior nervousness turned into irritation. 'They are perfectly respectable garments.'

'Even a schoolmarm would be hard-pressed to wear *that*.'

She let out a huff. She'd never admit that, even as they spoke, the cheap wool itched her neck.

'I have arranged for you to visit a Bond Street dressmaker,' he added gently. 'It's the one Claire's mother used and is frequented by the ladies of the *beau monde*.'

She pondered the request. 'I do need a wedding dress.'

'You need much more than that.'

Rather than continue to be offended, a knot formed in her stomach. A different kind of anxiousness. She may have had nice clothing in Lebanon as a child, but that experience was entirely different from an exclusive London dressmaker that served High Society ladies. When she attended the girls' school, the headmistress oversaw the students' clothing and oftentimes merchants would deliver items. She wasn't a lady by birth, and during her first marriage, she'd purchased clothing in shops far from Bond Street.

Her life was different now. Ravenwood may be known as a recluse, but he was still a duke, and she'd soon become his duchess. She'd need all the advice she could get, and if this dressmaker was as exclusive as he said, then the woman would know best regarding clothing.

'I shall escort you to the dressmakers, then leave you in her hands,' he said.

Could he read her nervousness? Was his offer to escort her to alleviate her concerns?

'I would think you are busy with other things.' Surely a duke would have a long list of more pressing obligations.

'I said I'd take you, not that I'd stay. I have business to attend.' He opened a desk drawer and handed her a piece of foolscap. 'As for other items you require, take this note and show it to any merchant. You will not be questioned and can make your purchases.'

Her brows gathered as she held the note. 'Is there a limit?'

'No.'

She looked up at him. 'No? You are offering me license to put you in the poorhouse.'

The scarred lip turned upwards. 'Highly unlikely. Plan to purchase whatever you require.' He raked his gaze over her. 'And then burn that dress.'

Ravenwood needed to stop thinking of his wife-to-be.

Sunlight streamed in the windows of the coach as it rumbled through the streets, taking them towards Bond Street. The light caressed Lena, highlighting her olive skin and mahogany hair. Her profile was lovely—thick lashes shielding dark eyes, a slender nose, and full, rounded lips over straight teeth. The more time he spent with her, the more he was convinced that she was far from governess material.

Of course, he'd noticed her the first time she'd appeared to fill the position. Dripping wet, he couldn't help seeing the shapely form beneath her 'uniform.' Had she lasted in the position, he'd have found it difficult to stay away. He never dallied with the servants or those in his employ, but he'd realized she was vastly different the moment he'd caught her from beneath the tree. If she knew his thoughts, she'd have the upper hand, and he couldn't allow that.

She was a complete mystery. One moment she challenged him, refusing to accept his decisions. She took Claire shopping even though he'd forbidden it. She insisted that he visit Claire's room to see her artwork, then suggested he let go the girl's pianoforte teacher and instead hire an art teacher. She'd faced him with more bravery than any junior officer.

'Do you think many ladies will be present in the shop?' she asked.

She faced him across the carriage. Just as he'd believed her fearless, anxiety crossed her lovely features—a sweet vulnerability that made him want to be a better man and ease her fears.

'Ladies? I suppose so. It is a modiste,' he said.

He took in her features, from the delicate arches of her eyebrows, thick lashes shielding entrancing dark eyes, to her full lips. He wanted to remove her hairpins and let down her tresses. Touch her hair as he kissed her. Unbutton the gown and bury his face in her breasts. Would her nipples be a darker shade or pale pink? He knew her curves to be ample, he had felt them when he'd briefly caught her beneath the tree.

Unease flashed in the dark depths of her eyes. 'Do you think they'll stare?'

Bloody hell. If she knew his wayward thoughts, she'd flee from the carriage before it came to a full stop.

They *should* stare. She was more beautiful than most. As Kent had pointed out, Lena may have proposed, but he never did anything he didn't want to.

'I think you shouldn't care,' he said.

'Why?'

She asked too many questions. 'They are not worth your concern.'

She pursed her full lips. 'Once we are married, I

will have to attend their balls and host dinner parties of my own.'

'You don't have to attend anything. And if you decide not to host a damned event, all the better.' His voice sounded harsh to his own ears. He was trying hard not to focus on her mouth and her pursed lips. They were full and pink and tempting and...

'But you are forgetting Claire,' she pointed out. 'And your agreement to help with her debut. Until then, acting the hermit is impossible.'

There it was again. Her spirit and defiance. She didn't call him a beast, like the gossip-mongers. Still, he'd rather have her irritated than vulnerable and anxious.

'You did it on purpose.' A tiny frown creased her brow, and she sat back on the bench seat. 'You agitated me because you know I'm concerned about the dressmaker.' A small smile curled her lips. 'You are not as cold-hearted as you want others to believe.'

He held his breath, not sure if it was her smile or her words that made his chest tighten. He couldn't allow her to get too close. It was for the best, for her protection. The truth was, he *was* a beast and the demons of war had never left him, never would. He deserved every damn nightmare.

The wheels of the carriage rolled to a stop.

Thank God. He glanced outside the window to a wooden sign with the image of a mannequin. Madame Nadine's Dress Shop. He wanted out of the carriage. He needed to put distance between them before she could ask more questions, before her sharp mind analysed him. Not waiting for his driver, he hopped down, lowered the step himself, and held out his hand for Lena. She slipped her gloved hand into his larger one as he helped her down. When her lowered eyes raised to meet his gaze, his heart thundered.

'You must not be concerned about cost,' he said. Before she could answer, he opened the door to the shop. A little bell chimed as they walked inside. Bolts of fabric from pale pastels to dark jewel tones were arranged on tables in a colourful array. Mannequins displayed day dresses, riding habits, and evening gowns. Two ladies flipped through sketches at the counter.

A back room curtain opened and a tall, red-haired woman with a measuring tape draped around her neck approached. 'I am Madame Nadine. How may I help you?' A hint of a French accent lingered in the modiste's voice. He wondered if it was real or affected. Either way, it didn't matter. She was supposed to be the best and he would settle for nothing less.

When Ravenwood turned to fully face her, the dressmaker flinched, first noticing his scarred side. A true professional, she was quick to recover. Unperturbed, he was accustomed to the reaction. However, Lena, by his side, stiffened. Clearly, she was not.

'My fiancée needs a wedding dress,' he said. 'She will also need a trousseau and a complete wardrobe.'

The dressmaker's gaze travelled over Lena from head to toe before returning to him. 'When is the wedding?'

'One week.'

She gasped. 'A week! I'm afraid that is impossible, sir. My schedule is full. You should visit a different dressmaker. I can recommend—

He expected the argument. 'My sister-in-law, God rest her soul, was Lady Ravenwood, and she frequented here.'

Madame Nadine's eyes widened. 'Your sister-in-law is…was—'

'I am now the Duke of Ravenwood, and this—' he touched Lena's gloved hand '—is my duchess-to-be.' He despised using his title. After all, the estate was never supposed to be his and was a constant reminder of his father's and brother's untimely deaths.

Once again, the dressmaker turned her attention to Lena, only this time the scrutiny was combined with keen curiosity. To be in charge of a successful shop catering to the *ton*, Madame Nadine must be a shrewd business-woman.

'I'm honored,' the woman said, 'but as I said, a week is too short a time and I have many orders to fulfill.'

'Money is not an object, Madame. My bride must have the best. Name your price.'

The dressmaker raised dyed red eyebrows that matched her hair. She glanced at the bolts of fabric on display before returning to his. No doubt she was calculating how much to overcharge him. Normally, he didn't tolerate being swindled. As an officer, he'd often had to negotiate to get the equipment he needed and the basics for his men. Coats, boots, and food. All were in short supply. But in this case, he'd told the truth. He wanted the best for Lena and he was willing to pay.

'I will have to hire an additional seamstress. It will cost,' Madame Nadine said.

'I have no doubt.'

'It will be at least double,' she warned.

'I expected nothing less.'

Standing beside him, Lena stiffened. He was aware of the movement but focused on negotiating with the dressmaker 'Very well. Do you have anything specific in mind, Your Grace?'

'I prefer bold colours. But a pale blue for the wedding dress.' He turned towards her. 'If that is to your liking…?'

Lena let out a gasp.

He lowered his voice. 'What is it?'

The heavy lashes that shadowed her cheeks flew up. 'I'm just surprised.'

He should know better than to ask but did anyway. 'Surprised I have an opinion?'

'Well…yes. I would never have guessed you had colour preferences for my dresses, let alone for the wedding gown.'

Hell, he was surprised himself. He longed to see her in lovely colours that suited her complexion. He didn't like going out, but when they did, he would be proud to have her on his arm…especially if she felt beautiful next to him.

Lena went through sketches with the dressmaker. 'A complete wardrobe requires morning dresses, carriage dresses, riding outfits, dinner gowns, and ball gowns.' Madame Nadine reached behind the counter to produce swatches of colourful silk, taffeta, velvet, brocade, damask, chintz, sarcenet, and muslin. Then there were the adornments—lace, spangles, and tulle.

'Oh, my,' Lena said. 'Everything is so lovely.'

He watched her as she touched swatches of fabrics, her

expression one of rapt wonder. He was jealous of the way she caressed each material, her slender fingers lingering on silk, satin, and velvets. What would it feel like to have her touch his flesh?

Jesus. He needed to get a better hold of himself. He forced his attention to the sketches.

'Her measurements need to be taken. Will you stay, Your Grace?' Madame Nadine asked.

He shook his head, clearing his throat. He'd accomplished his goal. 'I have business to attend to and will return in a while.'

Chapter Ten

As soon as the shop's bells chimed and Ravenwood departed, the dressmaker planted her hands on her hips, eyed Lena's dress once more, and clucked her tongue. 'Oh, dear. Could you have chosen a more unflattering dress?'

Did everyone believe her gowns were horrid? Her garments were premade, and selections limited. Nothing she owned was as expensive or luxurious as the garments displayed on the mannequins. Still, Lena grew defensive and felt the need to explain. 'Before my betrothal I was a governess.'

'A governess? Interesting. I never expected the Duke of Ravenwood to walk into my shop. You are quite special.'

'I apologize for how demanding His Grace was,' Lena said.

'Nonsense. At first, I was taken aback only because we have little time before the wedding, but it can be done.'

'He should still pay.' Not long ago, Lena was a working woman.

Madame Nadine's smile reached her eyes. 'Oh, I said

double, but since he has no idea what my prices are, I shall charge him exorbitantly.'

Lena laughed. The dressmaker was surprisingly candid.

'Now, as for your wardrobe.' Madame Nadine tapped her chin with a forefinger. 'As a governess, I can understand not drawing attention to yourself in an aristocratic household. But now you are entering a different part of your life. As a duchess, all eyes will be riveted upon you as soon as you step foot outside your carriage and into a room.'

Lena swallowed. She'd insisted Ravenwood attend events in preparation for Claire's debut in two years' time. She wanted to give Claire every possible advantage and she had the girl in mind when she'd drafted her list of requirements. She just hadn't thought through the consequences of those appearances for *herself*.

'You are nervous about becoming a duchess, no?' the dressmaker asked.

Lena understood why the modiste was one of the most sought-after by the *ton*. She had a shrewd intuition that made her successful.

'If you dress the part, confidence will follow,' Madame Nadine said gently. 'As far as I'm concerned, a working woman such as yourself will appreciate the title and everything that goes along with it more than those who have been born into the aristocracy.'

She was grateful for the woman's kindness. She expected the dressmaker knew how to cater to her clients, but she seemed genuine. Lena liked her.

'Now, how did a governess get tangled up with the elusive Duke of Ravenwood? You are aware of his reputation, of course?' the dressmaker asked.

'Do you mean why he isolates himself in his mansion? I suspect it has something to do with the war.' The evening he'd expected her for dinner, then failed to join her came to mind. When the housekeeper had told her not to ask questions, Lena hadn't understood *why*. She still didn't. She needed to inquire more from the staff as to the duke's behaviour.

As for Madame Nadine, the dressmaker served ladies far above Lena's station, and she must have heard rumours. She also knew that the woman's success depended on being discreet with her clients' private business. 'It must be strange for me to ask,' Lena said, 'since I'm his fiancée, but can you tell me why they call him a beast?'

Madame Nadine ran her fingers through her measuring tape. 'They say his regiment took heavy losses. And that Ravenwood himself was gravely wounded and did not return home straightaway. His scar is not the only injury he incurred.'

'What do you mean?'

'I do not have direct knowledge of Ravenwood. But I've heard of those returning from war only to have the army put them in institutions for war sickness. Others ending up as beggars on the street. And then some have thrown themselves into the Thames.'

Lena wasn't ignorant of this fact, and she'd seen one or two former soldiers in the street begging for coin. One in particular had been near her former home and had been a former sailor in the King's Navy. She knew of others closer to home as well. Ivan had mentioned his cousin suffered after returning from war and that his behaviour could be unpredictable at times.

'As for Ravenwood,' the dressmaker said, 'he has the means to—'

'To isolate himself and avoid society?'

'Perhaps, one day, you can ask him about his time in the army.'

Lena let out a sigh. 'Perhaps.' If she were brave enough to propose marriage, she should be able to ask him about his military experiences. But that seemed different, somehow even more personal, and the man was as approachable as a sleeping tiger.

The modiste slipped the measuring tape from around her neck. 'Now, we have little time and must get started at once.' Madame Nadine clapped her hands. 'Marie, Martha, Marion, and Marre!' On command, four young assistants rushed from a back room, halting before their boss. 'We have work to do. A duke's wedding is in less than a week's time. A full wardrobe and undergarments are needed.'

All four assistants simultaneously gasped.

Lena was whisked away to a back room and stripped of her gown. Garbed only in her shift, she stepped upon a pedestal in front of a cheval dressing glass. The dressmaker began taking Lena's measurements.

'Stand straight. Shoulders back.' Madame Nadine barked orders like a colonel herself. 'My job will be easy. With your raven hair, olive skin, and lush figure, you will look stunning in many colours.'

Stunning? Lena never sought to be the center of attention. But Ravenwood was turning out to be different than she'd expected. Her pulse beat faster whenever he was near, and he'd proved she was far from frigid with a single, mesmerizing kiss.

Madame Nadine snatched a scrap of red silk from an overflowing basket and held it up to Lena's face. She then swapped it for a bright blue, then pale yellow. 'Bright jewel colours as well as pastels both look lovely with your colouring.'

Feminine vanity surfaced and she experienced a slight thrill. She'd never had much opportunity to dress up in her life with Oliver. Would Ravenwood see her differently? Did she want him to?

Yes, I do.

He'd only thought of her as a dull governess, swathed in heavy, unattractive wool. What would he think if he saw her in one of the dresses on display in the shop? Would he notice her as a woman, not just a business partner who had proposed a marriage of convenience? An unsettling moment made her shift on the pedestal. Did she want the duke to see her as more than a bride of convenience? Desire could pose a risk to her heart.

Once her measurements were taken, the assistants left to work as swiftly as they'd appeared. 'You must go to a shoemaker for proper footwear and a milliner for matching hats and bonnets. There are also shops for leather riding gloves and satin gloves for balls,' Madame Nadine instructed.

'Is this all necessary?'

'You are fortunate the duke spared no expense. Each

piece of a lady's trousseau is exciting to select,' Madame Nadine said.

'Everything is lovely,' Lena said.

The dressmaker brought forth a nightgown made of a wisp of silk that would appear almost transparent in the candlelight. Lena felt herself blush. She'd never worn anything as tantalizing.

'The duke selected something similar,' Madame Nadine murmured. 'You will make for a lovely new bride.'

He had? She couldn't imagine wearing it for a man. 'I'm a widow.' She wasn't sure why she confessed this truth.

The dressmaker halted, a pin in hand. 'You must have been a child bride, one who had little choice in the say of your husband. Now you are a woman who can make her own decisions. A wise woman who will be a duchess.'

'You flatter me,' Lena said.

Madame Nadine waved a hand. 'A lady's wedding day is always special, no matter how many times she walks down an aisle. Now, the wedding will be here before you can snap your fingers, and we have no time to waste. Meanwhile, until everything is sewn, I have a dress for you that is much more appropriate than that that dreadful grey one. A lady never came back for her fitting. You are slimmer, and with a few quick alterations no one will be the wiser. I'll fetch it.'

The dressmaker slipped from behind the curtain, leaving Lena alone. She eyed her drab gown waiting on the hook, dreading putting it back on. She was grateful for whatever dress the dressmaker would wrap for her to take home today. Suddenly, a week seemed too long to own an entire new wardrobe.

Just then, the bell above the shop's door tinkled. Lena could hear two ladies conversing with Madame Nadine. They followed the dressmaker into the curtained area.

'Please wait here, ladies, until I will return with your gowns for a final fitting,' Madame Nadine instructed.

Lena peeked outside the curtain to see the backs of two women, one blonde and the other brunette.

'Did you hear the Duke of Ravenwood is betrothed?' the brunette asked as she perused a small table of Brussels lace.

Lena grew alert at the mention of the duke, ducking farther behind the curtain to shield herself from view. From her vantage point, she only caught glimpses of their hair colour.

The blonde looked up from the same table. 'Ravenwood? Are you certain?' The blonde's voice seemed familiar, but Lena couldn't quite place it. Her voice was a lower octave than the brunette's, almost husky.

'I forgot you had a *tendre* for the man before he'd inherited the title. And before he'd returned from war,' the brunette said.

'It was a little more than a decade ago.' The blonde sighed. 'Still, the man was hard to forget.'

Lena's stomach tightened at the mention of Ravenwood's prior experiences with the woman. Who was she? Lena could only see the back of the blonde's head and willed her to turn around.

'He was quite the rogue. I was envious of his attention

towards you. Rumours of his prowess were legendary.' This from the brunette.

The blonde laughed. 'In that instance, the rumours were true. I never left his bed unsatisfied.'

The brunette shrugged. 'Ravenwood has changed since his return from the Continent. Other than his clubs, the man is rarely seen outside his home and has a dark reputation.'

The fair-haired woman spoke with a facile tongue. 'In the past, Ravenwood could have his pick of women. He must be lonely now in that great house all by himself... I have a mind to seek him out.'

Lena's hands fisted at her sides. She'd known about Ravenwood's past reputation as a rogue, but to hear it from these women made her uncomfortable. She didn't like to imagine him with another, especially the cold blonde.

'What about his scars? His pretty face is not as it was,' the brunette said.

'I'm no longer fickle. Besides, his manhood was not injured, only his face.' The other woman chuckled. 'After tolerating two husbands' inadequacies, I can overlook the superficial.' The blonde hesitated. 'Who is the bride to be?'

The brunette scoffed. 'His lady is not a lady. My maid heard it from one of the servants in Ravenwood's home. His betrothed is a widow and was hired as his niece's governess.'

A gasp from the blonde. 'An ambitious, title-seeking widow?'

Lena took offence at that description. She was never after the duke's title or his fortune.

'Her mother was from some far-off country in the Middle East,' the brunette responded. 'She has mixed blood, not entirely English.'

Lena's chest tightened at the women's blatant prejudice. Her mother had been a loving, kind woman, much better than either of these two vipers.

'She must have learned harem tricks and is skilled in the bedroom for the duke to lower his standards and taint his bloodline to marry a half-Arab woman.' The blonde let out a cruel laugh.

Lena was aghast, and anger bubbled in her chest from the hateful gossip. She'd previously experienced this prejudice firsthand. Oliver had often insulted and looked down upon her heritage.

'Will you pay him a visit?' the brunette asked.

'Both of my husbands were unskilled and boring in the bedroom. Finally, as a widow, I want adventure and pleasure. What better way than to seek out a former lover?'

Not if I have a say about it! Lena's jaw clenched and her initial dislike of the blonde tripled. The fact the woman would even think to pursue a man engaged to another spoke volumes about her character. Lena felt she had every right to be incensed.

Only she didn't, not really. She had agreed to a marriage of mutual convenience with Ravenwood. They hadn't spoken of anything other than her taking Claire under her wing and the progression of the title. His life was his own. He hadn't insisted she stay faithful after an heir was born, nor had she insisted he not stray.

Then why did she have to restrain herself from bursting forward and confronting his former lover? Demanding she stay away from the duke?

Because Lena was now a different woman than the one she'd been in her first marriage, and she would not repeat the same mistakes from her past. Older, wiser, no longer meek, or beholden to her father's will or Oliver's machinations. She would fight for what she wanted.

'Wait!' The blonde's voice rose an octave. 'What did you say her name was? I wonder if…'

Sweeping the curtain aside, dressed only in her shift, Lena confronted the two startled women. 'You want to know my name? Mrs Lena Harper, fiancée to the Duke of Ravenwood.'

Both ladies gaped in surprise. The brunette pressed a hand to her chest. Lena turned to face the blonde for the first time.

She blinked. Once. Twice. A strange buzzing sounded in her head and her vision blacked in the corners. She resisted the urge to press a hand to her forehead. Was she fevered? Hallucinating?

No. She took a deep breath, and the woman came back into focus. As well as Lena's composure. She couldn't say who was more surprised.

'You!' was all Lena could muster. No wonder the voice had seemed oddly familiar. It had been years, and she'd shoved it out of her mind.

How could this be happening!

The blonde exhaled, seeming to regain her composure as well. 'Lady Beth, may I introduce you to my former stepdaughter.'

Francesca, Lady Powell, the wife of her father the Marquess of Grisham, was older, thirty-seven years compared to Lena's twenty-seven, but still beautiful. She wore what had to be one of Madame Nadine's creations, an exquisite form-hugging dress that artfully emphasized her slim waist. Honey-blond curls were piled upon her head. Her eyes were cornflower blue, and her lips painted pink. She was everything Lena was not. Fair, perfectly dressed, and bloody rich.

'Your stepdaughter?' Lady Beth, who was also well-dressed, placed a hand on the blonde's sleeve in support.

'Stepmother?' Lena nearly spat. 'I never called you by that name.'

From what Lena had heard, she'd swiftly remarried another aristocrat, the Earl of Powell, once her father passed.

The first time Lena had seen Francesca was when the marquess had brought her to his home at the tender age of ten. Lena's mother had died weeks before and it was her wish for her daughter to leave Lebanon and live with her English father in London. It could have worked.

If not for the woman standing before her.

I won't have your bastard living beneath our roof, Lena had overheard the lady tell her father when she'd arrived in England.

The last time Lena saw the marchioness was at her father's funeral. Lena was instructed not to sit with the family in the front row at the grave-site, but to stand in the back. She'd strained to see and hear the priest as he spoke, and she was not to place a rose on his casket before it was lowered into the ground.

Why did *this* woman have to be Ravenwood's former lover? It may have been well over fifteen years ago that they'd had an affair. Well before Ravenwood had joined his Regiment. Well before he'd advanced to Lieutenant Colonel. And well before Waterloo and her marriage to Lena's father.

Still, Lena's dislike of the woman remained. And if she intended to seduce Ravenwood, then Lena's feelings were more than justified.

Lena raised her chin and placed her hands on her hips. 'I overheard everything. Seek another lover.'

Francesca's eyes turned icy. 'You were a thorn in my side as a girl. As a woman you are trying to grasp a title far above your station. How dare you tell me what to do?'

Lena's temper flared bright and hot in her chest. Her mother was from a royal Arabian bloodline—she was just as good as any lady of the *ton*. She tossed back her head and glared. 'Because why would Ravenwood want you when he has me?'

Both ladies gaped in unison.

Just then, Madame Nadine burst into the dressing room with a garment draped over her arm. 'Apologies, ladies,' she said to Lady Powell and her friend. 'But there has been a delay and your gowns are not yet ready. I will have them in time for Holloway's ball.'

'It's for the best,' Lady Beth said. 'I must pick up a package from the jeweler. I dare not be late or he will close shop.' She tugged on Francesca's sleeve. 'Come along. We can return to the dressmaker's another time.'

Lena let out a long sigh and sagged against the wall as the two women departed.

Madame Nadine hesitated as she eyed Lena. 'Are you unwell?'

'I'm simply tired,' Lena said.

'Of course. You've had to pick out an entire wardrobe in a short amount of time. Now, one last dress for you to wear today and you can be on your way.' The dressmaker showed her a purple dress of fine muslin with a ruffled hem. Lena had never owned anything as pretty. Determined to put the distasteful scene behind her, she held up her arms as she slipped into the dress.

The woman who'd ordered the dress had larger hips and a thicker waist, and the dressmaker swiftly pinned and took in the garment where it gaped.

'I'll send word as soon as more pieces are ready for you to return for the fittings. Meanwhile, take this dress with you.'

When the purple dress was packed with tissue in a box, Lena thanked the dressmaker, then departed the shop with her purchase. The duke's crested carriage awaited her. He must have taken another conveyance home. Across the street, she spotted Lady Francesca and Lady Beth. Francesca was speaking with a gentleman with a hat, greatcoat, and walking stick. She laughed at something he'd said, her slender, ringed fingers drawing attention to her chest, then smiled coyly and touched his sleeve. The man's eyes widened in appreciation. Lena's gut tightened. Francesca might be older, but she was also the type of woman who knew her beauty and how to use it. Men must fall at her feet. Was that how Ravenwood had viewed her?

How could Lena compare? And did she want to?

Yes, yes she did. She'd asked Ravenwood to wait to come to her bed. Would he lose interest in her the moment his former lover returned into his life?

Not if I have a say about it. If that woman thought to intrude upon Lena's marriage before the vows were even exchanged, then she'd have a battle on her hands.

It wasn't just Lena who could be harmed, but Claire as well. Gossip could be cruel, and if Francesca dallied with the duke, Claire's coming out could be tainted. The girl had suffered enough from the recent death of her parents. Lena thought of her mother's jewels, the necklace and the bracelet with the *acht* that protected one from evil and jealousy and reflected the ill will back onto the onlooker. She'd failed to get the jewels back from Stanley Peterson. Now the need was imminent, and there was only one way to protect herself and Claire.

She must find another way to possess them before the wedding.

His office was well-appointed with a Wilton carpet, neat desk with blotter and ink-well, and sideboard with decanters of liquor he'd offer to his most valuable clients. She sat in a chair and clutched her reticule in her lap. 'I'm here for my fair share of the marital property.'

Stanley's broad brow creased. 'Pardon? You must be confused. I'm not certain what share you refer to.'

Lena raised her chin. 'The share Oliver promised me.'

Stanley's crocodile smile made her skin crawl. 'Now, Lena. We both know that is untrue. The legal documents were examined by the solicitor. As your husband's business partner, all his property and wealth reverted to me.'

She bit back a retort and said calmly, 'What of my mother's jewellery? I want it back.' Legally her property had belonged to her husband after they'd married. Of all her losses, her mother's jewels were the most painful. She hadn't thought to fetch them right *before* the funeral. Who would have thought all would be taken from her?

Stanley blinked. 'What jewellery?'

Hatred slithered deep in her gut. His man of affairs had emptied the house of valuables when she'd been out making funeral arrangements.

She wrestled with the urge to grab the silver letter opener and stab Stanley in his greedy hand. 'The turquoise necklace and bracelet belong to my mother and are rightfully mine.'

She didn't bother to explain the importance of the talisman in her culture. Stanley would scoff at her beliefs. She thought of the duke. Would he understand? Most likely,

Chapter Eleven

'Mr Peterson will see you now.' A young clerk drew Lena's attention and escorted her down a corridor and opened a door for her to pass. So, he'd agreed to see her today. Good. She was determined to leave with what was rightfully hers. If he'd refused this time, she'd plan to cause a scene and barge into his office.

Stanley stood from behind his desk as soon as she walked into his office. 'Lena, to what do I owe this pleasure?' In his late fifties, he was heavy-set with fleshy jowls and his round, shiny bald pate gleamed in the sunlight from the window. He'd acquired a polished veneer to deal with wealthy clients and hide his poor upbringing as the son of a fishmonger.

She'd worn one of her previous dresses, a green wool that complemented her colouring. It was far from the fine dresses of the ladies on Bond Street, but it was the prettiest one she'd owned. Her long, curly hair was free from her customary bun, and she'd tied the locks with a matching green ribbon. She needed confidence as well all her wits to deal with a snake like the man standing before her.

the battle-hardened man would think that believing the *acht* warded off evil and jealousy was silly superstition.

Stanley went to a sideboard and poured two drinks. 'Have a sherry, my dear. It will calm your nerves.'

Calm her nerves! She pushed back her chair and stood. 'I do not wish to drink.' *With you*, she wanted to add.

He shrugged and set her glass on his desk, then leaned against the desktop. 'I've always had a soft spot for you, Lena. I'd often stay up at night thinking of Oliver's good fortune. He was lucky to serve your father, the marquess.'

She'd been so young, and she'd wanted to please her father. Oh, what she wouldn't give to turn back time. She'd refuse the marriage. Run away if she must.

Stanley sipped his sherry as he stared at her. Standing close, his breath smelled like onions. 'I believe you need money, and I'd be agreeable to let you a townhouse, Lena. I'll be sure to visit as often as I can. I can be generous and will return your mother's jewels over time.'

Several heartbeats passed before she realized what he was suggesting. She didn't bother to point out he'd denied knowing of the jewellery moments before. Heart thundering in her chest, she met his eyes. 'And what of your wife?'

'What does she have to do with my proposal? She has gained weight and cares only for rich food, gambling, and her own family.' His black gaze raked her from head to toe. 'And she looks nothing like you.'

It took all her effort not to visibly cringe from his perusal. Instead, Lena's lips curved in a calculating smile. 'On second thought, I'd like the sherry.'

Satisfaction crossed his face. 'I knew we could come

to an agreement.' He picked up the glass from his desk and handed it to her.

She promptly tossed it in his face. 'Go to the devil!'

Ravenwood fired the pistol. A split-second later, the wood splintered in the red center of the target.

'Your aim is consistently accurate,' Kent said.

Ravenwood lowered the weapon. 'You need practice.' Kent's shot was close, but he had yet to strike the center of the target.

'It's unfair,' Kent said. 'You went to war. I went to the House of Lords.'

The pair had met at Manton's Shooting Gallery on Davies Street in Berkeley Square that afternoon.

As for today, he'd been more than eager to escape home, knowing both Lena and Claire were beneath his roof. He needed peace, and the satisfaction of shooting at a wooden target alongside his friend provided the perfect outlet.

Other gentlemen were at the gallery and the occasional sound of a pistol firing pierced the air. Betting was common practice at the gallery, and he knew of men who bet considerable sums of money on shooting contests.

As for the owner, Ravenwood admired Joseph Manton for his improvement of rifled artillery as well as the accuracy of a duelling pistol. Ravenwood was never so foolish as to duel, but nonetheless, he realized the value of the man's work.

'Control your breathing and focus on steadying your hand,' Ravenwood instructed.

After preparing their pistols, they both fired. Ravenwood hit the target's red center once more. Kent missed entirely and cursed.

Ravenwood set his pistol down on a bench and turned to his friend. 'I obtained a special license. My wedding is in a couple of days. The church is scheduled, and the staff has arranged the wedding breakfast. As my closest friend, you agreed to stand by my side.'

'I'm your only friend,' Kent pointed out.

Ravenwood ignored his friend's sarcasm. 'Your sisters are invited, of course.'

'Amelia and Audrey will be thrilled. It's not every day they are invited to a duke's wedding. And the wedding breakfast?'

'At the ducal mansion.'

'You haven't entertained there in how long? Your house-keeper may faint with glee.'

Once again, he ignored his friend's sarcasm. 'Things will change now. My bride-to-be expects me to entertain as well as attend a certain number of balls and parties.'

Kent gaped. 'Truly? And you agreed to her requests?'

Ravenwood let out a snort. 'I had little choice. Besides, it's best for Claire if we start to make appearances in anticipation of her upcoming Season.'

'I see. What else did your bride get you to agree to?'

Ravenwood kept his mouth shut. The last thing he'd admit to his friend was that he'd agreed to stay away from his wife's bed for a full week after the wedding. Knowing Kent, he'd hoot out in laughter in the middle of the shooting gallery.

As for Lena's demand, it would take all his restraint.

Hell, she was far from frigid and had a passionate nature. The kiss had shocked him in more ways than he'd like to admit. She'd been sweet and responsive. Curiosity had turned into enthusiasm and the experience was one he craved again. For a man who'd kissed his fair share of women, it was unnerving.

What if you decide to visit my bedchamber? He wasn't certain what led him to ask her that question. The stakes were high and titillating.

'I'll be at the church early,' Kent said. 'I anticipate watching you finally bind yourself to—'

'Your Grace!'

Both men turned at the sound of a booming male voice. A short, muscular, middle-aged man resembling a bulldog barrelled towards them. He wore a dark coat and carried a hat in his right hand.

'What the devil,' Kent muttered under his breath.

The man halted in front of them and looked directly at Ravenwood. 'Pardon the interruption, Your Grace. My name is Constable Burke. I'm here regarding a matter of importance and delicacy.'

Ravenwood eyed him. 'What is it?'

The constable's eyes travelled from Ravenwood to Kent then back to Ravenwood. Clearly, he was uneasy speaking of whatever 'delicate' news he had to tell.

'You can speak in front of the earl,' Ravenwood said.

The constable cleared his throat. 'A woman attempted to burglarize a Piccadilly townhouse this afternoon, Your Grace.'

Ravenwood's eyebrows snapped together as he looked at the man. 'And why is that my concern, Constable?'

'Because, Your Grace, the woman claims she is your betrothed.'

Of all the things Ravenwood expected, fetching his bride-to-be from a constable's office was not one of them.

Lena sprang to her feet as soon as the door opened, and he stepped inside the small office. The space was sparsely furnished with only a wooden chair and small desk, it's surface scarred. The wood floor was dull and scratched. It was a place to hold criminals for questioning.

'I can explain, Your Grace,' she blurted out, gripping her hands before her until her knuckles were white. Even her olive complexion appeared pale.

Clearly, she was in distress. What on earth had happened? He could not imagine Lena as a thief. Whatever had occurred, it must have been a big misunderstanding. He studied her face another moment. Rather than be appalled, angry, frustrated, or any other emotion that would seem logical in given circumstances, he found himself fascinated. But he couldn't allow that to show—this situation demanded he take another tack.

He approached slowly, not wanting to startle her. 'The constable told me about a reported robbery. I'd love to hear your explanation, but it's best if we leave straightway. The constable was kind enough to hold you here instead of Newgate until my arrival.'

She paled even further. 'I see.'

The two simple words made no sense at all to him. She

was wearing a dark cloak, and his first thought was that it was a good choice of attire if one planned on burglarizing a house. He also noticed her hair. She'd removed the pins and her long, dark curls were pulled back in a ribbon. The curls reached almost to her waist. Luxurious, lovely hair. He had to tear his gaze away.

'Pull up your hood,' he said, his voice hoarse. 'We will leave by the back entrance.'

When she made no move to obey, he stepped closer. She came alive then and tugged the hood over her hair.

He took her arm. The path was clear outside the door. He'd paid the constable a good amount to ensure privacy. A hackney was waiting by the back. Lest the crest of the ducal carriage be recognized, he'd left it at the shooting gallery. While still inside, Ravenwood looked for Kent across the street, and his friend waved to let him know it was safe to leave the building.

He wouldn't chance a scandal.

Only once they were seated inside the hackney, and the wheels began moving, did he ask her the question that had festered since the constable had found him at Manton's.

'Do you wish to end our engagement?' He gave himself credit for keeping his voice level.

'No.'

Relief flooded him from her unhesitant, straightforward answer. For a fleeting instant, he'd thought she was trying to escape their impending wedding. A moment of dread—unwanted and unexpected—had pierced his chest. It was a different fear than his nightmares from war. Either way, he didn't like it. Not one bit.

She looked up at him, her dark eyes shining with trepidation. She licked her lips and his gaze dropped to her mouth. Kissable lips, rose-hued and plump. Lips that were made to be kissed. Lips meant to travel over a man's chest and lower still…

She lowered her hood and, once more, his attention was drawn to her hair. He wanted to reach out and finger a lush curl, to test the silky texture. His fingers clenched by his sides. She looked different, lovely.

And she offered no justification. No explanation. Somehow that fact intrigued him even more.

It must be a misunderstanding. 'Did you try to steal from a home?' he asked.

'Yes.'

Now he was stunned by another straightforward answer. She truly must be in shock. Beneath the layers of wool lay a fascinating woman. A spark flared in her eyes. The first sign the shock was fading.

'Why?' he asked.

'Because the owner of the home stole something from me. I wanted it back.'

The constable had told him the name of the owner. Stanley Peterson. The name meant nothing to him, but obviously it meant something to her. 'Will you tell me what it is?'

She averted her eyes. 'You will think it silly.'

'Try me.'

'My mother's jewellery. A necklace and a bracelet. I want to wear it at my wedding.'

His jaw tightened. 'It's your property? And he stole it?'

She glanced outside the hackney window, then at her hands, then finally at him. The anger that shone in her dark eyes took him by surprise. 'Stanley Peterson was Mr Harper's business partner. After Oliver's death, his solicitor claimed everything reverted to him, including my mother's jewellery. I went to Mr Peterson and asked him for the jewellery, but he refused. It means nothing to him. But the jewellery means much to me. He offered to return them in exchange for…for something else.'

Anger flared hot in his chest. A picture formed in his mind of a greedy partner who sought to take advantage of a young, lovely widow. 'You should have come to me.'

She blinked, frowning. 'Why?'

'Because I am going to be your husband. Any wrongs done to you, I will right them.'

'Truly?' The hope in her voice made him feel special. He'd never had someone look at him like that before…like he could make everything right.

He pushed down the emotion. He was far from a hero. Others might call him one. Men in his Regiment and fellow army officers. As for Lena, there was something he could do for her.

'What about you? Do you wish to end our engagement?' she asked.

'No.' It surprised him how quickly he answered. He didn't want to examine how he felt about her, but he knew he wanted to marry her.

She let out a sigh. 'I'm glad to hear it.'

'Is there anything else you want from that house, anything at all?'

She shook her head. 'Only my mother's jewellery matters.'

'Are you certain there is nothing more?'

A long second passed. 'Well, I had a silver brush and mirror.'

'Make a list,' he demanded. He leaned forward, his hands resting on his knees. 'But first, tell me everything you know about this man.'

Chapter Twelve

Ravenwood knew his physical presence was intimidating. At six feet three inches, not to mention the wicked scar marring half his face, men stepped out of his path. His title, when used strategically, could also be an intimidating factor. He normally did not use either for personal advantage. Today was different.

Today he wanted Stanley Peterson to tremble in his boots.

The stockbroker's clerk, a thin man with a wiry mustache, looked up from his desk as soon the duke walked through the door. The clerk held a quill in his hand. 'Can I help you, sir.'

'Lord Ravenwood to see Mr Peterson.'

The clerk's eyes widened, and his mustache twitched. 'Raven—' The quill dropped to the desk blotter, and he pushed back his chair to jump to his feet. 'Your Grace! Allow me to summon Mr Peterson at once.' He looked back over his shoulder as he scurried down a corridor to knock on a closed door.

The door cracked open and Ravenwood could hear the

hum of words exchanged. Moments later, Stanley Peterson appeared. Short and portly, his face had an unmistakable flush of enthusiasm.

'It's an honor, Your Grace,' Peterson said. 'If you would please follow me to my office.'

Eagerness nearly oozed from the man's pores. No doubt, the stockbroker believed it his good luck when a duke personally sought him out at his place of business.

Once inside his office, Peterson motioned for Ravenwood to sit before he took his own chair. 'What can I assist you with, Your Grace?'

'You have some things that belongs to my fiancée. I want them back.'

Stanley gaped. 'Pardon? I have no idea to what you are referring, Your Grace. Perhaps if you tell me the name of your—'

'Mrs Lena Harper.'

The earlier ruddiness of his complexion faded. 'Mrs Harper is your fiancée?'

'We are to marry in a week. I believe you summoned the constable when she attempted to retrieve what was rightfully hers.'

Peterson's mouth took on an unpleasant twist. 'She attempted to burgle my home!'

He kept his voice level. 'Only to retrieve the jewellery her mother gave her.'

'Legally, I am the inheritor of everything from my business partner.'

Ravenwood's fist clenched and unclenched at his side. It had been a while since he'd resorted to violence. He knew exactly where to press against a man's throat to limit air supply, to strike against a chest to cause heart palpitations, or simply punch a man hard enough in the stomach to bowl him over. Hand to hand combat had been a last resort on the battlefield, but not uncommon. He hadn't felt violence towards another in a long time. The weasel before him was different. This man had taken advantage of Lena.

My Lena.

'Only because you stole the jewellery first,' he replied, keeping calm. Ravenwood stood. Peterson pushed back his own chair, and Ravenwood took satisfaction in the flash of fear in the man's eyes. 'And in either case, I don't care. You should have returned them to Mrs Harper long ago.' He took a step closer to the jackal. 'As for summoning the constable, I should seek my own punishment. One word from me about your dishonesty and no man will trust you as their stockbroker at the Exchange.'

Peterson held up a hand. 'Your Grace! Please! I shall tell the constable I made a dreadful mistake and to pursue it no further. Meanwhile, I shall return the jewels at once.'

Ravenwood removed a list from his coat pocket and placed it on the man's desk. 'There are more items. I expect them all within the hour.' He turned on his heel and left the stockbroker's office before he did something he'd regret.

A soft purring and the nuzzling of the kitten's nose woke Lena. She opened her eyes to find the cat, Bella, on her pillow. 'Sweet girl.' She scratched the cat's ears. She glanced at the mantel clock, then sat up in bed.

Ten o'clock.

Sweet Lord. Tossing the covers aside, she sat up as if she'd been jolted by lightning. She'd slept like the dead. Come to think of it, she woke feeling as if a marble was rattling around her skull. A low knock sounded on the door.

'Come in.' She managed with a raspy voice.

The door opened and a young maid entered sheepishly and bobbed a curtsy. 'Good morning, miss. I was unsure whether to wake you.' The kitten scurried out the door. 'That furry little one is on her way to the kitchens for a treat from Cook.'

Lena shoved her feet into slippers. 'I'm afraid I missed breakfast.'

'His Grace instructed us not to disturb you. He said you had a trying evening.'

Trying was one way to describe last night's debacle. The constable had been frighteningly stern as he'd arrived at Stanley Peterson's home and dragged her away like a common criminal. In hindsight, she had been one.

What had she been thinking?

She'd been thinking she wanted what was hers—and that her search was justified. She'd been so angry with Stanley Peterson, especially after he'd suggested she take up as his mistress. Getting into his home had been simple. So had her plan.

At least so she'd thought.

She'd informed the butler that Mr Peterson had invited her and would arrive soon to meet her. Then she'd asked for tea while she waited in the parlor. She knew Stanley took advantage of his ageing staff and paid them little.

After his crassness at his office, Lena had thought to take advantage of Stanley. While the butler had been preparing the tea, she'd sprinted upstairs to search Stanley's bedchamber. She'd looked in his escritoire, his chest of drawers, and an end table. She'd moved on to his wardrobe. Dammit, she'd even looked under his bed.

When she'd returned to the parlor, the constable had been waiting for her. The butler had not believed her story after all and had summoned the authorities. She'd been humiliated when Ravenwood had come to fetch her. She'd thought she'd be sick. But he'd been so kind…

Her maid opened the drapes, letting in the sunshine. 'Good morning, my lady.'

She'd learn the maid's name was Janine. Before returning here as the duke's fiancée, she'd never had a maid. She'd always been self-sufficient and dressed herself. But her life had changed, and as a duchess, she'd have to become accustomed to having servants.

The selection in her wardrobe was scant until the seamstress completed her order. The lovely purple dress from Madame Nadine hung beside her own drab dresses. Janine did not hesitate to select it. The purple gown hugged her curves and the silk felt luxurious against her skin. The bodice was lower than Lena was accustomed to, but flattering. Lena sat at a dressing table as Janine arranged her curls in a fashionable style. When she was finished, Lena stared at the cheval glass in amazement. She looked like a different woman.

Certainly not a criminal.

'His Grace awaits your presence in the blue drawing room,' Janine said.

'Not his study?' Lena expected the duke would want to address her in his domain. It seemed to be where he preferred to conduct his business, and that's what she was to him: business. He'd been kind to her in the carriage, protective. Vowed to get her things back. Her heart warmed at the memory. But just as quickly, nervousness tightened her stomach. Had last night changed everything? Had he, in the light of day, reconsidered their arrangement?

Her temple began to throb.

'No, miss. He was quite clear regarding the blue drawing room.' Janine curtsied and left.

Lena gathered her courage and headed down the grand staircase and into the drawing room. Ravenwood stood at the window, his hands folded behind his back. At the rustle of her skirts, he turned, and her breath stalled.

He was striking, formally dressed in trousers, a striped waistcoat, and snowy cravat complete with ruby pin. A different tension fluttered low in her belly.

'Did you sleep well?' he asked, his voice polite as if he were discussing pleasantries with a stranger at a ball.

'I missed breakfast.' It was all she could think of saying.

'You did.'

She took another daring step into the room. 'Did Claire rise on time?'

'She did.'

His short answers were not comforting. Perhaps he was angry. 'I apologize. It won't happen again,' she said. Was he avoiding the subject of her burglary or enjoying making her squirm with anxiety.

'The dress fits you well.' A flash of admiration lit his eyes.

She blinked at the change of topic. 'Madame Nadine does very fine work.'

He motioned for her to sit on a settee. Once she was settled, he chose a brocade chair across from her, his long legs crossing at his booted ankles.

She decided it was best if she addressed the concern that loomed between them. 'Are we to speak of yesterday?' Her breathing turned choppy.

He lowered his voice. 'I believe we said then all there was to say.'

'Truly?'

'I asked for you to join me here for another reason.' He motioned to the table where a rectangular black box sat. In her apprehensive state, she hadn't noticed it earlier.

'Please open it.'

Her brow furrowed as she reached for the box. She opened the lid, then froze.

Nestled in black velvet was her mother's jewellery, a gold filigree chain with a cross and the turquoise *acht*, along with a gold-and-turquoise bracelet.

Her throat tightened and she felt tears behind her eyes. She couldn't cry. Not in front of him. She'd fought back tears yesterday, only this was different. These were tears of joy. She looked up at him, her heart hammering. 'How did you get them?'

'I paid a visit to Stanley Peterson.'

'And he willingly gave them up?'

His lips turned up in a self-satisfied grin. 'He had no choice.'

She could only imagine how imposing the duke had been. Stanley Peterson was a weasel, and he must have crumbled when Ravenwood stepped in his office. 'I wish I could have witnessed it.'

He shrugged a large shoulder as he continued to watch her as if studying her every moment. 'If that's what you wished, then all you needed to do was ask.'

She laughed, then covered her mouth in horror. 'I thought you had reconsidered our betrothal.'

His expression stilled and grew serious. 'I told you I had no wish to do so.'

Lena lifted the necklace and bracelet from the box. Warmth spread through her chest, her limbs. The filigree chain slipped through her fingers, and she touched the cross, then the pendant with the *acht*.

The duke watched her, focused on her face. She should be conscious of his perusal. Instead, she could not tear her gaze away from the gold and turquoise in her hand.

At last. Her mother's items were where they belonged. *With her.*

She owed Ravenwood a debt of gratitude she'd never be able to repay. It was the eve of their wedding, and he'd retrieved her precious items. She slipped the bracelet on her wrist and sighed out loud at the familiar weight and feel.

She stood and offered the necklace to him. 'Will you help me with the clasp?'

He rose and she held up her hair and turned.

She felt his presence before his touch. The cool filigree chain slipped around her neck. His warm fingers brushed her skin as he secured the clasp. Her heartbeat rocketed and she turned and met his blue eyes, her fingers resting on the pendant.

'Thank you.' The simple words held more meaning than any other compliment her scrambled mind could conjure.

'I told you I would get you anything you wanted from that house.' Something shiver-inducing flashed in his eyes. Again, she was grateful for his efforts and wished she could have seen his dealings with Stanley.

'My mother's jewels mean more than the entire contents of the residence.'

His gaze lowered to the pendant. 'It's unique. What does the charm mean?'

'It's a protective eye, or *acht*. It wards off bad spirits. My mother purchased it from a travelling vendor in Lebanon. I feared marrying without its protection. It must sound like superstitious nonsense to you, but it has much significance to me.'

'It's not nonsense if it makes you happy.' His blue eyes were softer but still magnetic.

'You want me to be happy?' she blurted, then bit her tongue. She'd never been happy in her first marriage. Her husband hadn't cared.

'Why wouldn't I?' he asked gently. 'This marriage is not a gilded cage.'

'By happiness do you mean other lovers?' She could hear the strain in her own voice and pushed aside her trepidation. It was best if they set the rules from the beginning.

His tone turned gruff. 'No. I'd like to know my heir is my own.'

'Is that the only reason?' she pressed.

'Would there be another?'

The question did not warrant an answer. Besides, she had the answer she needed. He was not interested in pursuing an affair, and the news had warmth surging through her again.

Reaching out she touched his arm and smiled. 'Thank you again for retrieving these.'

Chapter Thirteen

Silence reigned in the church as the priest awaited Lena's response. Could she do it? Could she marry a man she barely knew? Could she perform her duties and keep the most important part of herself—her heart—guarded from risk? Panic gripped her and her voice caught in her throat.

Ravenwood stood by her side. Dressed in a navy coat and dark trousers, his presence was a force at her side. His eyes were warm, questioning, and her heart thundered. She resisted the urge to touch the *acht* talisman pressing against her skin beneath her silk bodice. Her wedding gown was a creation of pale blue silk and net overlay with a wisp of a veil.

She opened her mouth, and, thankfully, the words slipped out. 'I do.'

Ravenwood spoke his vows, his voice clear and unhesitant. He reached for her hand and slipped a ring on her finger. As if in a daze, Lena looked down at the simple gold band on her left hand. She still wore the betrothal ring on her other hand and had not expected another ring.

The priest closed the duke's family Bible. 'You may now kiss the bride.'

She turned to face Ravenwood. Their previously shared kiss was hard to forget. This kiss had to be different. Ivan, along with a dozen of the duke's close family and friends, watched them. It should be quick and for show rather than seduction. Still, her heart raced, and her breasts tingled against the silk bodice of the exquisite gown.

He lowered his head and a dark lock fell slightly forward on his brow. She resisted the urge to brush it back. The touch of his lips was expected. Yet, her skin grew warm, and a smattering of butterfly wings fluttered in her chest. The kiss unbalanced her and her hand rose to clutch his sleeve.

He lifted his head, his eyes roving her face and lingering at her lips. The sound of the guests clapping and cheering sounded distant to her overheated senses. As they faced their guests and walked down the aisle, she made certain to smile until her cheeks ached.

They were whisked away to the Berkeley Square mansion for an intimate wedding breakfast.

Ivan was the first to wish her well. 'If you ever find yourself in need, come to me.'

She knew what he meant, and she loved him for it. 'I won't. And my marriage will not change our friendship.' Ivan kissed her on the cheek just as Ravenwood came to stand by her side. He placed a possessive hand around her waist.

'Mr Abadi. Your presence today means much to my wife.'

My wife. If there ever was a man claiming what was his with words and touch, it was Ravenwood. It was all unnecessary and the duke knew Ivan was not a threat. Not in the way a husband would fear from another man. Still, the tension between the two men was palpable.

'I would not miss Lena's wedding.' Ivan offered a smart bow before departing.

'I will invite him to visit in a week's time.' She wanted the duke to understand that she would not abandon her friend now that she was married.

'It was part of our agreement, was it not?' Ravenwood said dryly.

Neither had time to speak further as the Earl of Kent approached.

'Congratulations!' Kent slapped Ravenwood on the back. He turned to Lena and grinned 'You are a lovely bride, Your Grace. My sisters are most anxious to meet you.'

Your Grace. Lena's shoulders tightened. Kent was the first to address her as duchess. Even though she'd understood the title came with the marriage, she was taken off guard.

The Earl of Kent's two sisters were a whirlwind of energy. Twins, they had both debuted this year and were in the midst of their first Season. Both Amelia and Audrey were pretty, slender, and of average height, but Amelia had brown hair and Audrey auburn.

'We will fetch you ladies lemonade.' Kent seemed eager to escape his sisters, and he headed to the refreshment table with Ravenwood.

'Your dress is stunning, Your Grace,' Amelia said when the men had left.

'We've never been inside the duke's residence. The house is huge. How many rooms does it have?' Audrey's eyes were as large as saucers.

Lena found them both friendly. 'Thank you, it—'

Amelia touched her sister's arm to interrupt. 'What is Ravenwood like? We've heard all sorts of stories, but we know not to believe everything. After all, he's our brother's good friend.'

'Was his proposal romantic?' Audrey asked.

'Will you come to our home for a special dinner?' Amelia this time.

'Yes! We will tell our brother to invite you,' Audrey said.

Both sisters spoke incessantly. Lena adored them. Without answering any of their questions, she embraced both twins and assured them she would soon have them both over for tea. They clutched their hands over their hearts in unison and vowed to come.

Across the room, Lena spotted Claire, sipping a glass of champagne alone in the corner. 'Pardon, me,' she said, 'as I seek out another.' As she approached Claire, the girl suddenly looked suspicious.

'Are you going to scold me for drinking champagne?' Claire asked.

'No. I was going to join you for one.' Lena waved over a liveried server carrying a silver tray to fetch a bubbling glass.

Claire sipped from her flute. 'I suppose you expect me to welcome you into the family.'

The girl's frankness was refreshing. 'It would be nice.' Lena sipped her own glass.

'Well, we have been getting along but I'm still not convinced.'

'Convinced about a warm welcome?' Lena asked.

'No, I'm not convinced you will stay for good.' Lately Lena had spent less time with Claire than she'd wanted. Her art lessons were still on her mind, and Lena hoped to make it up to the girl. She also planned on more shopping trips to escape the mansion.

Lena held up her left hand to show her ring. 'I am now family.' The girl had an understandable fear of abandonment. Lena vowed never to abandon her.

Claire pursed her lips. 'Hmm. But my uncle comes with that bauble, and he can be quite intolerable.'

Niece and uncle had a past, and Lena hoped she could somehow help. Before she could respond, Ravenwood appeared by her side. 'I can only assume my niece has welcomed you,' he said.

Lena did not hesitate. 'Of course, she has. Isn't that right, Claire?'

Claire set her flute down on a table and glanced behind Ravenwood's shoulder. 'Pardon me, Uncle. I have yet to greet Lord Kent's sisters.' She hurried away.

Lena watched a frown furrow the duke's brow. 'Give her time,' she said.

Ravenwood's jaw tightened. 'What if she does not change her ways?'

'You married me to help, remember?'

The intensity of his look riveted her. 'That's not the only reason for our marriage.'

At the reminder of her part of their agreement—the scintillating part—her bodice suddenly felt too tight. She didn't miss the obvious perusal and approval of her dress. He was so disturbing to her in every way, and she was aware of the increase of her breaths. She boldly met his eyes. 'And you recall one of my requirements?'

His lips curved into a devastating smile. 'Ah, yes. I am to devote a week to your wooing.'

When he determined to be charming like this, she feared for much more than the loss of her own will. She was beginning to realize how a sensible woman could lose all reason around a charming man. The duke was neither a rogue nor a rake, but he had been, and her cheeks grew warm under the heat of his gaze.

'Haven't I begun?' He leaned close. *Too close.*

His breath brushed the shell of her ear causing a tiny shiver down her spine. 'I liked our wedding kiss. I think you liked it, too.'

She had, and she wanted him alone more than she cared to admit. But she needed to temper her reaction to him. If she let herself fall too hard for the duke, she feared there'd be no coming back.

The meow sounded under her bed. Lena dropped to her knees and lifted the bed skirt to search for the kitten. 'Come out, Bella,' she enticed.

Weary with exhaustion after the stress of her wedding

day, she wanted to return the cat to Claire's bedchamber before she went to sleep. She yawned. Who knew weddings could be so tiring? Her first marriage ceremony had taken all of a half hour, and there had been no wedding breakfast afterwards.

Marriage to a duke was vastly different. She'd smiled during the wedding breakfast and accepted the well wishes of the guests, all the while aware that her feet hurt in her new shoes and the corset beneath her expensive wedding gown felt laced too tight. As for her new husband, her nerves had sparked at the brush of his lips at the altar, and when he'd touched her low back while they'd greeted guests, her pulse throbbed in her ears and her heart fluttered wildly in her breast. Though her attraction to the duke had increased, she was grateful to have more time to get to know him before consummating their marriage.

Hours later, she was finally out of her wedding dress and alone in her chambers. At last, she spotted the feline in the far corner under the bed. 'I see you!'

Cajoling the cat to come within reach, she scooped the tiny kitten into her arms.

She let out a long, exhausted sigh. The cat had been sleeping in Claire's room; she couldn't collapse into bed herself until she returned Bella. Not bothering with slippers, she left her bedchamber, holding a lamp in one hand and a squirming kitten in her other.

Barefoot, Lena padded down the carpeted hall. Just as she came up to Claire's door, the cat leaped from her arms.

'Bella!' she whispered as loud as she dared. The kitten looked back, her green eyes shining, before sprinting down the grand staircase.

Lena cursed under her breath and hurried to follow, her feet silent on the carpet runner. Stepping into the vestibule, the cold marble sent a chill up her spine. She wished she'd had the foresight to don a wrapper and wear slippers.

'Stop, Bella!'

The cat streaked down the hall, then darted into a room. Oh, no! She knew precisely which room Bella had entered. She only hoped it was unoccupied at this hour of the night.

Lena halted at the doorway to glance inside the duke's study. No such luck. A lantern illuminated the room, along with the light and heat of the coal brazier in the fireplace. She scanned the space.

The room appeared empty. No one on the sofa or at the desk. Maybe a servant hadn't yet doused the lamp and fireplace.

Then she heard it. A low moan. Ravenwood's distinctive deep voice. 'I told you to run!'

Was he speaking to her? A chill raced down her spine that had nothing to do with the cold. There was a slight movement, then she spotted an arm on the armrest of a leather chair and a half-empty glass on a side table.

'Your Grace?' she whispered.

'I said run!'

She stepped into the room, on pins and needles, expecting him either to summon her or send her away.

Nothing.

She crept closer to the chair, then peeked around the side.

Ravenwood was sleeping.

Lamplight flickered over him, illuminating his inky hair and sun-bronzed skin. He'd removed his coat, waistcoat, and cravat. The top two buttons of his shirt were undone, and she could see the muscular column of his throat and a sprinkling of dark hair at the open V of his shirt. She found herself riveted. She'd never seen a man's naked chest other than her first husband's, and it did not compare.

Even more startling, his feet were bare. Surprise siphoned through her at the sight of his feet, long and lean. She'd never seen a man's bare feet. Oliver had kept his stockings on, even when he'd crawled into bed.

'No. No. You won't make it. None of us will.' Ravenwood's mumblings caused gooseflesh to rise on her arms.

Perspiration beaded on his brow. His hair was in disarray as if he'd run his hand repeatedly through the thick locks in agitation. His broad shoulders heaved with each breath.

She realized he was in the throes of a nightmare. The man must be plagued by horrors of war—as if he were reliving an injury, a battle, or witnessing someone else's wounds. Her breath stalled in her throat. This was a private moment, one she wasn't supposed to witness, one she was not equipped to aid. She realized she knew even less about her new husband than she'd thought.

Her heart went out to him, and she wanted to help. To somehow ease his pain. She had no experience with what he'd witnessed on the battlefield or the suffering he'd endured.

But she knew about loneliness, and anguish seared her heart. Her fingers reached out to brush back the lock of hair across his forehead, then she pulled back her hand. Instinct told her not to wake him. He was strong and proud. He'd never want her to witness this or speak of it. Especially not on their wedding night.

She backed away. From the corner of her eye, she saw Bella sprint from the room.

'Have you changed your mind about our wedding night?'

Lena froze. *Good God.* She turned slowly, afraid to face him. 'How long have you been awake?'

'Long enough.' His voice sounded slightly sleep-dazed.

She turned to him. 'I was not spying. The kitten ran away.' Even though it was the truth, she knew it sounded like a silly excuse.

'Is the cat in this room now?' he asked.

The smart feline had escaped 'No.'

'Then why are you still here?'

Gathering her courage, she approached him. He stayed seated, his eyes raking her from head to toe. She'd worn the nightgown from the dressmaker's, the one he'd chosen. When her maid had placed it on the bed that evening, she hadn't objected. The servants had no need to know Lena was not to share the duke's bed tonight.

She realized her back was to the coal brazier and the sheer nightgown revealed much from the light. She felt suddenly naked. Her nipples tightened and an unbidden warmth spread though her limbs. She folded her arms across her chest and tried to decipher his unreadable features. She'd found him in the throes of a nightmare; now she was the one who felt exposed.

If he noticed, his only response was a huskiness in his voice. 'Have a drink with me.'

'A drink? It's well past midnight and I don't think that—'

'It's our wedding night. If we are not to spend it the way I'd prefer, then the least we can do is share a drink.'

Put like that, she had little to argue. She sat in a chair across from him. 'I prefer wine over whisky.'

He rose and went to the sideboard in the corner of the study. Without a coat or waistcoat, the linen stretched and molded over his shoulders. He returned with a whisky for himself and a goblet of Madeira for her. She accepted it and he returned to his seat.

'What did you see?' he asked.

She swallowed a gulp of wine. Even in her anxiety, it went down smoothly. The Madeira, like everything in the duke's cellars, was fine and costly.

He closely watched her, and her fingers tightened on the stem of the goblet. He was testing her with one simple yet difficult question. Her answer must be honest.

'You were having a nightmare.'

'What makes you think I wasn't dreaming of you?'

She shot him a disbelieving look. If he thought to lie or jest, then he'd best do better than that. 'Does it happen often, Your Grace?'

He swirled the amber-coloured liquid in his glass. He drained the whisky, then set the glass down on the table. 'Yes.'

One simple word and her sympathy returned. How long

had he suffered from nightmares? Ever since his retirement from the army? Questions plagued her.

Seconds passed. The intimate nature of the admission was not lost on her. He was not a man to confess weakness. She was not a woman to pry into another's demons, even if those demons haunted her new husband.

'My name is Brent. No need for formalities now that you have seen me in slumber.'

Brent. He'd given her leave to use his Christian name. Not because they were married or had an intimate long conversation before a lit fireplace. But because she'd seen him at his worst. It was another test of sorts. It was her turn to try to help him, to let him know she would not betray his secrets or what he believed was a weakness.

He didn't look weak now that he was fully awake. Every inch of him looked hard and merciless. She didn't fear him physically. But there were other types of trepidation. He was dangerously appealing. Like a scarred and muscled pirate.

Heavens. She lowered her lashes before he could read her thoughts.

'You are staring at my feet. Have you never seen a man's bare feet before?'

'No.' Another honest answer.

The crackle of a dying ember in the brazier drew his attention. 'Do you know how uncomfortable wet socks can be? Especially in soaked Hessians. It rained the night before and well into the morning and the ground was saturated. Our officer coats were wool, and they added ten pounds of weight, but I found the wet socks worse.'

He stared into the fire, and she didn't dare speak. 'We stood for hours, waiting for orders, then, when we finally marched, our toes were damp and blistered and it was uncomfortable to walk. It didn't matter that sweat rolled down my back and into my eyes. I wanted to remove my boots and march barefooted.'

Silence stretched between them. Something as simple as wet socks in soggy leather boots, and she could imagine the discomfort. Had he focused on something so mundane that he didn't have to think of the horrors hidden beneath his subconscious? Horrors that gave a strong man like Ravenwood, a battle-hardened officer, nightmares?

'Do you wish to speak more of it?' she asked gently.

'No.'

She interpreted his refusal as she thought best. *Not yet.*

Sharing wasn't part of their agreement. Easing one's nightmares was not on her list of requirements or his demands. Yet, she wanted to hear, to help, to soothe his pain. Perhaps it was her nature. Perhaps it was *him*. Either way, things could not be rushed, and time mattered.

She set down the goblet and rose from her chair. He watched her, his midnight blue eyes stalking her every movement.

'When I was a child, I had nightmares,' she said. 'I think all children do on occasion. My mother would ease my fears and my tension. May I try?' Without waiting for his response, she walked behind him and touched his shoulder.

He stiffened and turned his head to glare at her. 'I don't think—'

'Shh. Let me try.' For a pulse-pounding moment, she

thought he would refuse. Demand she leave. Instead, his steady gaze bore into her, then he turned to face the fireplace. She took that as consent. Gathering her courage, she placed both hands on his broad, warm shoulders.

Chapter Fourteen

Lena's lavender bath soap teased Ravenwood's nostrils. She bravely stood behind him, her hands resting upon him.

'I can help.' Her fingers were light as she began to massage him with long smooth strokes. His breath caught and he sat stock-still. The tightness in his muscles eased slightly.

'Am I hurting you?'

The concern in her voice made his gut tighten. *Hurt him?* Not even close. Her touch was too gentle, and he found himself wanting more.

'No.' His voice was gruff.

She increased the pressure. The tightness of his muscles eased a fraction more. He realized he was tense, much more than he'd believed, and her ministrations felt magical.

He'd yearned for more time alone with her since their meeting in the parlor yesterday morning. He'd never forget the look on her face when she'd opened the box and discovered her returned jewellery. She'd looked at him with wonder, with an appreciation that he did not deserve. Why wouldn't he get the items back for her? They were rightfully hers. He had the wealth, position, and physical strength to get her anything she desired. Yet, she made him feel like a goddamned hero.

And then she'd spoken of lovers.

Hell, no.

He was not interested. His response had been instantaneous and fierce. He had agreed to her proposal, a marriage of convenience. He did not have a right to dictate her life any more than she had a right to tell him what to do. But the thought of her with anyone else twisted his stomach.

She moved to his neck. He turned his head to the left, then the right, releasing the tightness. Her nails lightly scratched the base of his skull, sparking a startling need. It was a form of intimacy, a closeness he hadn't experienced with a woman in a long, long time.

As she ran her hands over his shoulders, he imagined her in the sheer nightgown. He'd have to be a monk not to notice the wisp of fabric when she'd first entered the room. And when she'd stepped in front of the firelight, he'd seen every delicious curve, every dip and valley. Her nipples had tightened, and his mouth had watered. The whisky hadn't been strong enough.

She lowered her head, and her breast brushed his shoulder. 'I knew it would help. You feel more relaxed already.'

Christ. Was she trying to seduce him? Was it her intention to tempt and tease? She wasn't a virgin, and she had to know the effect of her touch. The fact that it was their wedding night made it more arousing. Any red-blooded man would want to bed his bride.

But she'd asked for a week of wooing. And he'd foolishly agreed.

His voice was rough. 'It feels good.'

She continued to massage him. He continued to ache. He was glad he was sitting, or she would undoubtedly notice the hardness in his trousers.

At last, her hands fell away, and she moved to stand before him. 'Goodnight, Brent. I hope you can sleep peacefully tonight.' His chest tightened at the use of his name whispered from her lips.

Just as silently as she'd entered, she slipped from the room, leaving behind an enticing trace of lavender and a tantalizing glimpse of long, slim legs beneath the wispy gown.

He closed his eyes and ran a hand though his hair. Whatever her purpose, the result was the same. He thought of her, not a bloody battlefield.

Ravenwood sat alone in the breakfast room, suffering a throbbing headache from last night's whisky.

He could not decide which was more disturbing—that Lena had seen him in the throes of one of his nightmares, or that she'd cared enough to help him.

She hadn't pried or asked unwanted questions. Instead, her touch had released the tension he'd been carrying in his shoulders. She'd had a calming effect. But then she'd left, and he'd gotten little sleep after—only his thoughts had been of *her*.

He was on his second cup of black coffee when Lena walked into the dining room.

She took one look at him, and her lips tilted up at the corners. 'Good morning, Your Grace,' she said a bit too cheerfully. 'Claire is running a tad bit late.'

He gave her his fiercest frown.

She ignored it and went to the sideboard to fill a plate with eggs, toast, and bacon from the sideboard.

He watched her as she returned to sit across from him. Her rose day dress was feminine, and the bodice was designed to draw attention to the swell of her breasts. Her hair had been styled fashionably in a coronet of intricate braids that revealed her slender neck and golden skin.

'You appear different.' He inwardly cringed at his weak attempt at a compliment. Where was the silver tongue from his youth?

She opened her napkin and spread it on her lap. 'The rest of Madame Nadine's clothing arrived.'

The dressmaker's exorbitant fee had been worth every penny. He cleared his throat. 'What are your plans for the day?'

'I thought to go shopping with Claire.'

He would never understand the need for ladies to shop as frequently as they did. He visited his tailor when needed, not for the pleasure of the experience. 'Do you ride?'

She picked up her fork. 'Passably well. I rode when we travelled from village to village to visit family and friends in Lebanon.'

His calendar held no commitments until the Earl of Kent was expected for their weekly outing at the coffee house. 'I'd like to take you to the park.'

Her face brightened. 'Oh?'

'You asked to spend time together, remember?' His tone was brusque, more than he'd intended. What the devil was wrong with him? He'd charmed and seduced dozens of women in the past. Why was he acting like an inexperienced, fumbling youth now?

She gifted him with a smile that made his skin tighten. 'I have a new riding habit.'

'Is that a yes?'

'Yes. Riding is a splendid way to be seen together in society in anticipation of Claire's future debut.'

His niece's debut was the last thing on his mind, and he felt a pang of regret for not thinking of the girl. He'd actually given thought to Lena's advice of softening his approach with Claire, at least in regards to her schedule.

As for his bride, a week was too long not to share a bed with her. How could he quicken the wooing? Well, he could start by learning more about her. It was what she intended when she'd suggested they wait. He wanted to know her better, too.

And, surprisingly, he wanted to give his new wife everything she wanted.

'How often did you ride in Lebanon?' Ravenwood asked as they rounded a bend in the park.

Lena sat side-saddle upon a mare from Ravenwood's impressive stables. It was a lovely, cloudless day for a ride in Hyde Park. She wore a smart riding outfit of sapphire blue with gold braid. Her horse, named Grace, was an elegant bay with a high instep. Ravenwood had told her the horse was hers if she liked her. She'd never owned a horse, or a new riding habit…or ever dreamed of being called a duchess.

Ravenwood sat tall and proud, and handled his large, black bay with the ease of an experienced rider. Her gaze was drawn to his muscular thighs and his strong hands as he held the reins. It was clear he'd spent hours upon a mount.

He was watching her, waiting for her response. 'Like I told you, we left our bustling village to spend summers in the country, visiting family and friends. Girls were never permitted to ride in the city or the village, but no one paid attention in the country, and I rode though the hills and the fig orchards. I learned how to shoot. Even how to swim in a lake. Going back to the village was stifling after such freedom.'

He watched her, a gleam of interest in his eyes. 'What is the landscape like?'

'It's lovely. A large part of the country borders the Mediterranean Sea, and the water glistens beneath the hot afternoon sun. The water is warm and enticing for bathers. The countryside is lush with greenery. My mother's family owned orchards of fig trees. I used to climb the trees and stuff myself with ripe figs.' Her chest tightened at the memories. It had been years, but she could picture her homeland clearly in her mind.

A grin tugged at his lips as he led their horses on the winding pathway. 'Ah, it makes sense now.'

'What does?'

'How I found you up a tree on your first day of employment.'

She pursed her lips. 'To be fair, I was trying to bond with Claire.' She'd taken Claire shopping earlier and had returned for an afternoon ride in the park with him.

'By climbing out a casement?' he teased.

'Well, yes. To talk with her,' she said. Clearly, he was relaxed and in a good mood.

'As I recall, you couldn't climb down.'

'The fig trees were never as tall as that oak,' she protested. 'And I would have eventually climbed down on my own.'

He burst out laughing.

She arched a playful brow. 'You don't believe me?'

'I do not doubt you. But then I wouldn't have caught a glimpse of your lovely legs.'

Unsure how to respond, she felt her face grow warm.

They rode side by side. It was the beginning of the promenade hour and more riders appeared in the park. Ladies strolled arm-in-arm with parasols. Others rode in high-perched phaetons or on prime horseflesh around the park. It was a time to be seen just as much as it was to enjoy the outdoors.

'How old were you when you arrived in London, and what did you think of it?'

She shivered at the memory. 'I was ten and I hated it. I had a perpetual chill, and I was unused to the frequent rain.'

'What else?' he asked.

He was probing. She saw no reason not to be honest, at least about this. 'England may claim to be more modernized. But there is a downside as well. The factories put out black smoke that chokes the sky. The women dress differently, act differently, but their sovereignty is not absolute. I had to wait to become a widow to gain any type of freedom.'

His enigmatic eyes bore into her. 'And now you're a wife once more.'

'Yes, but this time I'm not a child bride,' she pointed out.

'A very grown woman indeed.'

His tone made her breath catch and her belly tighten. She found her new husband irresistible, but she must remind herself their marriage was a business relationship.

'I would think many of the items on your list would be honored by any gentleman and did not need to be written down.'

'You would think so, but I have learned from experience that all gentlemen do not do the right thing when it comes to women or their wives.' She shifted in her sidesaddle. She had firsthand experience. 'Why all the questions, Your Grace?'

'Is it wrong to want to know about my wife's past?'

'No.' It was on the tip of her tongue to ask about *his* past.

She shoved aside her maddening attraction to the man. The sun shone, and it had been a long time since she'd ridden for sheer pleasure. She wanted to enjoy the experience, not dwell on the past.

Or ask about him. If there ever was a man who was secretive about his demons, it was the duke. She was curious about him and hoped she would know him better over time.

She grew keenly aware of the attention of the other riders in the park as they circled the Serpentine. Both pedestrians and riders glanced their way. Some blatantly stared. A woman nearly fell from her mount while straining back to look at them.

Lena lowered her voice. 'Have you noticed that everyone is watching us?'

'Society wants to know more about the mysterious Duchess of Ravenwood.'

She'd spent the past years attempting to hide. Oliver never liked it when visitors noticed her, and any inquiries into her past 'could have adverse effects for my business,' he'd warned. An illegitimate daughter of a marquess, combined with her Middle Eastern blood, was hardly favorable. Keeping to herself and dressing as Oliver preferred, she'd grown accustomed to people's gazes passing over her without truly noticing her.

But things had changed, and her new title *did* make a difference. 'I'd hardly call myself mysterious,' she said.

'You are to them.'

'What about you?' she asked. 'You are not known to attend balls or garden parties or ride in the park during promenade hour.' In her opinion, he was just as mysterious. Even more so.

His eyes met hers, holding firm. 'I don't like the attention either. Not anymore at least.'

His tone, along with the admission, drew her attention to his face. He sat straight in the saddle. Proud and defiant, almost daring passersby to stare. For the first time, she'd wondered what it was like to bear the scar. Was he always conscious of his face? Did it bother him still?

Once more, she wanted to know much more about the war hero, the beast as some called him…more about her husband.

They approached a river and sunlight glinted off the water. 'Shall we walk? There is a bench by the river,' he said.

They secured the horses, and he offered his arm. The warmth of his skin radiated through her glove. Sunlight filtered through the leaves and glinted off strands of his dark hair. 'It's lovely here,' she said.

He ducked his chin in a nod. 'I thought it the perfect place for an afternoon to ride.'

He'd agreed to spend time with her before any intimacy. She hoped he truly wanted to know her as well. She'd asked for a week. Now it was their first day of wooing.

Before she could think of a response, he spoke up. 'The truth is, I'm enjoying myself this afternoon.' His expression looked genuine, and his free hand brushed her lower back as they drew closer to the water. Warmth followed the path of his hand, heating more than her back. It was the slightest touch and then gone, but it had the strangest effect on her. Her breath caught, and her belly tightened. A passionate fluttering arose at the back of her neck.

They both stopped and stood motionless. Her gaze dropped to his mouth, and she had a ridiculous urge to kiss him. From the way he was looking at her, she believed he was thinking the same thing. Good God, if he leaned down and kissed her in the public park would she protest or invite the intimacy? 'Your Grace, I—'

His head lifted. 'We are about to be put upon.'

'By whom?' Lena asked.

'Your Grace!'

Lena turned at the sound of the feminine voice. A blonde woman riding a white horse waved across the park. Lena's fingers stiffened upon his arm.

Francesca.

Of all the rotten luck! Lena had been enjoying herself, enjoying a perfect afternoon with her husband, when Lady Powell intruded.

Francesca halted her mount before them. 'What a wonderful surprise, Raven... Your Grace.'

'My lady,' Ravenwood said.

'Is this the new duchess?' From her mount, Francesca looked down at Lena.

Ravenwood made acquaintances. 'This is my wife, the Duchess of Ravenwood. Your Grace, this is Lady Powell,' he addressed her formally.

For a heart pounding moment, Lena thought Francesca would mention their confrontation at the dressmaker's. Instead, the lady's lips curled upwards.

'Your Grace,' Francesca said to Lena. 'My friendship with the duke has quite a history.' She looked at Ravenwood. 'In fact, I can't remember precisely where we met. Was it at Lady Higgins' picnic, Your Grace? Or Lord and Lady Kerwick's ball?'

Ravenwood waved a dismissive hand. 'No need to guess. Suffice it to say, we are acquainted.'

'Yes, we are *acquainted*,' Francesca said.

Had Lena not overheard her speaking at the dressmaker's she might have missed the true meaning behind her words.

'You both must come to a dinner party I'm hosting next Saturday. It will be fun to get to know your duchess.' Francesca's attention turned to Ravenwood. 'And to rekindle our friendship, Your Grace.'

Lena's muscles tensed. She had no intention of accepting an invitation from the woman. But what of Ravenwood? If he agreed, she had no choice but to accompany him.

'Thank you, but I fear we have accepted more invitations than we have days to attend,' Ravenwood said.

Lena let out a held-in breath. Had he sensed the woman's interest? Or had he refused because he disliked society events? They had yet to accept any of the many invitations they had received.

'I'm disappointed but must understand,' Francesca said, her mouth forming a playful pout. 'After all you are newly married and wish to spend time together.' Her eyes flicked to Lena before lingering on Ravenwood once again. 'However, my invitation remains open. Perhaps another time soon.' The lady turned her horse around and galloped away.

A myriad of emotions churned in Lena's chest. Anger. Anxiety. And unease. 'You should know Lady Powell was my stepmother,' she stated. 'Since my father, Lord Grisham, is long dead, I don't consider her that any longer.' In truth, she'd never considered her a stepmother.

Ravenwood nodded. 'It came up when I had my man of affairs look into you as a chaperone, but it never concerned me. You should also know we had a past, but it means nothing,' he said matter-of-factly.

His honesty surprised her. 'Good. Because today is not the first time we've been reacquainted since my childhood. She and I had a confrontation recently in the dress shop.'

Ravenwood arched a dark eyebrow. 'Oh?'

'It was unpleasant.' Lena would not say more. Francesca's description of her heritage had stirred Lena's own deeply hidden insecurities. Lena was aware of what wagging tongues would say of her mixed race, especially amongst the *ton*. It didn't help that she was the illegitimate child of a marquess. She could pretend the gossip didn't bother her, but the truth was different. And when she had a child with the duke, she would want to shield him or her from the world's cruel prejudice. Would it be enough for her son or daughter to have a powerful duke as a sire?

And then there was Claire's debut. She wanted to help the girl, not hinder her with gossip.

'You needn't worry about Lady Powell,' Ravenwood said smoothly. 'I won't tolerate her interference.'

Lena tightened her grip on her reins. He'd meant to reassure her, but she didn't trust the woman. She'd enjoyed their afternoon up until Lady Powell's intrusion. What was the woman's game? Did she believe Lena would simply step aside and allow Francesca to slip into the duke's bed under her watch?

But by her own demands to wait a week, Lena wasn't

even sleeping with her husband. Did she have a right to object if he wanted an affair?

Yes, I do. The weight of the ring on her finger said she had that right, and she'd exercise it.

Lena's mother often said the best way to solve a problem was to confront it headlong. She was not an Englishwoman by birth, and if Lady Powell believed her to be a harem girl, then she'd truly give the woman something to gossip about.

Lena glanced back. Sure enough, Francesca was watching them. Specifically, Ravenwood. Even across the distance, Lena could swear the woman's eyes were lustful.

Perfect.

Blood rushed through Lena's veins as she tugged Ravenwood's lapel. When he bent to her, she kissed him full on the mouth.

The brush of Lena's lush lips against his mouth was a shock. Blood surged in his veins as Ravenwood returned the kiss, his mouth covering hers hungrily. Her tongue tentatively ran across his lower lip, and he wanted to crush her against him in the middle of the park for all to see. He longed for her to part her lips, for him to kiss her the way she was meant to be kissed.

Whatever had come over his wife? If it was jealousy over Francesca, then she need not worry. In the back of his mind he knew this public kiss would cause wagging tongues and inflame the scandal sheets tomorrow.

He didn't care.

He was loath to break away but found himself lifting

his head. Without thinking, he brushed his thumb across her mouth. Her lips glistened and heat flooded his veins. 'I'm not complaining, my dear, but perhaps we should return home.'

Her brow creased and she bit her lower lip. 'You must think me brazen.'

The sight of her teeth on her full, pink lip made him harden uncomfortably in his breeches. 'As I've said, what others think does not concern me. Does this mean my wooing is working?' Dare he hope she'd welcome him into her bed tonight?

She squeezed his arms. 'Do not get ahead of yourself. I have a preference for red hothouse roses and chocolates.'

'I can manage both at once.'

'And poetry.'

He offered a half-smile. 'Now that is a challenge.'

Her eyes twinkled. 'Hmm. You lack inspiration.'

If she continued with her playful flirting, he'd toss her over his shoulder like a pirate seizing his booty and ride back to his home. 'Then you must inspire me.'

By the time they made it home, the Earl of Kent, was waiting for him. Blast! Ravenwood had completely forgotten about their plans.

Kent greeted his wife. 'Your Grace, it is a pleasure to see you again.' He lifted Lena's hand and pressed a kiss to the back of her glove. 'I apologize, but I do believe Ravenwood has forgotten our arrangement today. I cannot blame him. If I were recently married to such a lovely lady as yourself, I would forget my head were it not attached.'

Lena chucked. 'Then I apologize for the duke's forget-fulness.'

Ravenwood's frown deepened. 'Do not be fooled by the earl's charm. He often forgets his head *and* his place.'

Lena waved them both off and headed up the grand staircase.

Kent trailed behind Ravenwood to the study, where his friend peeled off his gloves and headed for the sideboard, then proceeded to fill two glasses with port. 'I understand now why you agreed to marry the governess. Like I said, you are not a man who does anything he doesn't want to do.'

'You are speaking in riddles.'

Ravenwood did his best to ignore his friend's smugness.

The truth was, he'd enjoyed spending time with Lena in the park. Her childhood experiences in Lebanon intrigued him, and he was genuinely curious about her. He looked forward to learning more, to uncovering all the layers of his wife.

'Not really.' Kent handed him a glass, then sprawled on the sofa and crossed his booted feet at the ankles. 'I believe you have met your match. I look forward to seeing the sparks fly between you two.'

Chapter Fifteen

'You sketched this?' Lena asked.

Claire shrugged and fidgeted with the pencils on the escritoire in her room. 'Do you think it's good?'

With Ravenwood occupied with the earl, she'd sought out Claire, who had been drawing in her room. As she looked at Claire's current artwork, she was captivated by the piece. The drawing was of a handsome fair-haired young man, who looked a year or two older than Claire, sitting on a bench in a garden. The detail was striking, including the eyes and the hands. The proportions of his body were perfect.

'It's amazingly lifelike,' Lena said as she stood by Claire's chair. 'And hands are difficult to draw.'

Claire swiveled in her chair and met her eyes. 'How would you know?'

'I had a friend in Lebanon from the same village. She was skilled at sketching with charcoal. She used to draw people at the marketplace.'

'Did your friend sell her artwork?'

Lena thought back. 'She did. I wish I had purchased

a piece and brought it to England with me, but I was too young to have my own money.'

Claire busied herself arranging her pencils by length. 'Selling even some of her pieces must have been exciting.'

Lena's eyebrows drew together as she recalled her artist friend. 'Yes, but her family was poor. She sketched to eat.'

'Still,' Claire said. 'I would like to sell my work one day.'

'There is nothing stopping you. Keep practising.'

Claire shoved the sketch aside and stood. 'You said you mentioned my artwork to my uncle.'

'I did.'

She planted a hand on her hip, and a frown appeared between her fair eyebrows. 'Well, it did no good. He never visited. Nor did he stop the pianoforte lessons.'

'He will,' Lena vowed. 'The wedding has occupied our time, but no longer.'

Dealing with Ravenwood was tricky. He was stubborn, especially when it came to his niece. But he'd been perfectly agreeable this afternoon on their ride in Hyde Park. He'd shown a true interest in her past. He could have spoken of the weather or other trivial topics. Instead, he'd been intrigued by her background and her life in Lebanon. It was startlingly different than Oliver, who'd refused to acknowledge her culture. Once again, Ravenwood had surprised her.

'Are you afraid of him?' Claire asked, drawing back her attention.

'Afraid? No.' *Not entirely.* The man could be charming one moment and painfully distant the next. Despite his pleasantness in the park and her resolve to be in charge of her life, she did fear being intimate with the man. Not so much the acts of intimacy, but the *aftermath*. Oliver's constant berating was hard to forget. What if she wasn't any good in bed? What if Ravenwood, afterwards, looked at her with the same disdain. A cold numbness spread in her veins just imagining it. She would never expose her heart again.

Lena grew aware of Claire watching her, and she forced her fears aside. 'How about we find you an art instructor? I'm thinking of a real artist from the art district.'

'Truly?' Claire sat back down. 'How? My uncle would never approve of someone from the art district.'

'Leave him to me. Meanwhile, please don't hide this piece—display it.'

'Where?'

'In your room. Right here.' Lena pointed to a prominent spot beside the window. If all went as planned, then Ravenwood would notice it.

Lena sighed in her sleep. She dreamed of Ravenwood. He came to her chambers in the middle of the night, stopping by her bedside. Leaning down, he brushed his lips to hers, causing butterfly wings to blossom in her chest. Her lips easily parted, inviting him to deepen the kiss. His mouth evaded hers, trailed a path down her throat and halted at her ear. His distinctive cologne, sandalwood and bergamot, teased her senses. His kisses stoked a gently growing fire. A delightful shiver of wanting ran through her, and her nipples tightened beneath the silk nightgown.

She grew restless, a delicious ache blossoming between her thighs. She arched towards him, wanting more, wanting…

She reached out to press a hand to his muscular chest, needing to feel his heart beat beneath her palm. The touch was real, so real…

Her eyes flew open.

Flesh and blood, the duke was kneeling by her bedside. 'Ravenwood!'

Her delicious dream was not a dream at all. Her mind was sluggish to comprehend. A candelabra sat on her nightstand, and candlelight flickered across the chiseled planes of his face. She could make out the shadow of his scar.

'Lena, are you all right?' His voice was low, tinged with concern.

As the last wisps of sleep disappeared, she raised herself on her elbows. The arousal she'd experienced while she'd believed she was sleeping returned in a rush at the sight of him so close.

She swallowed. It was impossible to steady her erratic pulse. 'Yes…yes…why are you here?'

'I was passing by and heard your moan of distress. I feared you were having a nightmare. I know how frightening they can be.'

She knew how guarded he was about his own nightmares. It must have cost him to make this admission. Warmth spread through her from the note of concern in his voice. But he'd mistaken her moan of desire as one of distress. The implication had her cheeks flushing. 'And you sought to help?'

'You came to my aid once. Why wouldn't I come to yours?'

He was referring to when she found him in his study, and she'd massaged his shoulders to ease his tension. Was he thinking of doing the same? Her pulse leaped at the thought of his touch.

'Thank you, but I'm fine,' she said, her voice more at ease now that she was fully awake. 'It must be well past midnight. Why were you awake?'

She could make out the breadth of his shoulders in the candlelight. 'I never sleep well, as you know. Now, you are worried about something. I can tell.'

Despite her denial, he was astute enough to sense something was wrong. She could never confess that her restless sleep was due to an erotic dream about him. 'I confess I did have a troubling dream.'

'Do you wish to speak of it?'

She shook her head.

'I have my own confession,' he murmured. 'All I could think about when I was out tonight was your enticing kiss in the park.' His tone had turned from concerned to husky with desire.

He had thought of her? 'And will you kiss me now?' The question slipped from her lips.

'Do you want me to?' He continued to look at her, his gaze turning heated.

She was in her nightgown, and he was mere inches from joining her in her bed. If she gave permission, one kiss could turn into much, much more. A dreaded, all-too-familiar sliver of panic rose in her throat at the thought of intimacy. She stiffened, her fingers gripping the coverlet. 'No. I fear allowing you to kiss me while I lay in my bed is unwise.'

He watched her, his eyes unfathomable. 'We agreed upon a week, and I will uphold my part of the bargain.'

'You will?'

'I would never force you.' He picked up her hand and placed a kiss in the center of her palm. 'To prove myself, I'm willing to wait longer.' His gaze softened. 'You can have as much time as you need.'

Truly? Her pulse pounded and she was momentarily speechless. Heat radiated from the touch of his lips in her limbs. She struggled to gain her senses. He felt just as enticing in her dream. 'Ravenwood, I… I—'

'You require more wooing.' He rose from the bed and held out his hand. 'Come with me.'

'Where?' Surprised at this development, she stared up at him.

'Outside.'

'Outside? But it's well past midnight.'

'It's a full moon and the gardens are illuminated. Come with me. Unless you'd rather we stay in your bed.'

She pushed back the sheet and rose. She donned her robe and followed him outside.

The gardens had an ethereal lunar glow. The moon hung low like a Roman coin, and she breathed in the sweet-smelling daffodils, forget-me-nots, and flowering shrubs. He walked a path along the hedgerows before halting near a stone bench by a pond.

'I used to come here as a boy and toss stones in the water.'

She imagined him as a dark-haired boy with blue eyes and an inquisitive nature. The pride and joy of his mother. 'Were you quiet or rambunctious?'

He chuckled. 'I tended to get myself into trouble. I'd run around the grounds, come home with cuts and scrapes, along with a frog or two. I'd often vex both my nanny and my mother.'

She smiled as she pictured him 'gifting' his mother and nanny with a frog. He must have been carefree and happy.

Quiet moments passed as they sat together on the bench, bathed part in moonlight and part in shadows from the tall oaks. The tension that had tightened her nerves when she'd woken to find him in her bed dissipated. Instead, she felt comfort sitting next to him in the silence.

He sighed deeply, then turned to her. 'Will you tell me what you fear about intimacy?'

Her reprieve was not to last. The intimate question was fraught with concerns. 'I never said I feared it. I'm a widow, remember?' It was humiliating to talk about such a private topic.

'What do you fear?' he asked again gently.

She sucked in a breath, her mind working along with her lungs. Dare she confess? Was she brave enough? 'Disappointing you.'

His low laugh took her by surprise.

A different unease made her stiffen. Her lips thinned and she glared. 'Are you laughing at me?'

He held up a hand and shook his head. 'No. Your first husband's incompetence was the problem, not you.'

Her mouth dropped open. 'How do you know? Eventually I will disappoint you and you will be angry with me.'

His brow furrowed. 'You won't. And I won't.'

'Again, how do you know?'

He shifted closer, his muscular thigh brushing hers. The thin nightgown provided little barrier. 'You once told me you believed you were frigid. You are anything but, remember?'

How could she forget? Her heart thumped erratically whenever she recalled that *first* kiss.

'From what I can discern, you possess a passionate nature,' he continued.

Even if he was right, and she could share his bed and unleash her passionate side, she needed to keep her head. She could never lose her heart to him. She was already more drawn to him than she'd intended—cared too much about what he thought—and she needed to protect herself. If a man could lie with a woman and not fall in love, so could she.

But as she looked up at the hard planes of his scarred face, nothing felt businesslike at this moment.

He picked up a stone and handed it to her. 'Toss this into the pond.'

'Why?'

'It's the first step. The stone represents your past and your fears. Throw it away.'

'Are you serious?' She considered his strange request.

'Trust me.'

Trust him. Why did he make it sound so simple when it was anything but. She looked down at the stone in her hand. It was an ordinary stone, dirty, not perfectly round or white. Just an ordinary stone. She scrunched her nose as she thought of all the ugly experiences of her past. She clenched her fist, the edges of the stone pressing into her palm. She raised her arm and tossed it into the pond. A light splash sounded.

'Now, think of that stone every time you doubt yourself. Start anew.'

'Anew.' Could it be that easy?

He reached out, his fingers raising her chin so she met his eyes. 'I cannot promise never to lose my temper, Lena, but it will not be because you disappoint me in bed.' He dipped his head and pressed his lips to hers. 'Goodnight, wife.'

The following afternoon, Lena found Claire in the music conservatory slouched over the pianoforte. The music was spread before her, and Claire sat on the bench with her arms crossed and a sour expression on her face.

'The horrible pianoforte instructor, Mr Tillsdale, is expected this afternoon. I refuse to leave my room to meet him!' Claire protested.

Lena paused for patience. 'Don't be so dramatic.'

Claire turned on the bench to face Lena. 'Dramatic? Perhaps you should take lessons with him. Did you know he raps the back of my hands with a ruler if I don't keep my wrists in the proper position?'

Her lips parted in surprise. 'Does Ravenwood know this?'

'Why bother to tell my uncle? What good would it do anyway?'

Lena believed it would make a difference. Ravenwood might have strict rules, but he wanted the best for his niece and wouldn't want anyone to harm her.

As for how to handle the duke, Lena considered the best tactic.

Her mother had often used an Arabic saying when it came to her father, the marquess.

Tackle a man with cheerful fearlessness.

Her mother had described her father as loving and giving. But from what Lena recalled of the marquess, he'd been a firm, reserved man. Had her mother conquered him with cheerful fearlessness?

Could she do the same with the duke—a man whose moods seemed ruled by nightmares?

If it would help Claire, then she'd try.

'Did you hang your sketch like I suggested?' Lena asked.

'It was a wasted effort.' Claire fidgeted with her skirts. 'He hasn't come to see it.'

'Today he will.' Determination sparked in her chest. She'd mentioned the painting to the duke, but he was currently isolating himself with his newly hired steward, managing affairs of the estate. He'd kept his word and spent time with her. Surely, he could spare a minute to see to his niece. 'Go to your room and wait for me there.'

Lena left the conservatory and hurried down the hall.

As she approached the study, the door opened, and the steward stepped out.

'Your Grace,' the man greeted her respectfully.

'Good day, Mr Riverton.' Lena had made an effort to recall all the servants' names, even the new steward. Before he could shut the study door, she slipped inside.

Ravenwood was standing behind his desk, his palms pressed flat on the desk's surface, his attention focused on open ledgers. Dressed in his shirtsleeves without a jacket or waistcoat, clearly he'd been working.

'Did you forget something, Riverton?' he asked without looking up.

'It's me,' Lena said.

Ravenwood's head snapped up. 'Lena. Is something amiss?'

Her pulse quickened at his perusal of her. She realized it was the first time she'd entered his study without being summoned. 'I'd like to show you something. Will you come with me?'

His dark eyebrows snapped together. 'Can it wait? As you can see, I have work before me.'

She understood he had duties, but Claire was one of them. And in her opinion, his niece was the most important. She took a deep breath to gather her courage and her resolve. In and out. *Cheerful fearlessness.* 'It's a surprise, and it will only take a few minutes of your time.'

She knew he was intrigued when he closed one of the ledgers and stepped away from his desk. 'Where is this surprise?'

'Claire's room.'

'You wish to show me her artwork before Mr Tillsdale arrives?'

'You never visited her room,' she pointed out.

'I've been busy with my steward.' He scrubbed a hand down his face.

'Oh, is something amiss?'

'*Amiss* is an understatement.' He was silent for a long moment, and she wondered if he would refuse to answer. Then he let out a sigh. 'My father and brother gave their stewards too much authority without supervision. As a result, theft occurred and the stewards fattened their purses while my father and brother had occupied themselves hunting, gambling, and entertaining. Items have disappeared— from bottles of fine French wine from the cellar to tea from the tea chest to supplies for tenants in their country landholdings. The theft has been both subtle and blatant. I've spent months trying to unravel it all.'

Her heart went out to him. Inheriting a dukedom came with a wealth of responsibility. Still, part of that involved his niece. 'I do not doubt you. But perhaps you could still take a break and spare a moment for Claire.'

Walking around his desk, Lena touched his sleeve.

He stiffened, his gaze lowered to where her hand rested on his arm.

For a pulse-pounding moment, they stood together. Awareness flared where her hand lay, kindling a foolish, feverish craving. Then his other hand covered hers where it rested on his sleeve, and his thumb drew slow circles over her skin. A tingling radiated from each stroke, and she grew a little breathless.

'I will go with you. But before we leave, will you give me something in return?' he asked.

Dare she ask? 'And what is it you desire?' As soon as the words left her lips, she knew she'd phrased it poorly. Had it been a slip of her tongue? Or had she really wanted to know?

His eyes never left hers. 'A kiss.'

Her breath caught in her lungs. 'We've already kissed. Three times if you include at the altar.'

'I don't think there is a limited number of kisses between a husband and wife. Do you?'

'I don't suppose so.'

'Good. I'll wait.'

Shock ran through her. 'You want *me* to kiss *you*?'

'Yes.'

Could she do it? Just the thought that they were bartering was outrageous. Then why did butterflies swarm in her chest at the thought of kissing him? She suspected his game. By giving her control, he was easing her fears about intimacy and seducing her at the same time. Her heightened senses were evidence it was working.

She felt like a breathless girl of eighteen. Coming close, she placed a hand on his chest and rose on tiptoe. He tilted his head to the side and waited, his eyes watching her every movement. The prolonged anticipation was almost unbearable. Heart hammering, she touched her lips to his. When he showed no reaction, she ran the tip of her tongue along his full, lower lip. It was soft, unlike the rest of the man. His scar was wickedly tempting, and her lips hovered over it, then she tentatively licked it.

At his low growl, she drew back. 'Aren't you going to kiss me back?'

'Not yet. Keep going.' This time when she kissed him, he parted his lips and her tongue slipped inside to softly brush against his. He tasted of rich brandy. His hands remained by his sides, and she wanted him to touch her, to hold her. It was wickedly arousing and frustrating at the same time. Both of her hands now pressed against his chest, and she felt his heart beat strongly beneath his shirt. She kissed him deeply then, lingering and savouring the moment, then nipping his lip with her teeth.

With another deep growl, he came alive and pulled her to him, taking her mouth with demanding mastery. Warmth followed the path of his hands, searing more than just her back. She felt it in the strangest places. A tingling in the pit of her stomach. An enticing warmth between her legs. The hardening of her nipples beneath the silk bodice. She met him just as fiercely, shocked at her own eager response. She had a burning desire, an aching need, to feel his skin beneath his shirt, for him to touch her breasts. Was that her moan or his?

He broke the kiss, his arm still around her. 'Your fear of disappointing me in bed is for naught. Come to me at night.'

'Tonight?' Her heart jolted at the traitorous coiling deep in her belly at the mere idea.

He stepped away and shoved a hand through his hair. He pulled back the strands and they fell back in place. 'Not tonight. When you're ready.'

He was being remarkably patient. He'd asked her to

kiss him, then held himself in check for longer than she'd have liked.

'Now, I'm a man of my word. Show me what you came here for,' he said.

With shaky hands, she smoothed her skirts, a tangle of emotions rioting inside her—fear, not so much of the man, but of herself. Could she be intimate with him and keep her heart safe?

Together, they mounted the grand staircase, Ravenwood slowing his steps for Lena to keep up with his longer strides. She was dressed in a form-fitting yellow gown. When she walked in his study, she was like a sunbeam, a breath of fresh air in his dark, sterile world. An unwanted deep longing tugged low in his gut. For a man with worldly experience, her kiss in his study had shaken him to his core. The tentative touch of her lips against his had been seductive in its hesitancy. He'd wanted to crush her to him, and it had taken all his control to keep his hands by his sides. When she'd nipped his lip with her sharp, white teeth, lust had spiraled deep in his belly.

Good God, what would she be like in his bed?

'I may not change my mind about piano lessons for Claire,' Ravenwood said as they reached the landing.

Her face brightened in a way that caused the pull in his low gut to tighten even more.

'We shall see.'

He was growing accustomed to her cheekiness as well. He anticipated and looked forward to it. Another surprise.

They reached Claire's door. Ravenwood knocked. 'Claire, it's me.'

Claire appeared, looking visibly surprised, and held the door open wide for them to enter. The cat, Bella, sleeping on Claire's bed, lifted her head, watching the newcomers.

The drapes were drawn open and afternoon sunlight brightened the furnishings of the room. Ravenwood scanned the walls, taking in the array of artwork. Each piece was uniquely beautiful. The still life bowl of fruit. The landscape of the gardens. A sketch of the London sky, showing the coal smoke from the factories. Another at Hyde Park during a sunny day, with carriages on the Serpentine and ladies carrying parasols as they strolled arm-in-arm during promenade hour. A charcoal sketch of a boy sitting on a bench. Each was different, not just the medium—one charcoal, another watercolour, one done in oils. She was creative without instruction, and even though he had no artistic ability, he recognized and appreciated her talent

At last, he spoke. 'You did all of these?'

'Yes.'

'The vase of pink and yellow flowers is nice.' It was the first work that he'd noticed. Cheerful and colourful, the brush-strokes added dimension in the afternoon sunlight.

'I was happy when I painted it,' she said softly. 'My mother was alive, then.'

A pang in his chest reminded him of her loss. If only he were the type of man who could offer comfort…who knew *how* to offer it. He had no idea how to help a six-teen-year-old girl, other than the way he'd found comfort for himself, in structure. Apologizing for all she'd gone through would come off as meaningless. He had to show it another way. He truly admired her work, and he was proud of her.

'Claire is brimming with talent,' Lena said, breaking the awkward silence. 'Imagine what she can learn with formal art instruction. Painting is just as socially acceptable for young ladies as pianoforte lessons.'

'I know my mother was pianist,' Claire said, 'but music and art are both creative in their own way.'

'Yes, they are,' he agreed.

'I'm happy to help find her an art instructor,' Lena said.

'Mr Tillsdale will not be coming today,' he announced.

'Is he ill?' Claire asked.

The duke shook his head. 'I shall send him a note telling him his services are no longer required.' After seeing his niece's passion for art, he knew he was making the right choice.

Claire stood stock-still, appearing not to immediately comprehend his meaning. Then her face brightened, radiant. 'Thank you, Uncle!' She threw her arms around him.

Stunned, heart pounding like a drum, he wrapped his arms around her in return. Her soft dark hair rubbed his cheek. It was the first time he'd hugged Claire since returning from war, and, as he returned her embrace, his gaze met Lena's over his niece's head.

Lena's smile was wide, her own lovely eyes bright with happiness.

Ravenwood placed a hand on Claire's shoulder. 'There's one condition.'

Claire sobered. 'What is it?'

'The vase of flowers is to be displayed in the vestibule,' he said.

Claire hugged him again.

Chapter Sixteen

Lena didn't have to think of Ravenwood that night. He had long-standing plans with the Earl of Kent at his home for an evening of cards and cigars.

Whether his absence was a reprieve or not, she couldn't say. She'd been more confused than ever over the past couple days. He'd showed consideration when she hadn't expected it. Her first marriage was hard to forget, and she'd told herself she'd protect her heart the second time. She was finding it harder than she thought.

With the duke gone for the evening, Lena had planned to spend time with Claire. She could watch her draw while they chatted. Her plans were waylaid when Claire claimed a mild headache and requested a dinner tray be delivered to her room.

It wasn't until later that evening that Lena decided to check on the girl. She softly knocked on her door and waited. No answer. She knocked again, louder this time. Still no answer.

Was she asleep? Or had her headache gotten worse?

Concerned, Lena reached for the handle.

Then stood stunned as she stared into the empty bed-chamber.

She was struck by a feeling of déjà vu from her first day as Claire's governess, discovering her room empty.

It was dark outside, a crescent moon offering little light. They'd been getting along, and together they had convinced Ravenwood to dismiss the pianoforte teacher in exchange for searching for an art instructor. She understood Claire was still mourning the loss of her parents and was navigating an entirely different world with her uncle and his new wife. But to feign a headache in order to slip out into the night?

It was reckless and dangerous.

If Lena could not find Claire—and fast—she'd have to tell Ravenwood that his wayward niece had gone missing. Again. Explaining another escape from the house would be highly unpleasant.

Lena hurried to the window in Claire's bedchamber and glanced outside. The tree had been cut down before the betrothal. So how had the girl escaped? Lena leaned farther out the casement. A narrow ledge led to a vine-covered trellis on the side of the mansion. Had Claire inched her way across the ledge and climbed down? Lena recalled how nimble the girl had been when she'd scurried down the tree and hopped to safety, leaving her stranded on a limb. Or had she silently slipped out the back French doors into the gardens?

Either way, why go to such lengths to leave the house at night? Her first thought was that this was a rebellion against the duke's rigid rules and forced pianoforte lessons. But that made no sense. The duke had relented on the lessons and the two had made a huge leap forward in their relationship. Claire had gone so far as to embrace Ravenwood. So why jeopardize that now?

Unless…unless there were more to it? What would make a sixteen-year-old girl risk her reputation and the wrath of her guardian?

A boy.

Lena had been her age once. It wasn't a far-fetched idea. It was more likely than not.

Lena left the room and headed downstairs, leaving the house from the servant's entrance. She paused when she got to the gravel drive. *Think, Lena.* How far could Claire have gone on foot? Going with her gut, she headed towards the gardens and opened the gate. A drizzle of rain had ceased, and the air was as humid. Crickets chirped in a lyrical orchestra, and a sliver of moon cast a faint glow across the vast lawn. Her steps slowed at the sound of low whispers. The voices came from deeper in the gardens.

Creeping along in the shadows, her footsteps were muffled by the lush, well-kept grass. Her slippers had gotten wet and would be ruined. She spotted Claire in the far corner of the property. Standing on a gardener's crate, Claire clutched the top of a wooden fence that separated Ravenwood's property from his neighbour's. Dressed in her nightgown, her feet were bare, her toes curled over the edge of the crate.

Who was Claire speaking with?

Then Lena spotted him.

A tawny-haired boy, or young man, rested his hands on the fence, his head bent close to Claire's, as they whispered to each other. From Claire's low chuckle and slight smile, Lena suspected this was not the first time the two had met.

She likes a young man. A neighbour.

A slight tug centered in Lena's chest. Claire was old enough to notice boys, and this young man was certainly of the age to notice her.

Lena's first instinct was to charge forward and demand Claire return to the house.

Instead, she stayed hidden in the shadows. Her thoughts tumbled as she observed the young couple. Maybe their clandestine, late-night visits helped Claire through her mourning? What if Claire were able to share her pain with the boy in ways she could not with the adults in her life? What if he made her *happy*? Even if the crush were just a young lady's fancy, Claire had already lost her parents. Why tear this away from the girl as well?

Still, Lena knew she had to speak with her. The girl was her responsibility, and she must warn her against secret meetings with a neighbour boy in the middle of the night. If Ravenwood found out, he would have a fit and their recent tenuous relationship would be broken. Meanwhile, Lena would inquire as to who their neighbours were and decide on a way to properly meet the family in the light of day.

It was a plan, and in her mind, a good one. She'd draft an invitation tonight and have it hand delivered early tomorrow morning.

The couple's soft laughter made Lena smile. She'd deal

with this on her own. Why cause conflict between uncle and niece when the two were getting along for the first time?

The perfume of the two dozen pink roses wafted to Lena as soon as she descended the staircase the following morning. She'd stayed up late, waiting for Claire to sneak back into the house and safely close her bedroom door. As she'd waited, she'd drafted an invitation and given it to her maid. As a result, Lena slept through breakfast. It was a wonder Ravenwood hadn't sent her maid to wake her.

'The flowers arrived for you this morning, Your Grace,' Barnes announced.

Lena reached for the embossed note by the flowers.

These roses match the hue of your lips.
R

Poetry. Ravenwood had written a line of poetry. He'd mocked poetry when she'd first mentioned it, but he'd given her roses and written her a sweetly romantic line.

Oh, he was smooth. She envisioned him as a charmer in his youth. A lady wouldn't stand a chance.

'Where is His Grace, Barnes?' she asked.

'The duke is currently in his bedchamber with his valet.'

He must be rising late today as well. She hurried up the stairs and found his door ajar. She could see Ravenwood's valet tying the duke's cravat.

Both men looked up at her short knock. 'May I have a moment of your time?' Lena asked.

At Ravenwood's nod, the valet bowed and left.

She stepped into his room. It was a masculine chamber with mahogany furniture and a large four-poster bed. She avoided looking at the bed, highly conscious of Ravenwood's hooded eyes watching her. He was dressed in a navy coat that accentuated his broad shoulders and fawn-coloured trousers that hugged his muscular thighs. His cravat was now expertly tied after his valet's ministrations, and he was clean-shaven. The drapes had been opened and his dark hair gleamed in the sunlight. His scar was a white slash across his cheek.

'The roses are beautiful,' she said. 'The poetry was unexpected.'

He took a step forward. 'It's not as good as Lord Byron.'

A fluttering stirred deep in her chest. 'It's perfect.' She didn't need a fourteen-line sonnet. The fact that he'd taken the time to write it himself made it special.

There was a slight pause as he regarded her. 'Are you afraid of the water?'

The question took her by surprise. 'No. I used to swim in the Mediterranean Sea when I was young. I loved the feeling of freedom and weightlessness.'

A humorous glint lit his eyes. 'I didn't mean swimming, although I would enjoy that activity with you. What I meant to ask is if you fear being on a rowboat. I'd like to take you boating on the Serpentine at Hyde Park.'

Her pulse leapt. 'Yes, I'd like that very much.'

Soon after, they were at the lake. Several rowboats lined the lake-shore, and, after Ravenwood spoke with the boat-master, he helped her inside one of the rowboats. With a push away from shore, he then climbed inside the boat and joined her. He'd taken off his coat, and his shoulders strained against his shirt as he rowed. The oars rhythmically skimmed, then entered the water. Lena lifted her head towards a cloudless blue sky as the sun kissed her cheeks.

'Tell me about when you last swam,' he said.

'It was back home. We'd travel to the Mediterranean Sea on holiday. Many Europeans travel to Lebanon to enjoy the sea as well. The water is blue and warm and filled with bathers during the warmest months. My mother would often call out and tell me not to venture too far. One of my earliest memories was of my father, the marquess, holding my hand as I played in the surf.'

'What else did you enjoy there?'

'I loved market day. All the colourful tents of the vendors, the smells of cumin, cloves, Aleppo pepper and sumac and the scent of grilled lamb. I would admire all the trinkets and gifts for sale, like jewellery, hand-woven rugs, pottery, and perfumes. I even liked to watch the haggling between buyers and sellers.'

'It sounds fascinating. And loud.'

'It's both.' She smiled.

They came to the center of the lake, and he stopped rowing and lifted the oars from the water. 'And you? What do you enjoy?' she asked. He'd taken such a keen interest in her during their outings. She wanted to know more about him.

He leaned forward on the bench, his eyes bright in the sunlight. 'Coffee.'

'Coffee?'

'I never drank it until the Earl of Kent recommended a coffee house near the Exchange. We meet at Jonathan's Coffee House once a week to read the papers and listen to the jobbers and stockbrokers discuss the latest investments.'

This was an interesting fact about him. 'It sounds like you enjoy the company as much as the beverage.'

'I suppose so. They are used to me there, even the servers, and no one stares.'

He must be referring to his scar. She couldn't imagine what it was like to bear it. If her face was marred, would it affect how she acted? Would she become a recluse? Avoid her own friends? Never glance in a looking glass? She wasn't vain, but could she bear it?

The boat slipped beneath a canopy of trees. His dark hair caught the ray of sunlight sneaking through the canopy of leaves, framing his strong, chiseled cheekbones. 'You did not meet Lord Kent there the past two days,' she said.

'I've been meeting with my steward. As I mentioned, the estate was not left in order, and it has taken me longer than expected to right it.'

'I appreciate the time you are taking away from the estate ledgers today.'

'There's nowhere I'd rather be right now.'

Her heart did a pitter-patter. When he said such things, she felt her heart slipping. She'd sworn never to let another man into her heart. Love only led to heartbreak.

When they returned, Barnes approached Lena. 'A letter was hand delivered for you, Your Grace.' Barnes held out a silver salver.

Lena tore open the sealed foolscap. Her eyes widened at the quick response from next door. Her maid must have delivered her invitation at daybreak. Her first invitation as duchess and the guests had accepted!

'What is it?' Ravenwood asked.

He was in a pleasant mood and she hoped he would be receptive. She cleared her throat. 'Would you mind if I invited our neighbours over?'

'Why?'

'They are our neighbours. We should become acquainted. In addition, it will be good practice for Claire.'

'How will inviting our neighbours help my niece?'

She'd expected the question and was ready with her answer. 'They have a son her age. She must learn how to speak with young men. The entire purpose of her debut is to find a marriage match.'

His lips turned down. 'I'm aware. I still recall Claire as a little girl. Now that she's older, it will be a form of torture watching Claire with young gentlemen and not discouraging them, but rather, encouraging her to find a worthy one.'

'I believe it's what many good fathers—or in your circumstances—uncles must face. As for our neighbours…' She bit her lip, unsure how to tell him.

His gaze dropped to the letter in her hand. 'If you have something else to say, it's best if you just tell me.'

'The Marquess and Marchioness of Billingham and

their son have agreed to come tomorrow afternoon,' she blurted out.

His brow furrowed. 'Agreed? Then you already invited them?'

'I didn't think it would be a surprise. Inviting guests and attending functions are both on my list—'

'Of requirements. I remember.' He leaned closer, his eyes bright.

'So you are agreeable?' she asked.

'I find myself agreeing to more than I expect to when I'm with you,' he said in a low murmur.

Heavens. Her heart thumped in her chest. He was being charming *and* agreeable.

He offered his arm. 'Now shall we enjoy the rest of our afternoon?'

Her heart made a pitter-patter. 'There's more?'

'It's a warm day and I plan to take you to Gunter's for ices.'

Her breath caught and tangle of traitorous emotions knotted in her chest. She did not fear him but herself. And her heart.

It had been a perfect day for Lena. She and the duke had sat beneath a shaded tree while enjoying lemon and pistachio ices. She'd learned more about Ravenwood, and although he hadn't been thrilled at the prospect of their neighbours visiting, he'd acquiesced. Was he coming to understand the benefits for Claire? Or was it to please his wife? A selfish part of her wanted it to be to please her.

It was Wednesday, the middle of the week, and she

looked forward to the rest of his wooing. When they'd returned to Berkeley Square, Ravenwood's steward was waiting for him. Now, with the duke conducting business in his study, she had time to focus on another matter. She found Claire in her bedroom, working on a pad as she sat on a cushion of the window seat. The drapes had been pulled aside and tied with a gold cord to allow for the best possible sunlight. Bella sat on the bed, the cat's lovely green eyes watching them.

'I see you are hard at work,' Lena said.

Claire held a piece of charcoal in her hand as she sketched. 'The best light is in the afternoon.'

The face of a handsome boy took shape on the paper. Lena recognized the face. She'd glimpsed the same boy's face in a moonlit garden.

Lena settled beside her on the window seat, folding her hands in her lap. 'I want you to know that you can confide in me.'

'Confide in you? What do you mean?' Claire asked without looking up. She worked on the figure's hair.

'I have your interest at heart. I want you to be happy.'

Claire kept on sketching. The boy's nose took shape, strong and fine. 'I see. And if I decided to confess a secret—and I'm not saying I have one—would you tell my uncle?'

'Only if I thought you were in danger.'

Claire let out an unladylike snort. 'Forgive me if I'm not convinced.'

'I have faith you will trust me.' Lena watched the work-in-progress. 'On another topic, I've arranged for us to have tea with our neighbours.'

That finally got Claire's attention. She dropped the charcoal and looked at Lena for the first time since she'd walked into the room. 'You did what? Why?'

'I told your uncle that it's important for us to begin to become acquainted with members of society. After all, your debut is right around the corner. What better way to start than with our own neighbours?'

A flash of panic crossed Claire's delicate features. 'Are they coming?'

'Yes, they've accepted my invitation.'

'All of them?'

Lena bit the inside of her cheek to prevent a knowing smile. 'Yes, all of them—the Marquess and Marchioness of Billingham and their son. As ladies of the house, I'd like you to stand by my side as we greet them.'

Claire swiped a hand across her forehead and a smudge of charcoal marred her brow. 'I… I… I don't know.'

'Why not? You are a charming young lady, and this will be good practice.' Lena reached for an embroidered lace handkerchief in her pocket. 'Goodness. You've smudged your forehead.'

Claire stood still and allowed Lena to wipe away the black streak.

'There haven't been guests here since I've arrived,' Lena said. 'I'd like to change that.'

'Are you certain this is a good idea? My uncle does not like guests.'

'He's already agreed. Now, I'm happy to help you select a dress.'

'Yes. A dress,' Claire said absent-mindedly.

Lena rose and went to the wardrobe. She began sorting through gowns. 'I like this pink one.' She held it up for the girl to see.

At Claire's silence, Lena asked, 'What's wrong, darling?'

Claire bit her bottom lip. 'Do you think pink makes me look childish? I don't want to look like I'm just out of the nursery.'

Lena made of show of studying the dress. 'Hmm. Perhaps you're right. It is a little young.' She reached for another and handed it to her. 'What about the lavender?'

Claire rose and crossed the room. She held the dress up to her and looked in the cheval glass mirror. 'What do you think?'

Lena held her tongue at Claire's anxiousness. 'I think you will look beautiful. Our neighbours will be enchanted.'

Claire turned left and right as she held up the dress. 'And you're certain the entire family is coming?'

'Yes. I'm certain. Our neighbours must be curious about the duke.'

Claire turned away from the dressing glass. 'They are more likely more curious to meet the new Duchess of Ravenwood.' She tossed the lavender dress on the bed. 'Will you help me with my hair when they come? I'd rather you do it than a maid.'

'I'd love to. If you want, we can practise hairstyles now.'

The girl beamed. 'Yes, I'd like that.'

Claire sat at her dressing table, and Lena picked up a silver-handled brush and began to brush Claire's dark locks. 'I understand they have a son a year or two older than you,' Lena hedged. 'His name is Peter.'

The slight stiffening of Claire's shoulders was a telltale sign. 'You know, don't you? Is that why you asked me to confide in you?'

'There is another way that holds no risk to your reputation.' She needn't say more. Claire was intelligent and knew.

'Does my uncle know?'

Lena had already decided. 'I see no need to tell him, not if you stay in the house at night.'

'I—'

'When our neighbours arrive, you can show Peter our gardens while we have tea and scones by the terrace. It will be perfectly acceptable.'

She nodded. 'I suppose I can do that.'

Lena brushed Claire's hair to the side and reached for a ribbon. 'It's never too early to think about a lady's first dance at her debut.'

Claire bit her bottom lip. 'What if the Marquess and Marchioness dislike me?'

Lena set down the brush and squeezed Claire's shoulders. 'They could never! Be yourself, darling, and they will be just as charmed as young Peter is.'

Ravenwood looked up from where he stood at the bottom of the grand staircase. His wife, wearing a white silk dress, held the railing as she descended the stairs. A delicate scarf lay around her neck. His gut tightened. Their neighbours were expected at any moment. He disliked meeting strangers, and in his experience their reaction was always the same. They would try not to stare at his scar and their discomfort only served to heighten his own anxiety and, in defence, his own anger.

Surprisingly, the dreaded anticipation he should have experienced as they waited for the Billinghams was absent. Instead, all he could do was stare at his wife.

Lena looked lovely in the form-hugging silk. Her olive complexion was radiant against her white gown, and her glorious mahogany hair was swept back in an elegant chignon. Her silk scarf drew his eye. Peacocks and flowers embroidered in colourful thread added a touch of colour to her dress.

'You look lovely.' His voice was gruff.

Her dark eyes, slanted at the corners, smiled up at him. 'You look fine today as well, Your Grace.'

He stood straighter, like a lovesick boy craving a compliment from a beautiful girl. His valet had fussed over him and had expressed his pleasure that guests were visiting. He'd frowned through dressing. He'd reached his limit, however, and had come close to tossing his valet out when he'd attempted to style his hair in the *à la brutus* fashion favored by dandies.

Lena came close and he breathed in the scent of lemongrass. Without a thought, he reached out to touch the scarf.

Her eyes were bright. 'It was my mother's. They sold these in the weekly Lebanese market in a local village.

The peacocks are a symbol of angels and immortality in Armenian culture and belief.'

'It's lovely as well.' His chest tightened at her smile. He enjoyed how effortlessly she shared her past and culture with him. He was fascinated and wanted to know more. If only he could share his past as easily.

'Our guests are expected at any moment,' she said.

For some reason, meeting their neighbours was important to her. She'd even insisted Claire be present. He'd never bothered to inquire who owned the neighbouring property. If he'd never met them, he'd be content. But today he'd push aside his misgivings, welcome strangers, and act the proper host. He rationalized that a small gathering in the comfort of his own home had to be better than a crowded ballroom.

'Do you know anything about them? I'd like to be prepared,' he said.

She gave him a sidelong look. 'The Marquess and Marchioness of Billingham have a son, Peter, who is two years older than Claire.'

'How do you know this about the son?'

She smoothed her skirts. 'I inquired when I returned to the dressmaker for my fittings. When Claire shows him the gardens, it will be perfectly proper since they will be in eyesight the entire time we are seated outside on the terrace.'

'I see you have given this visit much thought.'

Her smile brightened her lovely features. 'It's my first-time hostessing as a duchess. I also want to be prepared.'

He should be used to her bewitching smile. It shouldn't affect him each time.

A knock on the front door alerted them that their guests had arrived. Claire joined them just before Barnes opened the door and took their neighbours' hats, cane, and cloaks.

'It is a pleasure to meet you, my lady.' Lena glided forward to greet the Marchioness of Billingham.

The marchioness smiled. 'We were pleased to get your invitation, Your Grace. This is our son, Lord Peter.'

Peter was a handsome lad, tall and lean, with a swath of fair hair and green eyes.

Claire stepped forward and Peter bowed. 'It is a pleasure to meet you, Miss Claire.'

Claire curtsied, and a faint blush stained her cheeks.

Ravenwood watched the exchange. Claire's shy, polite behaviour was interesting. Was it due to an interest in the marquess's son or because the young couple was under scrutiny from four adults?

Lena seemed at ease, as if she thought Claire's reaction perfectly normal. Perhaps he was reading too much into it?

The party settled on the terrace and servants brought tea and scones for the ladies. The marquess followed Ravenwood to a sideboard as he served the marquess his favourite whisky from the cellar.

'Good, smooth Scotch whisky.' Billingham sipped his drink.

Ravenwood reached for his own glass, but before he could drink, Billingham spoke.

'The battle was all in the papers. It was a magnificent win for Wellington,' Billingham said.

Ravenwood's throat grew tight. *Magnificent?* Thousands of British soldiers had perished. Many others were injured. There wasn't anything glorious about war. He should have anticipated the comments. It wasn't uncommon for civilians to bring up the war. Their ignorance was not to blame. They regarded him with curiosity and believed it was all honor and glory.

'You came home a hero,' Billingham said.

He'd come home a mess, a battle-worn, guilt-ridden mess.

'Plenty of good men died.' His voice sounded far off and rough.

Thankfully, Lena called the men over to join the others at the terrace table. Billingham enjoyed his whisky without further dialogue.

'We were pleasantly surprised at the invitation,' the marchioness said. 'We have resided next door for over a year.' She smiled.

'We plan to attend more society functions,' Lena said, then looked up at him. 'Isn't that right, Your Grace?'

Ravenwood cleared his throat. 'Of course,' he said, even though he had no intention of appearing more than necessary.

The marchioness lowered her teacup, her expression one of elation. 'Wonderful! We are hosting a ball this Saturday and we would be honored if you both would attend.'

Lena met his eyes over the rim of her teacup. 'We would be delighted, wouldn't we?'

Ravenwood gave her a forced smile. 'Delighted, indeed.' He hadn't been to a ball in five years—not since he'd left for war. He'd dread the crush of people, the pungent smell of perfumes used to mask sweat, the expectations of him as a new duke. The questions from other men about his war service. *Jesus.* He'd rather walk on hot coals. Still, if Lena was determined to go, he'd accompany her.

A movement out of the corner of his eye distracted him. Claire and the young lord, Peter, strolled together around the vast gardens. The couple stayed in sight, most likely conscious that they were being observed by their elders. He had expected some kind of scene, or an inappropriate or rude comment from his niece, but her behaviour so far had been exemplary. Had Lena had that much of an effect on the girl already?

When it was time for their guests to depart, Ravenwood shook Billingham's hand and bowed over the marchioness's hand.

'Thank you for coming,' Lena said. 'We shall look forward to the invitation to your ball.' When she turned to him, his wife's smile was all sweetness. Her dark eyes, however, were full of challenge.

With a start, he realized he looked forward to their battle of wills once they were alone.

Chapter Seventeen

Once they had seen their guests off in their carriage, Claire headed to her room, looking delighted. Lena returned to the terrace, aware of Ravenwood trailing behind.

'I worried that Claire would behave improperly,' he said.

The servants hadn't yet had a chance to clear away all their glasses, and Lena picked up her teacup. She sipped the rest of the drink as she thought how best to reply. He had no idea it was not the first time Claire and Peter had met.

'As for the ball,' he said, 'I've given it thought and assume it will fulfill my obligation.'

She whirled to face him. 'Nonsense. I never said *one* ball. And our neighbour's does not count.'

His frown deepened. 'It's a ball. It counts.'

'It would be horribly rude to refuse after the marchioness invited us in person.'

He dropped his gaze. 'You know how I feel about that many people gathered beneath one roof.'

'I would not ask it of you if it wasn't for Claire.' *And me.*

He closed his eyes momentarily as if having an internal

debate. She dared not say the full truth. Yes, as the Duke and Duchess of Ravenwood, it was important for them to be part of society. But Lena also wanted to attend simply for herself. As a stockbroker's wife, she hadn't been invited to balls hosted by the *beau monde*. There were other parties and dances that the middle class hosted for themselves. As her marriage had deteriorated, Oliver had not even allowed her to attend these. She had wasted too many years isolated and squirrelled away, without friends or society, in their home. Now that her life had changed, so had she. She hadn't expected that, but she was enjoying her new position in society and wanted to be part of this world.

'If I must attend on my own, I shall,' she said. 'However, I'd prefer to be escorted by my husband.'

'Why is that?'

Must she voice it? And how to answer without revealing too much? 'I was not born into the aristocracy and the *beau monde* is foreign to me. You, however, were born into a noble family and are familiar with the inner workings of the *ton*.'

He reached out to touch a loose curl that had escaped her pins. Heat simmered low in her belly at the simple touch and his closeness. 'The *ton* is nothing. They have not experienced hardship. Their superfluous manners are beneath you.'

She parted her lips. 'So you've said. Still, I fear walking in for the first time.'

His fingers moved to her cheek. 'If you feel that strongly, then I shall escort you.'

The gesture meant more than walks in the park, boating, ices at Gunter's, and gifts.

'Is that all?' he asked.

'Yes.' Did he fear she'd ask for another society event so soon?

He continued to watch her, his gaze deep and intent. 'Then I have a request of my own. I'd like to take you and Claire on a picnic in the park.'

Her lips parted. 'A picnic?'

'You mentioned you liked them when we first discussed spending time together.'

He'd remembered? She took a deep breath and let it out silently.

'Mrs Higgins will pack a basket and a bottle of wine,' he said. 'I think it's best if you ask Claire. Our relationship has improved somewhat, but she seems more agreeable with you.'

Awareness rushed through her at his request. He'd thought of this on his own? She could not have been more surprised. Or pleased. 'Yes, yes… I'll ask her.'

'Good. Tomorrow afternoon then.'

Lena sat on a checked blanket spread across soft grass and leaned over Claire's shoulder to peek at her sketchbook.

Claire hugged the sketchbook tightly to her chest. 'It's not ready.'

Ravenwood stretched out beside Lena on the blanket. 'Be patient. Let her finish.'

'Very well,' Lena said with a smile. 'I'll set out our food while we wait.'

It was a pleasant spring day with birds chirping and wildflowers scenting the air with their delicate fragrance. When Lena had told Claire that Ravenwood had planned a picnic and that he wanted her to accompany them, Claire had looked at her in astonishment as if she'd performed a miracle. Then she'd smiled brightly. Lena had noticed changes in the girl. She was happier. The art lessons and the afternoon tea with the neighbours had made a difference. Ravenwood must have noticed as well.

Cook had prepared a picnic basket for the three of them. Lena spread out the cheese, bread, cold meats, and fruit— strawberries, apples, and oranges—on a plate. Lena had added her own surprise to the basket. On a separate plate, she displayed the baklava she'd prepared herself in the kitchen. Finely chopped walnuts mixed with sugar were layered between thin sheets of dough, baked, then drizzled with a sugar syrup. It was one of her favourite childhood desserts and she'd craved it. Cook had been astonished when the new duchess wanted to spend time in the kitchens, but once Lena had explained how she'd missed the sweet from her childhood, Cook had relented.

Would Ravenwood like it? Her nerves jittered as she placed the plate before him.

'This is a delicate dessert from Lebanon,' she explained to him. 'Cook helped me prepare it.'

'You made this?' He gazed down at the little plate in surprise. 'In our kitchens?'

She'd previously cut the baklava into small squares. He

appeared intrigued as he picked up a piece. Rather than take a small bite, he popped the entire piece into his mouth.

She waited, fingers clutching the plate, heart pounding.

His eyes widened as he chewed. 'This is delicious. What is it?' He licked the sugary syrup from his fingers.

'Baklava. Finely chopped walnuts are mixed with sugar and cinnamon and then layered between fine layers of buttered dough. It's then drizzled with sugar syrup.'

'How many pieces did you bring?' He eyed the rest of the serving, then peeked in the basket.

'Just the one plate.'

His eyes twinkled. 'Do I have to share?'

'I want to try a piece!' Claire set down her charcoal pencil and reached for a square. After her first piece, Claire nodded. 'Uncle is right. It's delicious.'

Lena held away the plate before Ravenwood could snatch it from her. She smiled like a simpleton. She couldn't help it. Happiness made her giddy. 'I thought you would turn up your nose at it.'

His brow furrowed. 'Why would you think that?'

How to explain? Oliver had hated anything to do with her culture. Letting go of these things or putting them out of sight was easier than putting up with his prejudiced comments and scorn. She'd read the books in private and sneaked into the kitchens to prepare the food she'd craved at night. But by hiding her past, she felt as if she were betraying her mother and a part of herself.

She was aware of Ravenwood's attention as he waited for her answer. 'Baklava is from the Middle East, not something you would find at Gunter's.'

His intense look made her shift on the blanket. 'So? If you want to prepare cuisine from your homeland or any other dish you desire, why would I stand in your way? I only have one request. I ask that you allow me to sample it.'

She gaped. His reaction was not what she'd expected. She watched as he reached for another piece of baklava and slowly chewed, as if he were savouring the sweetness.

He'd known about her half English, half Middle Eastern heritage. He'd admitted to obtaining the services of a private investigator to look into her background before hiring her as a governess for Claire. He'd known, but still…

Knowing and *accepting* were two different things entirely. His simple trying of her dessert, and her insides warmed and fluttered.

'Now hand me the wine so I may pour for us.' Reaching into the basket, he removed two glasses.

They dined on fruit and cheese for the rest of the afternoon. He refilled her wine glass, and they sat back on the blanket and basked in the warm sun.

'I'm ready to show you now,' Claire said.

Tentatively, she turned her sketchbook around. She and Ravenwood gasped in unison. Claire had sketched them together. The detail was remarkable, and she'd captured their image lounging on the blanket with the lovely park landscape behind them. Their eyes were bright and their smiles happy. Even more startling, Lena saw affection the duke held for her in the drawing. Did he really look at her that way?

'I'll hang your work in the hall.' Ravenwood grinned.

'Why only hang the masters when I have a niece with such talent?'

Claire's lips formed an O. Her eyes shone bright and then she cracked the largest smile Lena had ever seen on the girl. 'Thank you!'

She lunged across the picnic blanket to hug him. Ravenwood froze, then his arms went around the girl. It was the second time she'd embraced him and still as shocking as the first time. Once again, his gaze met Lena's over Claire's head. Only this time, he mouthed the words she never thought she'd hear from him, *Thank you.*

Lena's heart swelled. This was the way it should be between them. Their hair glimmered beneath the afternoon sun, the duke's dark locks and Claire's curls, their blue eyes bright. They'd both suffered loss. The duke more than just his immediate family, more than any man should suffer.

As for herself, she placed a hand over her chest as if a small crack pierced the protective shell surrounding her heart. She feared she was powerless to prevent it from widening and making her vulnerable.

Even more frightening, did she wish to fight it?

Lena clutched her belly as she laughed out loud. 'I've missed this, Ivan! I'm glad you visited.'

The two were in the drawing room. Later that afternoon, Ivan had visited with a backgammon board tucked under his arm. After a lovely day picnicking with Ravenwood and Claire, a visit from her friend made her happiness complete.

'I've missed you, too,' Ivan said.

Ivan looked handsome in a bottle-green wool coat which emphasized his olive complexion, jet hair, and deep, brown eyes. She rested her cheek against his chest—he sat next to her on the settee—and inhaled his familiar scent of woody amber cologne from the Middle East.

She'd always loved playing backgammon, also known as *tavlou*, with Ivan. The game had been played since ancient times and was popular in Greece, Armenia, Turkey, and throughout the Middle East. When she was young, players could be found on many Lebanese street corners and in homes. Ivan's board was lovely, with mother-of-pearl inlay and white and black stone markers.

'My aunties asked about you,' he said as he rolled the dice.

She loved his two aunties and considered them family. Both were a bit meddling but always meant well. 'I do plan to visit soon. I've just been busy.'

'You mean with the duke? What has it been like to be his duchess?' he asked.

'My marriage has been quite…unexpected.'

Ivan visibly stiffened beside her. 'Has the duke mistreated you?'

'Goodness, no! Please don't think that.' She covered his hand with her own and spoke earnestly.

His brow creased. 'Yet you're conflicted. I can tell. What has the duke done?'

Lena considered how best to answer. He'd always been a good listener when she needed one most. 'It's not something he's done, but something he suffers from.' She shifted on the couch as she recalled Ravenwood's nightmares. 'Ivan, you once told me of a cousin who had returned from war on the Continent.' He'd first mentioned this when they'd walked in the park one afternoon.

Ivan's dark eyebrows drew together. 'Vartan was with the Dragoons, a heavy calvary regiment, during the Peninsular Wars.'

'What happened to him?' she asked.

'He'd lost an arm. Vartan had a hard go of it when he returned home. He finally obtained work as a shopkeeper's clerk.'

'Has he suffered in mind?'

'You mean other than his lost limb? Vartan never talks about his days at war. His mother, my aunt, complains he's not the same man he once was.'

'What do you mean?'

'He's sad one moment, angry the next.' Ivan hesitated as he fingered one of his black backgammon markers. 'The duke's face is scarred. I can only assume he's also scarred inside in some way.' Ivan's voice took on a serious tone.

'Maybe if I spoke with your cousin, I could ask what has been helpful.' If she could aid Ravenwood in any way, she would try.

Ivan inclined his head in compliance. 'I shall inquire for you to meet Vartan.'

'That would be most helpful. I knew I could count on you,' she said.

They resumed playing and Lena's laughter returned. It felt so good to be with her friend.

* * *

The invitation to the Billingham ball arrived the following morning. Ravenwood lifted the embossed foolscap from the silver salver held by his butler. Without opening it, he knew what it was, and his stomach clenched. For a pulse-pounding moment he thought to tuck it into his coat pocket without a mention. Cowardly, he knew, but it would solve his dilemma.

'Is that the invitation for the Billingham ball?' Lena descended the grand staircase and glanced over his shoulder. She held the cat, Bella, in her arms.

Too late! He handed it to her, and she followed him into his study. The cat leapt from her arms to jump up on the sofa. The feline's green eyes watched him. He should have minded the animal, but he didn't. He was too preoccupied with his wife.

He'd enjoyed their picnic—more than he cared to admit. And what had happened after their return yesterday afternoon rattled him even more.

After he'd left her to finish some work in his study, his wife's distinctive laughter had reached him hours later. What or who was making her happy? He'd handed the ledger to his steward, pushed back his chair and strode down the hall to find Lena in the drawing room with her friend... Ivan. Lena's laughter had increased in volume as he'd halted in the doorway, out of sight.

She sat side by side with Ivan on the sofa, smiling and laughing—a husky laugh, not a high-pitched one, and full of joy. He wanted her to be that way with him.

Carefree. Beautiful.

The two had been playing a game and neither one noticed him standing in the corner of the doorway. How could he compete? Ivan was a rival. Not in the way a man was towards a woman. But a rival, nonetheless. He couldn't offer her the easy friendship this man could give her—he was much too guarded for that and always would be.

He'd stepped back, then turned away before either could notice him. And the realization of just how much he *wanted* to let her in had shaken him. He couldn't stop thinking about it.

He saw Lena shift out of the corner of his eye. She reached for a letter opener from his desk to open the Billinghams' invitation.

Her smile was captivating as she broke the seal and silently read. He'd lain in bed the night before, thinking of her.

'The Billingham ball will be our first event together as duke and duchess,' she said, clearly unaware of his thoughts.

As duke and duchess.

Regal and beautiful, she looked like she'd been born for the role. Her pretty jade dress was cut to fit her figure and her magnificent breasts swelled above the artfully cut bodice. She bit her lower lip as she glanced down at the invitation once more. 'I've never been to a ball.'

He had no doubt she'd charm and entrance society as the Duchess of Ravenwood. Just as she'd entranced him.

He, on the other hand, had attended countless balls and parties in his youth. He knew what to expect and how he was expected to behave. Yet, five years later, he had never been so terrified at the prospect of a crowded ballroom.

Do not think too much of it. He could do this. He could survive one night.

'Are you certain you will attend?' Her brown eyes were large as she watched him.

It was one ball. As a military man who had fearlessly faced death on a bloody battlefield, he was disgusted with his cowardice. His gaze dropped to her long, slender fingers on his sleeve, and he dragged her light lavender perfume into his nostrils.

Maybe if he made her his focus, he could walk into a ballroom and not panic. He could dance with his wife, speak with their hosts, and escort Lena onto the terrace for air.

He nodded. He could do this. He *had* to do this. And he would do it on his own terms.

His jaw felt stiff when he spoke. 'Send our acceptance.'

Chapter Eighteen

The evening of the Billinghams' ball Lena dressed in a sapphire silk ball gown. This gown was different than anything she'd ever owned. The jewel tone was vibrant, and the cut flattering. The design emphasized her breasts and long legs. Her maid had styled her dark curls in a chignon and placed a touch of rouge on her cheeks and lips. Her matching satin slippers were made for dancing.

Lena twirled in front of the dressing glass. For the first time, she'd chosen her own gown at the modiste, and she'd never felt so beautiful.

She twirled and the silk skirts floated about her legs. A shiver of excitement skittered down her spine. How would Ravenwood see her?

A low knock on her door sounded. Her maid must have returned. She hurried to open the door to find Ravenwood standing outside. Dressed in formal black and white with a silver-threaded waistcoat and a diamond pin in his cravat, he looked stunningly handsome. He reminded her of an image of Adonis she'd seen in a book of Greek Gods. Butterflies swirled in her belly.

The corner of his scarred lip twisted upwards. 'I have something for you. I couldn't wait until you appeared downstairs.' Reaching into his waistcoat, he removed a box and handed it to her.

Her hands felt limp as she held the box, and her heart-beat, already pounding, escalated. She opened the lid to find a stunning necklace of sapphires and diamonds nestled in black velvet. She'd never received such a costly gift. She looked up at him. 'It's...it's exquisite.'

'I asked your maid what colour your dress would be for the ball before visiting the jewelers.'

He'd gone to the trouble? She couldn't imagine Ravenwood seeking out her maid to ask about his wife's gown.

He lifted the necklace from the box she held. 'May I?'

As if in a dream, Lena turned. The air stirred with excitement as he stepped closer and placed the necklace around her neck. The stones were cool against her skin, but his touch was warm. His fingers brushed her nape, light yet with intent, to secure the clasp. Every muscle in her body tightened with anticipation. The butterfly wings fluttered fiercely. She longed to lean back, to feel those strong hands around her.

Ravenwood had surprised her more times than she'd ever thought with his kindness and compassion.

She turned to face him instead. Her fingers touched the precious stones. 'Thank you.'

He offered his arm, the perfect escort. 'Shall we?'

The air was humid and heavy as Ravenwood escorted Lena out of the carriage in front of the Billingham mansion. A line of well-dressed guests streamed up the sweeping stone steps to enter the residence. Torches blazed with light, and footmen helped men and women alight from their carriages to join the parade of revelers.

Brent glanced to Lena at his side. She looked lovely in the sapphire gown, and the jewels he'd selected at Rundell & Bridge paled in comparison. Her upswept dark hair revealed her slender neck and décolletage. Her brown eyes were wide as she took in the scene, her full lips parted.

With Lena's gloved hand on his arm, the couple made their way into the mansion to halt at the top of the ballroom stairs for a liveried and bewigged majordomo to announce them. Ravenwood surveyed the crowd below. The last time he'd been amongst this many people was on a field in France waiting for dawn and his regiment to march into battle. It had poured rain the evening before battle; tonight felt just as humid to him.

The couple before them was announced. 'Lord and Lady Wentworth!' The majordomo's voice boomed.

Ravenwood and Lena shuffled forward. Lena's fingers tightened a fraction upon his sleeve. 'Will you be all right to—'

'Yes.' He managed to grin.

The majordomo with a towering white wig and powdered face turned to them. A split-second later, the deafening voice announced them. 'The Duke and Duchess of Ravenwood!'

Dozens of pairs of eyes were drawn to the top of the stairs. With Lena's hand upon his arm, Ravenwood escorted her down the sweeping staircase. Dread did not encompass him, rather he was proud to have her by his side.

He knew these people. Years may have passed but they were the same. Wealthy, entitled, entirely unaware of what common soldiers sacrificed on foreign soil to keep them in their comfortable lifestyle.

Lord and Lady Billingham welcomed them. 'Your Grace and Your Grace, we are thrilled you could attend,' the marquess greeted.

'Billingham.' Ravenwood addressed their host.

'We are happy to be here,' Lena said to the marchioness.

After exchanging pleasantries, as Ravenwood led Lena away, he was aware of the attention they drew. Ladies whispered behind fluttering fans and gentlemen stared. Ravenwood fetched two glasses of bubbling champagne from a passing servant's tray and handed one to his wife. She was achingly beautiful. She was also pale. Nerves. He shoved any of his own uncomfortable feelings aside and gave her his attention. It was her first *beau monde* ball. He knew how snobbish these people could be. In his opinion, she was better than any of the high-born ladies.

'I envisioned this scene a thousand times in my head,' she whispered behind her fan. 'It is different in the flesh.'

'You are perfect. They are all jealous of me.'

She looked at him then. 'That's the nicest compliment you have ever paid me.'

Truly? Once more, he'd have to try harder.

She sipped the champagne. Her tongue passed over her full bottom lip to lick a drop. His gaze was drawn to her mouth. She had to stop doing that.

Her expressive dark eyes met his. 'What about you? You are here only because of me and—'

'I'm fine.' It was the truth. He felt no panic, no sickening tightening of his gut at the noise or the number of guests. It was warm outside and even warmer in the crowded ballroom. Expensive French perfume comingled with perspiring bodies. Ladies fanned themselves and men stayed by the open French doors for a wisp of air. He believed he would find it cloyingly overbearing. He didn't. Lena was by his side, and he drew strength from her presence.

The Earl of Kent approached along with his twin sisters.

Amelia brushed back a stray brown curl. 'Isn't this exciting! We were thrilled to get an invitation.'

'Do you think Lord Francis will ask me to dance?' the auburn-haired Audrey asked.

'She's had her eye on him for the entire Season,' Amelia said with a sly smile.

Audrey whirled to her sister. 'That's not true!'

Lena tapped Audrey on her shoulder and whispered something into her ear.

The young Audrey smiled brightly. 'Would you?'

'It would be my pleasure,' Lena said.

Audrey fanned her flushed face. 'I feel warm already and need a glass of lemonade.'

The sisters giggled behind fluttering fans as they traipsed off to the refreshment table.

Ravenwood watched, not surprised at the easy way Lena spoke to the young ladies. She had a similar manner with Claire. Kent must have noticed as well.

'What on earth did you say to Audrey to make her flush and rush off?' Kent asked Lena.

'Only that Ravenwood would introduce me to Lord Francis's family, and I would put in a good word for her,' Lena said.

'I will?' Ravenwood said.

Lena gifted him with a smile. 'Or course! Hopefully, the young lord will ask the lovely Audrey to dance.'

Kent grimaced as he watched his sisters across the room. 'Good God. They will put me in an early grave before they are both married.'

'It can't be that bad.' Ravenwood grinned. He couldn't help himself. Kent deserved a bit of taunting.

Kent shot him a disparaging look. 'You will be in my position soon enough.'

His friend's comments were precisely why he'd enjoyed teasing him when the chance arose.

The strains of the orchestra changed, and an excited murmur travelled through the ballroom.

'The waltz!' a group of ladies cried out.

'I must do my duty,' Kent said as he walked off towards a red-haired lady across the ballroom.

Ravenwood turned to Lena and offered his hand. 'Shall we?'

Her dark eyes widened. 'I thought you did not waltz.'

He'd once told her this. Things had changed and he wanted to escort her onto the floor. 'Forget what I said.'

Panic flashed across her features as she glimpsed the couples assembling on the ballroom floor. 'But I've only practised the waltz in the privacy of my room.' She shook her head once and a fat curl bounced saucily by her cheek.

He took her hand. 'Follow my lead.'

The truth was he'd waltzed more times than he could recall in his youth. He'd danced at every society ball with debutantes, widows, and even wives. He'd even waltzed in Vienna when he'd first arrived as a young officer in his freshly minted officer's coat.

But this time was different. *She* was different.

He led her to the floor, rested his hand on her slender waist and waited. Her eyes were huge in her face as she placed a hand on his shoulder and slipped the other into his hand. Her lips were parted and her breathing slightly labored. He caught the music, then spun her across the floor. Other couples joined them. It didn't matter. All eyes were upon them. Before he arrived, he'd worried about the reaction to his scarred face. He needn't have worried. Both men and women watched his wife. Beautiful. Vibrant. And Fearless.

'You are a wonderful dancer. You should have told me,' she said, a little breathless. 'Are they all watching?'

'Does it matter?' His fingers spread upon her waist.

Her breasts rose and fell above the bodice of her silk gown. 'I suppose not.'

The dance continued. Out of the corner of his eye, he spotted The Earl of Kent dancing with the red-haired lady. Another couple danced close by. He tore his attention away from Lena for a split-second to see Lady Powell partnered with a viscount. Ravenwood pivoted away, returning his attention to Lena. She was breathless in a way that caused a pull in his stomach. From the day she'd first appeared, she'd turned his life upside down.

The dance was over far too soon. He loathed to part from his wife.

Lena's face was felt warm as Ravenwood escorted her off the dance floor. 'Who would have thought waltzing was so vigorous?' Waltzing with the duke had been an exhilarating experience. She'd initially been highly conscious of the stares of the well-dressed lords and beautifully coiffed ladies, then she could think only of the man who had flawlessly whirled her across the dance floor.

'I shall endeavor to quench your thirst.' He winked, then was off to the refreshment table.

His charm caused her pulse to quicken. She waited by a potted palm in the corner of the ballroom.

At a slight movement of one of the fronds she turned, finding herself face-to-face with Lady Powell. Francesca wore an emerald gown with a lace overlay and her fair hair was arranged in ringlets that framed her face. Diamonds glittered at her throat. A heavy floral perfume wafted from her.

'You will never be able to satisfy him,' Francesca said, her voice low but firm.

Lena's skin prickled with warning. 'Pardon?'

'Ravenwood has particular needs.' She smirked. 'From his expression on the dance floor, I believe you have not met them.'

She'd been on the dance floor? Lena had been focused

on Ravenwood and hadn't noticed. The woman's rude comment made her blood heat. 'How dare you!'

Francesa's lips thinned. 'I dare because you are not his type.'

'And what type is that?'

'A high-born blue-blooded English lady.'

The barb struck deep. Lena should not care what this woman thought of her. Her prejudice should not hurt her or cause a deep-rooted insecurity to rise. It shouldn't matter that this woman had rejected her as an illegitimate child of tainted blood all those years ago.

Lena's fists clenched at her sides. She refused to let the woman's cruel words make her lash out in public. She faced her, chin high. 'My father was a marquess.'

'Ah, yes. And yet your first husband was a stockbroker. Who do you think suggested that match?'

Lena stood stunned as the full impact of the woman's words struck her. She'd suffered seven long, miserable years married to Oliver. Even if what she said was true and she'd suggested the match, her father had the final say. He should have refused and protected Lena. Instead, he'd married her off and washed his hands of her.

A smugness lit Francesca's eyes. 'As for Ravenwood, if you cannot give him what he desires, then he will seek out another.' She snapped her fan closed and walked away.

The woman, no matter how selfish, spoke the truth. Lena had not shared the duke's bed. He was a warm-blooded male who had needs. And according to his former lover, Ravenwood had a fierce appetite.

Doubts about Lena's marriage to Ravenwood resurfaced

anew. She'd resisted opening her heart after her disastrous first marriage. The men she'd trusted, her father and her first husband, had never truly protected her or unconditionally loved her. Oliver had treated her as a possession, never an equal, and he'd been ashamed of her background and insisted she keep it hidden.

Ravenwood knew of her Middle Eastern roots. He'd enjoyed her baklava at the picnic, but would he feel the same if she shared her culture in public? Would he be ashamed of her mixed blood when they had a child and she taught him or her about her mother's culture? Or as the heir to a dukedom, would her son have to deny it entirely?

Despite knowing better than to allow Francesca to ruin her evening, the woman's words crawled beneath her skin.

There were other fears as well, even more deep-seated ones. Despite her best efforts, Ravenwood had already breached her defences and made his way into her heart. The thought terrified her. He alone had the means to hurt her more than anyone, much more than Lady Francesca.

Just then, Ravenwood approached with two glasses of champagne. 'For you, my dear.'

In the midst of her inner turmoil, she tingled at the endearment. Lena accepted the flute and took a sip. The champagne tasted overly sweet. 'The ballroom is warm.'

He immediately offered his arm. 'Shall we take a stroll in the gardens?'

She nodded—she needed air.

The open French doors loomed ahead, and they stepped outside. Clouds filtered the moonlight, and the air was humid with the threat of impending rain. It was still cooler on the terrace than inside the ballroom, and Lena dragged fresh air into her lungs. Ravenwood led her down the terrace steps and into the garden. Crickets chirped their nighttime music. Another couple waved as they passed.

They halted by an isolated stone bench, and she sat. 'Do you regret marrying me?' she asked.

His brows drew together. 'Pardon?'

'Marrying me. Do you regret it?'

'Why would you ask me that?' He set a booted foot on the bench and rested an elbow on his knee. 'What happened?'

'Lady Powell confronted me,' she admitted. No use hiding it.

His mouth set in a grim line. 'We already spoke of her. It was ages ago. She means nothing to me. What did she say to upset you?'

Most likely the truth. They had yet to share a bedchamber. She lowered her voice. 'She claims that you have particular needs.'

He cursed, then released a long sigh.

'Is she right?' Lena asked.

His eyes flashed. 'It's true. I do have needs. I need my wife beneath me. Soft. Willing. And quivering with desire.'

Oh my. Whatever she'd expected, it was not *that.*

'Lady Powell claims I'm not your type.'

He arched a brow. 'And what is?'

'A full, blue-blooded Englishwoman.'

He set his foot down from the bench, his face hardening with anger. 'What does she know? Shall I show you what my type is?'

Lena stood and took a step closer. She'd promised herself she would not back down from what she wanted. 'Yes. Show me.'

Her consent must have been what he was waiting for. He pulled her to him and swooped down to capture her lips. He wasn't gentle but kissed her openly, fiercely, with a passion that heated her blood and made her toes curl in her satin ballroom slippers. She kissed him back, her tongue tangling with his.

He was not satisfied with just kissing for long. His mouth ravaged a path down her throat and his hands cupped her breasts, his breath hot on her flesh, his thumbs teasing her nipples over her bodice. Her nipples pebbled and she longed for his tongue to tease her naked skin. She clung to him, shamelessly arching into his touch. At his growl of approval, she grew more aroused.

'Wait,' she said panting. 'I need to tell you something.'

'What?' he murmured against her skin. 'Jesus,' he said. 'You are on fire.'

His hand lowered and bunched her skirts, lifting the hem of her gown. His fingers slid up her calf, her knee, and then past her thigh to finger her garter. If he didn't touch her soon, she'd go crazy.

'Tonight, I will come to your bedchamber.' She'd never been more certain of her decision.

He lifted his head, and a carnal fierceness sparked in his gaze. 'Let's leave. Now.'

He kissed her again and her tongue rubbed against his

while she tugged at his waistcoat to bring him closer. His leg shifted between her skirts. She arched forward, her moist center pressed against his trousers. She wanted him, desperately needed what he offered.

He broke away, tugged on her arm and began leading her out of the garden.

She felt a thrill as she followed. Their home was next door and she wondered how fast they could summon a carriage.

A loud crack of thunder pierced the air, startling her. It was followed by a jagged streak lighting up the dark sky.

Ravenwood's fingers tightened on her arm.

Painfully tight.

His breathing turned ragged, and he abruptly released her. She stumbled backwards and caught herself on the back of the stone flowerpot.

She stared at him. 'What is it? What's wrong?'

He threw out a hand. 'Stay away!'

He stood still, panting. He was looking at her, not the lightning streaking across the night sky. A wheezing sound reverberated from his chest. Something was wrong, very wrong.

'Your Grace?'

'Ravenwood!'

Nothing. Sweat beaded his brow and his gaze appeared far-away. His brow creased, his lips pulled slightly back from his teeth, and his chest rose and fell with labored breaths. He had recovered swiftly from his nightmares. Now he was somewhere else. In a dark, dreary place. He looked fierce and more than a bit frightening, and for a pulse-pounding moment she could envision him on the battlefield just before he charged the enemy.

In the distance, lightning streaked across the night sky again, illuminating his chiseled features and the cruelty of his scar. Her heart jolted with the following rumble of thunder.

'Ravenwood!' She approached hesitantly, afraid to startle him. 'Brent!'

It was the sound of his name that finally reached him. He ran a hand down his face, his eyes clearing slightly.

'It's only thunder,' she said. 'See the night sky. See the faraway lightning. It's a storm.'

'Thunder?' he whispered.

'It often rains in London, remember?'

'London?'

Did he imagine he was still on foreign land, on the battlefield? 'Yes…yes… London.'

He was coming around. She approached him now, less fearful. She pressed her hands against his chest and his heart raced beneath her palms. When he did not resist, she stepped closer and cradled his face in her hands. Her thumb travelled over his scar. He didn't flinch from her touch.

'You should go,' he said.

She shook her head. 'No. I won't leave you.'

'Go back to the ball. I need to leave before anyone sees me.'

He meant in his condition. He must feel terribly alone. Alone and helpless.

She understood both emotions far too well, and a heaviness tugged in her chest. What was wrong with him and how long had he suffered? A strong desire to help him arose within her that had nothing to do with him being her husband. But as a worthy man in need.

'Let me help you.' A note of urgency laced her voice. 'No one will know.'

'*You* know.' His tone was empty, sad.

She ignored it. 'I'll summon the coach at once.'

He jerked his head. 'No coach. Servants gossip.'

'Then we'll walk.' Only a fence separated their own gardens from the Billingham's property. She'd seen Claire and Peter secretly meet over it. There was also a garden gate not far from where they'd met. She'd lead Ravenwood there.

They could do it. She'd make sure they weren't seen. This time, when she held onto his arm, it was to support him as much as to support herself on the grass. Her slippers were made for a ballroom floor, not a wet lawn. A rock pierced the soft soles, but she bit her lip and did not cry out. Thunder boomed and lightning cracked. The sky opened up and it began to pour.

The rain had a calming effect, and he no longer seemed panicked. As for herself, her satin gown was ruined, and her slippers destroyed. Puddles splashed her hem. Her hair slipped from its pins to hang in a riot of curls, dripping down her back. She didn't care, her only concern was for the duke. Brent. She pushed forward as they skirted the perimeter until they found an opening in the fence where they could slip inside Ravenwood's gardens.

Lena was shivering by the time they entered through

the servants' entrance. She led him to the nearest room, the library. Mrs Hollins rushed forward, took one look at Ravenwood, then turned to Lena.

'Please light the brazier. Then leave us,' Lena told the woman.

Mrs Hollins didn't need any urging. Once the coal brazier was bright, the housekeeper shut the door behind her. Brent collapsed on a sofa.

How could a night of heaven turn into one of hell?

Chapter Nineteen

Once Brent was seated on a sofa in the library, Lena poured him a glass of whisky from the sideboard. He raised the glass, a tremble in his hand, and swallowed.

She crouched at his feet and reached for his right boot. She tugged and removed the Hessian. When he didn't protest, she did the same with the left boot, then peeled off his wet stockings. His skin was cold to the touch, and she pressed her hands against his feet to warm them.

Ravenwood dragged in a breath and reached for her hands. Wordless gratitude flashed in his gaze.

She still knelt before him, looking up into his eyes. 'Will you talk to me about what just happened?'

His gaze dropped to their hands. 'You will look at me differently.'

'No, I won't.'

He let out a ragged breath. 'It's not that simple.' His eyes met hers again. 'What I tell you is between us, and us only.'

She realized what he was asking. Ravenwood was a private man and for him to confess his secrets to her was profound. She was determined to help him and wanted him to know he could confide in her. Her fingers tightened over his, willing him to believe in her. 'I understand and I promise.'

He ran a finger down the jagged scar on his face. 'Do you wonder how I received this?'

'How?' The scar had fascinated her the first time she'd seen him. He was an enigma, a survivor.

He stilled. Even his breathing went quiet. 'It's not an easy story to tell…or to hear.'

She lowered her own voice. 'You can trust me.'

Trust her.

Trust was not easily given. Ravenwood had requested the same of her when he'd handed her a stone and asked her to toss it into a pond. Now she asked it of him. He knew it was his weakness, his vice, to never trust another. His immediate impulse was to shake his head and not speak. He dragged in a deep breath instead. Lena was different, and she deserved to know. She'd witnessed his nightmares and his waking episode.

Her eyes were dark and mesmerizing in the light of the brazier. 'It rained the night before Waterloo and well into the morning. Napoleon had decided to hold off his attack because he was worried about moving his artillery and his men in the soggy, muddy earth. His hesitation helped Wellington by permitting the Prussian army to arrive in time.'

'Where were you then?'

He let out a breath as he envisioned the day. She must have sensed his hesitation. She rubbed his feet again, warming them. He didn't want her by his feet, but by his side. Reaching out, he gently pulled her up. Only when she was sitting beside him on the sofa did he continue. 'I was in command of my men. My second-in-command was a man by the name of Harley, a father of six. Once we were in position, I waited until we received orders. Harley was to receive them first, then ride and deliver the orders to me. At last, we were able to march. I knew it would be bad just looking down at the French forces assembled. But I had no idea then just how bad.'

He squeezed his eyes shut, not wanting to continue, knowing he must. She rested a hand on his shoulder, her touch light, yet supportive. He opened his eyes and looked into hers—warm, welcoming chocolate. Long, dark lashes. She nodded her encouragement for him to continue.

'The battle was fierce. After hours, we appeared to be defeating the enemy forces, but not without sustaining heavy casualties. I quickly lost count of the number of Englishmen who fell as well as the bodies of enemy soldiers who littered the battlefield. The booming of the artillery was deafening. The wounded cried out. Screaming war horses fell. The already damp earth grew slippery with mud and blood.'

He stilled and shoved a hand through his hair. She rubbed his shoulders, calming him. 'Go on,' she urged, her voice low. He could do this with her by his side.

'After what seemed like hours later, the battle slowed. I was exhausted, parched, and drenched in sweat. We believed the worst was over. Then, despite our vigilance, a French soldier broke the line to hide behind a hill and began picking off my men. I headed for the Frenchman when Harley called out in warning. That's when I saw him out of the corner of my eye.'

'Who?' she asked. 'Harley?'

He shook his head. 'No. A second French soldier. I realized too late it wasn't just one that broke the enemy line, but two. I made a grave mistake by underestimating the enemy. The second Frenchman's musket fired and took down another of my men. I hollered in fury, pulled a blade from my boot, and launched myself at him with the single-minded focus to kill. We fought hand-to hand, both splattered in blood, no better than animals, knowing only one of us would survive.' A raw and primal grief overwhelmed him as he recalled the scene. His misery was like a steel weight, dragging him down. He struggled to continue. 'I stabbed him in the gut, but not before he struck my head with the butt of his own blade and lashed out, carving my face. The last thing I recall was him falling by my side, his dead eyes boring into me. Then blackness.'

He let out a shudder. She continued to rub his back as she sat beside him. Her dripping hair hung around her shoulders. Her dress was destroyed. She'd never looked more beautiful. He focused on the curve of her smooth cheek. His heart beat steadily now and was not racing as it had in the gardens. He was in control of his faculties and not in fear of another fit.

'Then what happened?' she asked.

The words came more easily now. 'When I woke two days later among a field of corpses, the constant throbbing pain of my face was a reminder that I lived. The constant *chink…chink…chink…*was a torment.'

'What was the noise?'

'The sound of the teeth robber's chisel chipping away and stealing the teeth of the dead. It wasn't just clothes, boots, rings, or snuff boxes that were pilfered from the dead, but teeth, which are in demand for false teeth.'

Lena's eyes were wide. 'Oh my goodness. I had no idea.'

How could she? 'I was too weak to cover my ears. I prayed for death, not from my injuries or that I lay in a sea of dead, but from that infernal noise. It reminded me of my failure, of not staying with my men. I later learned only half survived the battle that day. Even Harley, who left behind his six children without a father. I send them money every month.'

They sat in silence. He dragged in a deep breath and ran a hand down his face. 'I hear that chisel in my nightmares. Now that you know, do you think less of me?'

She placed a steady, comforting hand on his shoulder. 'No,' she whispered. 'I think you are the strongest man I know.'

The strongest man she knows.

Never did he imagine she would speak those words. Not after he'd talked of the war. Not after he'd admitted to letting down his men. Not after failing his second-in-command.

'It's not your fault,' she said, her voice calm and steady. 'None of it. The war was not your fault. Without your leadership, the losses of your men would have been greater. If you had not taken out the Frenchman, more men would have died. Don't you see? Cast aside your guilt.'

Cast aside my guilt.

Could he do it? Did he have the strength? Her faith in him, her utter confidence, gave him a sliver of hope. A chance at redemption.

'Lena, you must understand that what happened tonight will most likely happen again and—'

'Shh.' She pressed a finger against his lips. 'I understand.'

'Do you truly?'

'Yes, and I still want to be with you.'

His heart beat soundly at her words. 'What are you saying?'

'You should know I have my own confession.'

'Oh? Tell me.'

'You are not the one who lied tonight. I am.'

He shook his head, not understanding her meaning. 'When?'

She shifted on the couch and squarely faced him. 'I said I'd visit your bedchamber. I'm here instead. Make love to me now.'

His mouth went dry. She'd listened and still desired him? He'd wanted her for so long now, but never had his own desire been this fierce. His pulse throbbed and his hands shook with a need to claim her as his own. To truly claim her as his wife.

Leaning down, he kissed her.

If Lena hadn't been sitting beside Ravenwood on the couch, his kiss would have made her knees buckle. He cradled her face and covered her mouth with his own, with a sense of urgency that called out to her. She clung to him, her fingers travelling over his shoulders before caressing the back of his neck and stroking his hair.

He'd opened up to her tonight, confessing a deep part of his soul that she'd treasure. He'd suffered and survived when others would have given up and perished. Ravenwood was worthy.

He pulled back to look in her eyes, the fierce desire in his expression causing a swooping pull low in her stomach.

'Are you sure?' he asked. 'I don't want you to be with me out of pity.'

Pity? That was the last word she'd use to describe her feelings for him. He was brave and loyal. There was so much more to him, more that she wanted to learn and explore. 'I've never been more certain.' She stood and offered him her back. 'Help me with my gown and stays.'

He was by her side in a flash. 'Gladly.'

The sodden satin ball gown slipped off her shoulders, then gaped at her waist before dropping to her slippers. His fingers worked her stays and she soon turned to stand before him in her shift.

'I've imagined undressing you. Dreamt of it. Now the reality is much more arousing.'

The dark depths of longing in his eyes exhilarated her and gave her confidence. Slowly she lifted the shift over her head and stood naked before him. Her skin pricked from awareness and from the heat of the fire.

His gaze travelled over her body. 'My God, you are perfect.'

A knot loosened in her stomach at his words and the admiration in his eyes. 'I admit to being curious about your body as well.' Boldly, she reached for his shirt and tugged it free of his trousers.

The unscarred corner of his lip turned upwards. 'Truly? All you had to do was ask.'

He helped her lift the wet shirt over his head and tossed it aside. Her gaze greedily took in the hard planes of his chest and the corrugated muscles of his abdomen. She'd never imagined that just looking at a man's naked chest could make her quiver with anticipation. A trail of dark hair led down his stomach and disappeared into the waistband of his trousers. Her eyes widened at the impossibly large bulge of his manhood.

Even more arousing was the fact that he was her husband. *Hers.*

A knot rose in her throat. She ran her hands down his chest as she'd wanted to for so long. His skin was warm and hard, the sprinkling of hair teasing her palms. She could touch him forever.

'May I?' She reached for the placket of his trousers.

His hand covered hers. 'Not yet.'

Her gaze flew up to his and she bit her lower lip. 'Why?'

He shook his head, and a dark lock fell rakishly across his forehead. 'I don't want to frighten you.'

Her lips curved up. His concern for her touched a buried part of her. 'You won't.'

She reached for him again. This time, he did not stop her. Her fingers loosened the first button of its mooring.

Then the second. One more and his manhood sprang free. Her eyes widened at the size of him.

Oh, my.

Reaching out, her fingers ran the hard, veined length of him, then grazed the crimson head. He released a groan that heated her blood. Growing bold, she clutched his full length in her hand. She could almost feel his heartbeat beneath her fingers.

'Lena.' His voice was hoarse. 'I'm not made of steel.'

Kicking aside his trousers, he picked her up and carried her to the sofa, his body covering hers. Skin to skin, he was hot and hard.

He ran kisses down the column of her throat then lower still, and worshipped first her right breast, taking the nipple into his mouth and swirling his tongue around the turgid tip. Lena could only hold on to him as a pulse of heat radiated down her body and pulled low in her groin. Everything was new and wondrous and devastating at the same time. He moved to the other breast, and she whimpered with need. Restless beneath him, she ran her hands down his back and dug her fingers into his buttocks.

His steely length slid down the most sensitive part of her body and she gasped as desire streaked through her. 'Ravenwood.'

His voice was hoarse. 'Yes, tell me.'

'Please.'

He moved against her, harder this time, and she breathed in soul-drenching gasps. She was building towards something…something earth-shattering.

'You are a gift,' he whispered against her skin. 'A treasure. It must be good for you.'

It was good for her, and she'd never felt this depth of arousal, this type of need. She wanted more. She wanted *him*.

Miraculously, he understood. The undisguised longing in his eyes made it hard to breathe as he entered her slowly. Her body was already slick for him and greedy. He held back but she was beyond waiting. She arched beneath him.

A harsh breath exploded from him as he thrust deeply inside. She gasped. She wasn't a virgin, but he was large.

'Are you all right?' He stilled and inhaled through parted lips, his face tight above hers.

Their eyes locked, and she knew it took great will for him not to move. A dangerous tug centered in her chest at his concern. 'Yes. Yes.'

He exhaled, his breath shuddering on the way out. Her body molded to his and accepted him, all of him. He began to move, and she revelled in the power of each stroke. She loved the hardness of him and the feeling that they were joined as one. It was incredible, like nothing she'd ever experienced or expected. Soon, she was building, reaching for the stars, until with one more stroke, she climaxed.

'Brent!' she cried out.

His lips found hers, smothering her cry, then he lifted his head, his gaze meeting hers. She watched, fascinated, as he thrust twice more, then threw his head back. The pleasure on his face would forever be seared into her memory.

* * *

Ravenwood held Lena in his arms. The sofa was small, too small for his big frame, but he was reluctant to leave her. Dark crescent lashes framed her eyes. And her heart beat close to his chest. The coal in the brazier was dying and he wanted to be sure she stayed warm.

'Tonight was special,' he murmured against her cheek.

Her brown eyes captivated him. 'It was special. You opened up to me.'

He knew she meant his past. For a surprising moment, he hadn't even thought of it. Not when she stood bravely in front of him and told him she wanted him. Not when she'd removed her clothes and stood before him appearing as perfect as Venus.

Her lush curves were pressed against him, and he wanted her again. He swallowed. She had to be tender, and he did not want to hurt her.

She moved against him, her palm running down his chest. 'I've longed to touch you.'

Touch me more. Everywhere. He'd been starving for human contact. Not just sex. But a connection. One he'd felt when he'd spoken of the war. And one he'd felt when he'd touched, teased, and taken her.

He raised her fingers and kissed the back of her hand. 'I would not dream to deny you.'

At least for now he had his faculties. With Lena in his arms, the episode with the lightning seemed far, far away. In truth, he was not worthy of her. She was worth a hundred dukes, certainly to be tied to a better man. He shoved his insecurities aside, focusing on his wife in his arms.

Her rosebud lips curved sensually upwards. 'Good. Because I am persistent when I want something.'

As she climbed on top of him, he prayed she would always want him.

Chapter Twenty

Lena woke up alone in her bedchamber. After last night's bout of lovemaking in the library, Ravenwood had carried her to her bedchamber, kissed her forehead, and left for his own chamber. She'd been too exhausted to protest that she'd wanted him to stay and had fallen into a deep slumber. She spotted the folded foolscap on her end table.

Lena,
Rest well. Until tonight.
R

She held the note to her chest. She'd wanted him to stay with her last night, to hold her in his arms so she could wake alongside him this morning. Was he worried he'd have another nightmare? Or another waking episode like he'd had during the thunderstorm?

Would it be like this forever? Together, yet separated? With Ravenwood holding a piece of himself apart from her out of fear?

She wouldn't allow it. He'd let her in, and his confessions of what he'd gone through, were heartbreaking. Now that she better understood him, she was even more determined to help him.

She pulled the bell and her maid hurried inside and parted the drapes and opened the wardrobe. After dressing, she'd learned that Claire was visiting a friend and Ravenwood was out with Kent. Having both Ravenwood and Claire out of the house served her purpose.

Escaping the house was simple. She slipped out the servants' entrance, walked to the end of the street and hailed a hackney. Summoning the ducal carriage was out of the question. Soon, the hackney entered a different part of the city. Here the houses were closer together and not large.

She paid the driver and headed down the street. She stopped at a small brick house in the middle of the street. Without a knocker, she raised her hand and knocked directly on the door.

The door opened. Ivan took one look at her and broke into a broad smile. 'Lena! Everyone will be excited to see you.'

Arabic music sounded from inside the house. Lena stepped inside Ivan's family home and the delicious perfume of roasting lamb wafted to her. It was Sunday and the entire family would have gathered to eat and spend the day together.

'I'm starved. Are your aunties cooking?' Lena asked. Both were fabulous cooks.

'They finished cooking and are in the parlor, but I'm certain they will fix a special dish for you,' Ivan said.

Lena's stomach grumbled. In her opinion, English fare

did not compare with the spices and delicacies of Mediterranean and Middle Eastern food.

But first, she needed to ask her friend for help. 'Ivan, there is another reason for my visit. Remember how I mentioned wanting to speak with your cousin, Vartan, the former soldier? Is he here?'

Ivan nodded. 'Yes, I remember. Vartan is not here but is expected to be home soon. Meanwhile, come eat.'

'Lena!' Two older women, Auntie Norma and Auntie Anoush, called out as soon as Lena stepped into the small parlor. Norma was short and thin, with hair fading gently to grey. Anoush was short and plump and had reddish hair dyed with henna. Both wore wire-rimmed spectacles.

The house was full of Ivan's family. Arabic flowed from room to room and the familiar language seeped over her like a warm, welcoming blanket. Hospitable and friendly, his tight-knit family stirred a pang of jealousy. An ache centered in her chest. She longed for the family dinners back home in Lebanon with her mother and grandparents. Her family would spend hours around the kitchen table recounting tales of their youth and sharing stories about Lena's mother as a girl. After becoming a widow, she'd wished to return but wasn't able to afford the trip.

Ivan came from a large family, and there were twenty relatives and friends in the house each Sunday. Auntie Norma patted the sofa beside her. The cushion was worn and sagging. 'Tell us about your charge.'

They meant Claire. 'She will turn seventeen next month, and she is an artist.'

'Ah. It's good for a girl to have a talent,' Norma said.

'Posh! The English ladies cannot do anything,' Anoush sat across the way in a wooden rocking chair and waved a dismissive hand. 'They do not cook. Or clean. Or care for their own children. They hire nannies, nursemaids, and governesses. What kind of life is that?'

Lena hid a smile. Home and motherhood meant much in their shared culture. Lena was also half English and torn between two worlds. She acknowledged her English side and had respected her father. But her mother's roots ran deep in her blood.

As for her first marriage, Oliver had never permitted her to come here. She'd sneak out to see Ivan or visit market day in the diverse section of the city and stuff herself with grape leaves filled with meat and rice, falafel, and date cookies.

Anoush set down a plate of sweets on a table. Without hesitation, Lena reached for a date pastry. She shut her eyes as she took a bite. The sweetness of the dates and the buttered dough danced on her tongue.

'You are too thin and must eat more,' Auntie Norma said.

'She's right. I made a batch of date and fig pastries. I shall send some home with you,' Anoush said.

Fig! 'I adore anything with figs as well as dates,' Lena said.

'Is that Englishman treating you well?' Norma asked.

'All is well with Ravenwood.' The aunties meant well, but they were notorious for meddling.

'He is titled,' Anoush pointed out.

'He is a duke,' Norma said.

'So?' Anoush said, her razor gaze focused on Lena. 'Their titles are confusing and mean nothing. A man is a man. The way he treats his woman is what matters.'

'What she means,' Norma said, 'is that we pray Ivan finds a woman as loyal you.'

Oh, no. Lena swallowed her mouthful of pastry. She did not want to talk about Ivan. She knew Auntie Anoush prided herself as a successful matchmaker. What neither of the aunties knew was that Ivan was not interested in women but pined for another man.

Just then, a younger woman poked her head into the room. 'The lamb is ready.'

Lena entered the kitchen where a mountain of food was spread out before them in a spectacular display. The kitchen was much smaller than the one in Ravenwood's home but could produce just as much food, enough to feed two dozen guests. Aromatic scents of allspice, paprika, garlic, parsley, and sumac wafted to her. Her mouth watered as she filled her plate with lamb kebabs, rice pilaf, hummus, skewers of cooked vegetables, of tomatoes, eggplant, and onions. The homemade pita bread was soft and warm. It had been too long since she'd indulged in Middle Eastern food.

As she ate, Ivan returned to join her. 'Cousin Vartan has arrived and is in the other room. I'll take you to him when you are done eating.'

She set down her fork. 'I'd like to meet him now.'

Ivan led her to a small back room where five men played *tavloo.* One sat in the corner smoking a hookah. Ivan gestured to him. 'That is Vartan.'

Vartan's hair was longer than what was fashionable, and his beard unkempt. His right arm was missing at the elbow, and the sleeve of his shirt had been tucked and pinned. Lena dragged a wooden chair across from him and sat. 'May I?' she asked.

Vartan looked up, meeting her eyes, then glanced at Ivan. When Ivan nodded, Vartan shrugged and offered the hookah to her. She took it and inhaled. Then slowly exhaled. It was not her first time. She'd spent afternoons with her grandfather as a girl overlooking the fig orchards. Once, when he'd been tired and napped for the afternoon, Lena had mischievously smoked his hookah. When he woke, she suspected he'd known, but he'd never told her mother.

Vartan nodded in approval when she handed the hookah back to him.

The smoke gave her confidence to ask what had been on her mind. She hadn't forgotten Ravenwood's promise not to speak of his past, but if she didn't mention him by name, was she breaking that vow? She wanted desperately to help her husband, and the man sitting before her might hold the key.

'You were at Waterloo,' she said. It was a statement more than a question.

Vartan's watery brown eyes met hers. 'So?'

Another might be fooled by his apparent disinterest. Lena wasn't. Deep wrinkles set at the corners of his eyes and lips, and his fingers tightened on the waterpipe.

'I know an Englishman. He suffers from nightmares. And daytime episodes as well.'

He nodded, his eyes turning distant. 'Living nightmares,' Vartan said.

It was an accurate description of how Ravenwood had reacted to the thunderstorm. 'He is triggered by certain sights and sounds,' she said. 'Booming thunder reminds him of cannon fire.'

Vartan took another deep breath from the hookah. He exhaled, and smoke curled around his face like a snake. 'He cannot be helped.'

Lena's stomach dropped. 'I don't believe that!'

Vartan lowered the instrument and looked at her. 'Why do you care for this Englishman?'

Lena was aware of Ivan by her side. If she wanted this former soldier's help, she understood one thing: she had to be truthful even if she revealed the duke's identity. If she lied or dodged the question, he would see through her in an instant. She could not risk it. She *needed* his advice.

Her eyes never left Vartan's. 'Because he is my husband and the future father of my children.'

She was aware of Ivan stirring beside her. Vartan exhaled a long puff of smoke. 'Your Englishman is not alone. There is a group of former soldiers that gather in private.'

She sat forward on the chair. 'Where? Tell me.'

'We meet at a tavern.'

'How many?'

'It depends on the day. It is not a classroom. We do not require attendance.'

Her shoulders sagged. 'It may not matter. I don't think he will go.' She couldn't imagine Ravenwood joining a group of soldiers at a tavern and sharing his war experiences. He would consider asking for help a sign of weakness.

Vartan shrugged. 'Then he will suffer. God will not help the unwilling.'

The Arabic saying made Lena's gut clench. 'There must be another way.'

'If there is one, I am at a loss to aid you. The only way your Englishman's nightmares—day or night—will ease is if he shares his experiences with others. There is no medication, no army physician, no amount of bloodletting that will aid him. He must face his demons.'

Ivan spoke for the first time. 'Lena, there is nothing more you can do for the duke.'

Her spine stiffened and her jaw set with determination. 'Tell me when and where you meet. I will do the rest.'

Chapter Twenty-One

The tavern was a hubbub of activity. As soon as they stepped inside, the odor of smoke and unwashed bodies in too small a space overwhelmed her senses. It was a busy night and almost all the tables were occupied. Men wearing corduroy jackets and scuffed boots occupied tables beside middle-class merchants dressed in waistcoats and tailored coats. Buxom barmaids rushed from table to table with tankards of ale. A cloud of smoke wafted to the black rafters.

Lena looked to the back of the tavern where the group of former soldiers were to meet tonight. The door to the small room was currently closed.

Ravenwood rested his hand possessively at her back as they entered. 'Are you certain this is the establishment?'

'Yes, of course.'

Getting Ravenwood here had taken scheming. By the time she'd returned home from Ivan's house, she'd come up with a plan. She'd waited until Brent had come back from an outing with the Earl of Kent to ask him to take her to the tavern. His surprise had been evident.

'You want ale?' he'd asked.

'There is a tavern in the city where Arabic traders and their wives gather. I miss hearing the language and crave a good cup of *tsipouro*. You needn't worry. They also serve fine English ale,' she'd said.

He'd rubbed his chin with a thumb and forefingers. 'This is an unexpected request.'

'I cannot go alone. Unless you'd like me to ask Ivan to escort me.' It had been a lie but had the desired effect.

He shook his head. A muscle had leapt in his jaw. 'No, as your husband I shall accompany you.'

And here they were. Ravenwood eyed the crowd. 'I don't see any of these men drinking anything other than ale and cheap gin.'

She bit her lower lip. 'Perhaps there is another evening when the Arabs gather.' It was a poor excuse, and from his sidelong look she suspected he knew it as well. She tugged on his sleeve. 'I'm thirsty. Since we are here, why not order.' She motioned to an empty table near the rear of the tavern.

She held her breath, wondering if he would agree or march her out of the tavern and back into the carriage. Her eyes flickered to the back room, and she wondered if the former soldiers had already gathered and begun. Vartan had told her the day and time to come, and she hoped they weren't late. If they sat nearby, she could see if anyone came or went. Once they were seated, she could explain her true reason for coming.

She took his hand. 'Come. One tankard.'

He led the way as they wove through the space. She was

conscious of the looks they received from the patrons. At well over six feet tall and with the confidence of a man who was accustomed to being in command, Ravenwood looked every inch a nobleman. His scar gave him a dangerous look.

A barmaid came over and set two tankards before them. 'Anything else, m'lord?' She was buxom and blonde and bent forward, her breasts nearly spilling from her low-cut bodice.

Ravenwood shook his head, not bothering to give her a second glance.

Lena sipped her ale. Brent drank, all the while watching her closely over the rim of his tankard. Her heart thudded and she squirmed in her chair. Out of the corner of her eye, the back door opened, and a fair-haired man dressed in a dark coat and trousers entered. The door closed behind him.

Ravenwood lowered his mug, his eyes meeting hers, holding firm. 'Why are we really here?'

'I… I told you.' She inwardly cringed at the nervousness in her voice. 'I craved a certain drink.'

Ravenwood raised his hand, and the barmaid approached within seconds, as if she had been waiting nearby for his needs. 'Aye, m'lord?'

'*Tsipouro*,' he said.

Her pretty brow furrowed. 'Tis…what?'

'*Tsipouro*. Greek liquor.'

'Nothin' that fancy 'ere, m'lord. Not since I've worked 'ere over five years, now.' She propped an ample hip on the table. 'Anything else?'

'No. You've been most helpful.'

The barmaid smiled and flitted away to the next table.

One dark eyebrow arched as Ravenwood turned his attention back to her. 'It seems she's not familiar with your drink at this fine establishment.' He leaned forward, pressing his palms on the rough surface of the table. 'I'm listening.'

Lena felt light-headed. 'If I tell you, will you promise to consider what I say with an open mind?'

He sat back in his chair. 'How can I promise when I have no idea to what you refer?'

She sat on the edge of her seat and took a breath. 'I met a former soldier who suffers from war sickness. Nightmares. Daytime episodes. He meets other soldiers at this tavern, and they talk. He says sharing his war experiences with other soldiers has helped.'

She watched every tick and flash across his face. Narrowed eyes, a tightened jaw. She spoke quickly now, before he could refuse her. 'There is no judgement, no fear that what they say will leave the room or reach the army.'

'That's because they fear the army will call them weak and put them in asylums where surgeons use knives for bloodletting as if it's a sickness in our blood that can be drained.'

She felt dizzy once again. 'My acquaintance lost an arm at Waterloo. He says you must face your greatest fear.'

'I did. The battle is over.'

'That's not what he meant. You must talk about that day. Relive it. Every detail.'

'You are asking the impossible. Some things are better kept inside. It is my punishment.'

'I don't believe that. Not one bit. You must forgive yourself. Others need you. Claire needs you.' She hesitated and caught her breath before speaking. 'I need you.'

His eyes were dark and unfathomable. 'And this group meets here tonight?'

She waved a hand. 'In the back room.'

'You should have told me beforehand,' he said.

'I'm sorry. I was afraid you would not come.'

'And if I refuse to step into that room?'

She reached across the table and grasped his hand. 'I cannot force you.'

His eyes met and held hers, a strange sadness in the blue depths. 'I do not choose to be this way.'

'There is an Arabic saying. No one chooses what misfortunes befall them. They can only choose which way their future path will lead.' Her fingers slowly entwined with his. 'What path will you choose?'

What path would he choose?

Lena's lovely eyes looked at him with a need that simultaneously drew him like a lodestone and frightened him to his core. He should be angry, or at least perturbed, at her subterfuge to get him here. Deep down, he'd known there was something suspicious about her request. What lady would ask him to accompany her to a London tavern after dark?

He'd come to acknowledge that his wife was different from most English ladies. Her affection for Claire, her bravery—or stubbornness—to stand up to him, and the strength she'd needed to survive her own past made her singular.

He understood her reasoning for bringing him. His nightmares and irrational behaviour were alarming. The army would consider men like him weak.

Even worse. *Mad.*

The former soldiers behind the closed door must understand this and more. In a strange way, he wanted to hear them, to learn if their stories were like his. If they suffered from sleepless nights and envisioned bloody battle scenes while they walked down a crowded street. Or if they found peace in a bottle of whisky. He wanted to know.

He pushed back his chair and offered his hand. 'You may as well come inside with me. I cannot leave you out here with this riff-raff.'

Her smile gave him a strange sense of confidence.

'I most likely will not stay.' His voice sounded gruff to his own ears, as if he was convincing himself more than her.

She watched him, her dark eyes never leaving his. 'I understand.'

He knocked on the door and it cracked open. A grey-haired man with a grisly, unkept beard eyed them with suspicion. Unsure what to say, he introduced himself as he would have in the army. 'Lieutenant Colonel Ravenwood.'

'Rank doesn't matter 'ere,' the man said. 'Either do names.'

Brent gave a curt nod.

The man opened the door wide, and they stepped inside.

The room was dim with two lit lanterns. The only other faint light came from a coal brazier. The flames flickered, causing shadows in the corners of the room like looming spectres. It was enough illumination to see the occupants sitting in chairs.

A dozen pairs of eyes turned to them. 'We 'ave a new man,' the host said. His gaze flickered to Lena, then back to the duke. 'Will she be stayin'?'

'For now, if it's all right?' Lena asked, glancing around the room. They were entitled to just as much privacy as the duke.

Only after the men nodded did she settle into a chair in a corner.

Brent did not recognize any of the men, but he recognized their expressions. Aged beyond their years with deep wrinkles surrounding eyes that had seen too much and robbed them of their youth and joy. For the first time, he felt kinship.

They'd interrupted a tall, thin man who'd been speaking. His eyes were red-rimmed, most likely from both too much gin and lack of sleep. He'd lost a leg and leaned on a crutch.

'I lost more than me leg that day,' he continued, his speech uneven with an awkward cadence. 'I lost me friends, over a dozen of 'em. They were the lucky ones. Others, like me came home less of a man.'

Silence sounded. The brazier crackled with heat in the small room, sending sweat down Brent's spine.

'What's 'yer story?' The grisly bearded man looked to him.

His throat was dry as ash. He opened his mouth, shut it. Looking around the room, he saw eyes watching him. His lips parted again, and when he spoke, his voice was steady. 'I cannot get that sound out of my head. The sound of the chisel, a soft *chinking* that grew louder and louder, until it was all I could hear for two blasted days of hell.'

The man grimaced. 'Tooth robbers.'

'Yes.' An unexpected sense of relief caused him to sag in his chair. He tapped his ears with his forefingers. 'I hear that sound when I shut my eyes at night. I'm powerless to stop it. I despise myself for my weakness.'

Lena froze as a sickening sensation settled in her stomach. She hated that Brent considered himself weak. She wanted to step forward and place a hand on his shoulder. To assure him he was one of the strongest people she knew. Instead, she stood and slipped from the room. Once Brent began talking and she felt it was safe to leave, she sought to give him privacy as well.

She returned to the table they'd previously occupied. The barmaid who had looked upon Ravenwood with lascivious intent approached with a tankard, not full of ale, but water.

'Drink. It will help,' she said gently.

Lena's fingers trembled, just for a second, before she raised the cup to her lips. The cool water eased her dry throat. 'Thank you.'

Her gaze darted to the closed door. Many of the men inside were young, too young to have witnessed the cruelties of war. How many others had perished? How many women had lost their sons, brothers, husbands, or lovers?

'Yer man should come again. Most do. It helps,' the barmaid said.

'You have a husband?'

'A brother. He's inside. You're pale and should eat. I'll bring you fresh stew. Our cook made it today.'

Lena didn't think she could eat anything but was grateful for the barmaid's kindness. An hour later, Ravenwood appeared at the table. 'I didn't notice you leave.'

It was a good thing. It meant he had been engrossed in what the others had to say.

Lena set her spoon aside. She'd barely eaten. She hoped he didn't notice. 'I'm ready to leave if you are.' She pushed back her chair.

He cocked his head to the side, studying her. She met his eyes. She needed to be strong. For him. If he noticed her distress, he said nothing, only offered his arm.

He escorted her to the waiting carriage. He waited until she was seated across from him before taking her chin in his hand and tilting her face to his. 'Ask me what you want to know.'

Her breath caught at the intensity of his gaze. She shifted a little, settling deeper into the padded bench. 'How did you survive in that field?' The question had nagged her since hearing his story.

'A young Frenchwoman took mercy on me. Instead of stealing my clothes, she noticed I was still breathing. She helped me onto a wagon and took me to her family's farm. Nursed me. Let me leave when I was well enough. Like many others, I took more time to recover in Brussels. My men were not as fortunate.' He let out a shuddering breath. 'So, you see, I am no hero.'

She looked at him, a hot ache growing in her throat, her defences crumbling as she acknowledged how much she wanted the strong man before her, her husband. 'I do not see it the same way as you.'

He shook his head. 'Lena, you misunderstand—'

She placed a finger across his lips to silence him. 'I understand perfectly well. You could not control the war, the enemy, or the loss of your soldiers. You had no way of knowing you would be ambushed, and without your skill and bravery more soldiers would have perished. You were remarkably strong to survive, not just in body, but in spirit. You *are* a hero.'

He clenched his jaw, making the bones of his face tighten. 'Jesus,' he hissed. 'You weren't supposed to be like this.'

'Like what?'

His blue eyes blazed. 'A miracle.'

Ravenwood's chest knotted, and his skin grew hot. Lust and possession wound in his gut, a dangerous combination. He'd known for a long time that Lena was special. Kind, loyal, and forgiving. And now, his gratitude towards her for caring for him in his time of need, his most vulnerable moments, only increased. His head lowered, and he captured her mouth in a searing kiss. His desire ratcheted when she kissed him back, her arms rising and her fingers clutching his broad shoulders, then inching upward to slide into his thick hair.

He pulled back, his breath hot against her lips. 'No one has ever looked at me the way you do.'

'Then they all are blind.'

Her words were as arousing as her beauty—in and out. He secretly longed to be seen the way she looked at him. It was rare and intoxicating. He growled and ravished her mouth as he lifted her from the bench and pulled her onto his lap, his palm caressing her lower back. His scar pulled tight as he travelled down the column of her throat. Denying himself was no longer an option. 'I want you, Lena.'

'I want you, too.'

Her consent was an aphrodisiac.

Her gown loosened and he eased a breast out of her bodice and sucked a nipple full into his mouth. She tasted like strawberries and pure woman. When he cupped her second breast to his mouth, her moan fueled his lust.

'Oh, my.' She sighed. 'I fear I'll combust before we reach home.'

His hand lifted the hem of her dress and his hot palm slid up her stocking, past the frilly garter, and found the soft curls between her legs.

She squirmed. His groin grew harder beneath her. Would he make it to the house? 'God, to be inside you.'

She clutched his shoulders. 'I ache.'

'Where? Here, my love?' He pressed harder against her.

'Yes, yes. You know where.'

'I do.' His forefinger swept across the sensitive folds

of her body. 'I want to suck on this bud until you cry out my name in pleasure.'

Her dark eyes opened wide. 'You can't be serious.'

'I am. You'll love it.'

His forefinger drew a circle against her nub, and her eyes fluttered closed. 'Please, I—'

'I know what you need. God, I know all about need.' He drew out her climax until she was roused to the peak of desire, then she came in long, surrendering moans.

She was still shaking as he lowered her skirt and helped refasten her gown. Then, he took her into his arms, holding her tight and relishing the feel of her there. She sighed and settled against him. He wanted to hold her like this forever—why did that scare him?

He didn't know how long they remained that way—but suddenly the wheels of the carriage came to a halt.

They entered the house, then came to an abrupt stop at the sight of Claire in the vestibule.

'Uncle! Lena!' Claire's foot rested on the bottom step of the grand staircase, her hand clutching the banister. She was in a nightgown and wrapper.

'Where are you going this time of night?' Ravenwood asked.

A flash of panic lit Claire's eyes. 'I had a bad dream about my parents.'

He felt a stab of pity for his niece. He knew all about bad dreams. He turned to look at Lena and noticed a glance between her and Claire. He wasn't sure if there was an unspoken meaning between them.

Lena touched Ravenwood's arm, drawing his attention. 'It's all right. Go sit with Claire.'

His niece smiled. 'That would be nice, Uncle.'

The moment of passion he'd had with Lena earlier had been doused over his concern for the girl, and Ravenwood was grateful for his wife's understanding. He lifted Lena's hand and placed a kiss on the back of her palm. 'Thank you for an unforgettable evening.'

He carried a lamp and followed Claire into her room.

'Let's sit by the window seat.' He set the lamp on the chest of drawers.

Claire's eyebrows knit together. 'Am I in trouble?'

'No, I simply want to talk.' He couldn't blame the girl for thinking he was going to discipline her. Her anxiety made him cringe inside. Had he really been so intolerable? Had he turned into his disciplinarian father?

He sat and patted the seat beside him. She joined him.

The cool breeze from the slightly open casement felt good against his neck. He took a breath. 'I also had a troubling evening…remembering my time on the battle-field.' He'd start with a confession. Something personal he'd never shared with his niece.

Her eyes widened. 'Oh, I suspected you had bad memories. I… I just never understood.'

'Sudden sounds send me back to war. I cannot explain it. I can only say that I am unable to control my reactions.'

Claire tucked her legs beneath her and fully faced him. 'Is there anything I can do?'

He was touched by her concern. 'Yes. Just give me

time.' He reached out to touch her hand. She didn't pull away.

Claire rubbed her eye. 'I still miss my parents. Sounds remind me of them as well. Not jarring, like you. But the tinkling of glasses reminds me of the parties they used to have. And scents, too. I have a bottle of my mother's perfume that I often smell when I miss her.'

His chest tightened. 'I'm sorry for your loss. I should say it more,' Brent said. 'I also want to apologize to you. I inflicted a military schedule on you, thinking it would help you cope. I was wrong.'

Her lips parted. 'Oh, Uncle.'

'Let me finish. Just because routine helped me does not mean it will help you. I understand that now. I'm glad you enjoy your art lessons, and I promise to take your opinions into consideration in the future. I may not always agree, but I'll try.'

She nodded. 'Thank you, Uncle.'

They sat together for a full hour before he tucked Claire into bed and kissed the top of her head.

Chapter Twenty-Two

As the mantel clock in Lena's room struck midnight, Lena tossed and turned in bed. Every time she closed her eyes, she dreamed of her husband. She'd relived the velvet touch of his lips against her skin. Who would have thought she would grow to desire a man so much? Her past sexual experiences had been lukewarm at best, painful most times. She'd known she'd have to share a bed to get with child.

She'd never expected she'd *want* to.

Things had changed the prior evening. Brent had finally spoken of his past, finally explained his battle experiences. She'd assumed he'd suffered at war, but never in her wildest dreams, had she expected his confessions. He was a strong man to survive physically and mentally. She wanted to help him. He'd come to mean much more to her than a marriage of convenience. She'd stopped thinking of him that way a while ago, hadn't she?

Which frightened her. He'd called her a miracle, a gift, and her heart had turned over in her chest. She'd vowed to protect her heart, and now she found herself caring for him, falling for him, over the course of the prior week.

She threw her covers aside and sat on the edge of the bed. There was no sense staying awake. Whenever she had trouble sleeping as a child, her mother would fix her a warm cup of milk. She'd continued the practice when one of the young girls at the school woke up crying from a bad dream, or from missing a deceased parent. Whether it was from the hot drink or the comfort of a sympathetic friend, most times it helped, and the girl was able to sleep. She hoped Ravenwood had helped Claire earlier—the two needed more time together. Though, Lena suspected that catching Claire on the front steps wasn't the result of a bad dream but rather a nighttime visit to her beau. She'd noticed the girl was wearing shoes, as if she'd been out.

Stuffing her feet into slippers, Lena carried a lamp down the staircase and into the kitchen. She poured herself a cup of milk from the larder. Then, opening a cupboard, she reached for the wrapped pastries Ivan's aunties had prepared for her the other day and set them on the table. She eagerly unwrapped the package.

A mold had been used to press an intricate design of roses with vines into the dough before baking the pastries. She reached for a small, round pastry and took a bite. Her eyelids fluttered closed. The combination of the sweetness of the date filling and the flaky pastry danced on her tongue in a sweet ballet. She reached for a second pastry.

'What do you have there?'

She jumped at the sound of Brent's voice to see him standing in the entrance of the kitchen.

She swallowed and held up a pastry. 'Date-filled pastries.'

He walked forward, stealthy as a jungle cat, and stopped at her side. 'Hmm. Where did you get them?'

She pondered whether to tell him she'd visited Ivan's home, then decided to be honest. 'Ivan has two aunties. They are fabulous bakers and cooks of Middle Eastern cuisine.'

'You visited his home?'

'I did.'

He hesitated and her stomach lurched. 'Perhaps I will meet these two aunties one day.'

She let out a sigh of relief.

'You have flour on your nose.' He reached out to rub the tip of her nose with his thumb. The unexpected touch made her nerves tingle.

'The pastries have a light dusting of flour so they don't stick together.' She placed one on a plate and handed it to him. 'Would you like to try one?'

He accepted the plate and took a bite, his eyes widening as he chewed. 'The dough is soft and the filling is sweet. I've never had a date.'

'Truly? I've purchased them from travelling merchants at a Middle Eastern market.'

'In London?'

'There's a flourishing section of the city. Arabic traders arrive with goods from all over the world. The locals prepare food and pastries on market day.' London had a thriving diverse community that the *beau monde* was not aware of. Even if they were, many would consider it beneath them to visit.

He finished the pastry and his eyes held hers. 'I've never known what delicacies I've been missing.'

More nerves flickered to life at his words. Was he speaking of her or the pastry? She reached for another sweet for herself. This time, he watched as she took a small bite.

She swallowed, suddenly nervous at his perusal. Her already warm cheeks flushed hotter. 'You shouldn't stare.'

'Why? You are my wife.'

She was. And he was her husband. The cookie lost all taste as she stared at the attractive and virile man standing close.

He set his half-eaten pastry on the plate and his gaze dropped to her mouth. 'We never finished what we started in the carriage.' His strong hands spanned her waist as he picked her up to set her on the worktable, then stepped between her open thighs. He lowered his head slowly, torturously slowly, to brush her lips.

Reaching up, she pulled his head to her. 'Kiss me. Hard.'

'Sweet Jesus.' He obliged and captured her lips in a searing kiss. He was ravenous and hungry, and she met him with her own fervor.

With her bottom on the edge of the worktable and Brent between her thighs, the rigid length of his hardness rubbed against her. Her body hummed with excitement, and she grew wet between her thighs. She shifted, arched, wanting to pull him closer. Every fiber in her being ached for him.

He grasped her long hair. 'Tell me again. I need to hear the words from your lips.'

She narrowed her eyes. His face was fierce. His scar was stark in the lamplight. She experienced a thrill that she could make such a man desire her as much as she did him at that moment.

'I want you. I want this.'

His growl reverberated through her bones, seemed to echo off the kitchen walls. Blood coursed hot and thick in her veins.

His hands went to the tiny row of buttons at the front of her nightgown. Without a corset or shift, her breasts were free to his hungry gaze. He cupped both breasts and lifted them towards his mouth. He laved and suckled one nipple, then the other. The pleasure was intense and radiated to the thrumming center between her thighs.

She arched her back, greedy for more. Her body sang with desire, desperate for his skilled mouth and fingers. He lifted the hem of her nightgown, and his hands skimmed her naked legs. The garment bunched at her waist and her bare bottom touched the rough wood of the worktop.

His voice was hoarse. 'I want to taste you.'

His wicked words aroused her. The table was high, and he lowered his head and kissed her between her thighs, then he was *there*.

In her wildest imagination, she'd never believed a man could love a woman that way.

She grasped his hair and tugged. 'Brent—'

He lifted his head. 'Let me. I've dreamed of this, too.'

She was powerless to resist. He licked, swirled his

tongue, then gently sucked. Leaning back, she grasped the end of the worktable as shivering sensations turned her to molten lava. She cried out as her body tightened like a bow. He drew out her climax until she was crazed with lust, painfully close to the precipice before she careened over the edge and cried out in ecstasy.

Her body was still shivering from the aftermath as he rose and unfastened his breeches. He tugged her to him, then with one powerful thrust, he was inside her.

Her body accepted his length and breadth. Still, he was large, and she was still sensitive. He gently placed a soft kiss on her lips. 'Are you all right?'

Looking up into his eyes, she was lost. His face was tortured with both desire and concern. He was holding himself back, waiting for her. Unable to deny the truth in her heart any longer, she realized she was falling in love with him. She was no longer young and full of idealistic notions. She was a grown woman, and the love she felt for Ravenwood was more real than any youthful infatuation. It was also frightening. She'd never meant this to be about love.

Never love.

She bit her lip, keeping her emotions inside. If she didn't confess it, then part of her was still safe. She *needed* to be safe.

'Yes,' she said. 'It feels incredible.'

'You feel incredible,' he hissed. 'Tight as a fist. And as hot as a forge.'

His erotic words tightened the pang in her chest. As he pulled out and then thrust back, he touched a deep spot in her womb and her own passion grew. Desire combined with love posed infinite risk. But she was no longer willing to waste a moment more of her life denying herself pleasure.

She lifted her hips to meet him, her fingers digging into his shoulders. He was striking in his passion. The dark slash of his brows, the chiseled cheekbones, his half-scarred lip. The rising need grew, and she kept her eyes open as he pumped inside her. Too soon, her climax built and she was overcome with euphoria.

His growl of approval was fierce. 'God. I can feel you grip me.' He thrust once, twice more, then threw back his head as he poured himself into her.

They stayed together, forehead to forehead, breathing hard. Her limbs grew stiff, and he lifted her gently and placed her on her feet. 'I'll crave dates forever.'

She laughed. 'Does this mean you expect sweets in the kitchen?'

'I expect sweets from you.'

Oh, my. 'What kind?'

'I expect you in my bedchamber. Now. Tomorrow. And the next night.'

Why did his words cause a thrill down her spine? 'Now you sound demanding,' she teased.

'Never. What are your demands?' he asked.

'To be pleasured.'

His lips twitched. 'And did I please you?'

'Devil! You know you did.' She flushed as she recalled his dark head between her spread thighs.

Leaning down, his breath brushed her ear. 'There's more I can teach you.'

She slipped her hand in his big one. 'Lead the way to your bedchamber, Your Grace.'

His smile was devastating. 'As you command, wife.'

Chapter Twenty-Three

Parenting a sixteen-year-old young lady was a much more difficult task than Lena had imagined.

It was the following afternoon and she was walking beside Claire along Bond Street. The two were on a mission to find art supplies and headed to a shop known to cater to artists. As they walked, Lena pondered how best to bring up Claire's behaviour last night.

She decided upon a straightforward approach. 'You were sneaking out of the house to visit with the neighbour's son last night, weren't you?'

Claire looked at her in surprise. 'How did—'

Lena's lips twitched. 'Do you deny it?'

Claire let out a huff. 'No, I don't deny it.'

'You promised not to do it again.'

'I never promised.'

Warning laced Lena's voice as she said, 'Claire, I—'

Not waiting for Lena to finish, the girl hurried forward. 'Is this the place?'

Lena quickened her pace to catch up, then noticed a print shop's sign swinging in a slight breeze. 'Yes, this is the shop, but we are not done speaking about this, young lady.'

The little bell above the door chimed as they entered. The small shop was crowded with tables overflowing with brushes, oil paints, watercolours, charcoals, blank canvases, and sketchbooks. Prints from aspiring artists hung on the walls. One was a colourful watercolour featuring ladies with bright dresses and matching parasols walking on a sunny day in Hyde Park. Another of a sporting gentleman with his hunting dog. A third was a landscape of the Thames on a cloudy day. The shopkeeper—a middle-aged man with dark hair peppered with grey and black charcoal beneath his fingernails—looked like a mad artist himself.

Claire's eyes widened as she took in the array of brushes—some for watercolours, some for oils, those with pointed tips and others wide and flat. She picked up a brush that resembled a tiny lady's fan. 'Am I free to purchase what I'd like?'

'Yes.' Brent had waved Lena away that morning when she'd announced she was taking Claire shopping and requested a budget. 'Use your discretion,' he'd said without looking up from one of his ledgers. Lena took that to mean his niece could buy whatever art supplies she fancied.

Claire's excitement increased as she flitted to another table displaying cakes of varying shades of watercolours. 'Whatever you have done to lighten my uncle's mood, please keep doing it.'

'I'm not sure what you mean,' Lena said.

Claire looked up from the paints, her expression incredulous. 'Don't you? He's allowing me an art tutor and freedom to purchase supplies of my choosing. Even more inconceivable, for the first time, he sat with me last night and talked about my parents.'

She was happy they continued to get closer, and her heart warmed for them. As for after midnight, the time Brent spent with her had been unforgettable. Her cheeks heated at the memory of their encounter in the kitchen. It was a magical evening she would not easily forget. It had been frightening as well. She'd sworn never to fall in love with another again. Looking back, she didn't love Oliver. Not true love. But she *was* falling for her husband, especially after he'd opened up to her. But what if he never opened up again? His demons might not allow it. Then where would that leave her?

She wanted to rub this emotion from her chest. Only she couldn't. For the first time, she imagined a real marriage, not just one of convenience. She'd wanted children for so long and now thought of raising them *together.*

When had things changed? Was it during the picnic? Or when he'd confessed his past war experiences after the thunderstorm? Or after an especially tender bout of love-making? She only knew her expectations had changed, her feelings had grown, and she wanted *more* than a businesslike marriage.

'Are you going to tell the duke about Peter?' Claire asked.

The question drew Lena's attention back to the present. 'I only agreed to keep your secret if you agreed to stop sneaking out.'

Claire set down the cake of watercolour she'd been holding. Her eyes were earnest as she lowered her voice. 'I cannot! How else will I see Peter?'

Lena raised her hand when Claire opened her mouth to protest again. 'You will still see the young man. I will arrange more afternoon luncheons. Or walks in the park. Or to meet at Gunter's. There are ways. Soon, you will have your debut and Lord Peter can request to dance with you at a ball and properly court you with flowers and chocolates. Ravenwood would approve.'

Claire's brow creased. 'Promise that you will not tell my uncle about last night? He was kind when we talked, and he even shared. I don't want to upset him or go back to the way things were.'

Lena sighed. They had been getting along, and she treasured that relationship. What harm was there as long as Claire obeyed this time? 'I promise for now. Meanwhile, I'll send invitations to the Marquess and Marchioness of Billingham for—'

'Did someone mention Lady Billingham?'

At the sickeningly familiar feminine voice, Lena turned to see Lady Powell near the shop's entrance. She was dressed in the height of fashion in a silk, sapphire gown that enhanced her blue eyes and fair complexion. Matching sapphire ear-bobs dangled from her ears, and a necklace the size of a small pigeon's egg rested between her breasts. Even her reticule had been dyed the exact shade of her gown.

Lena's gut immediately tightened.

Francesca approached. 'Good day, Your Grace.' She looked at Claire. 'And who is this charming young lady?'

Lena wanted to grasp Claire's arm and leave the shop. She refused to give the woman the satisfaction. Not to mention it would cause unwanted questions from Claire.

Lena raised her chin a notch. 'This is the duke's niece, Miss Claire,' Lena said. 'Claire, this is Lady Powell.'

Claire bobbed a proper curtsy. 'Hello. It is a pleasure to make your acquaintance, my lady.'

'I couldn't help but overhear you mention Lady Billingham,' Francesca said. 'The marchioness is a close friend. We went to finishing school together.'

Lena's fingers twisted the strings of her reticule. Exactly how much had the woman overheard? Had she heard Claire confess to sneaking out of the house to meet the neighbour's son, or, worse, that Lena had agreed to keep the girl's secret from Ravenwood?

She didn't believe so. Still, it was bad enough that Francesca was acquainted with their neighbours. Lena regretted that she'd started this conversation with Claire at the shop. Lena's smile was brittle. 'I did not know you had an interest in art, Lady Powell.'

'Oh, I'm here to purchase one of the paintings for my own dear niece, who is the tender age of eight and is staying with us.' Francesca pointed to a small oil painting of a garden bursting with flowers. 'She spotted one of the paintings when we last strolled by.'

The knot in Lena's stomach tightened. The woman had turned her away at the nearly same age when she'd arrived in England, grieving the loss of her mother.

Do not think of the past. Lena shoved the painful memories aside.

'Now, which painting do you fancy?' Francesca asked.

'None,' Lena said. 'I'm here on Claire's behalf. She is the one with the artistic talent.' Now that the pleasantries had been exchanged, how fast could they escape from Francesca's presence?

The lady tilted her head to the side as she regarded Claire. 'Such a lovely young woman. You will have your debut soon, won't you?'

Claire smiled. 'A little over a year.'

Francesca sighed. 'I remember my debut. I was a bundle of nerves and so excited. I recall my first dance. Looking back, I do believe the young gentleman must have been just as nervous.' The lady's gloved hand fluttered to the sapphire between her breasts.

'I admit to being anxious, my lady,' Claire said.

'It's to be expected, of course,' Francesca said, 'but I do recall that my second dance went better than my first.'

'Do you remember him?' Claire asked, clearly interested in whatever the woman had to say.

She flashed a mischievous smile. 'A lady always remembers. My second dance was with your uncle, the duke.'

Lena's nerves sparked. What on earth was her game?

'Now, dear,' Francesca addressed Claire. 'Is there a gentleman you wish to dance with first? It is always best to know in advance. Others leave it up to chance. I was never one of them.'

Oblivious to the manipulative woman, Claire's face turned a telltale pink. 'Oh, there may be one.'

Francesca arched a well-plucked brow. 'Of course, there

must be. Whoever he is, he is fortunate to have caught your eye. Your neighbour's son, perhaps?'

Every muscle in Lena's body tightened. Once more, her suspicions arose as to just what she'd overheard.

'Why make a suggestion at all?' Lena asked.

Lady Powell turned to her. 'As I said, Lady Billingham and I are old school friends and confidantes. She has a son a year or two older than the lovely Miss Claire.' She turned back to Claire. 'Have you met him, dear?'

The girl stood still, at a loss for words.

'As a matter of fact, she has,' Lena said. 'We invited the family for afternoon tea, and Claire had the opportunity to meet their son, Lord Peter. Isn't that right, Claire?'

Claire swallowed. 'Yes.'

Francesca flashed a crocodile smile. 'Charming. Perhaps he will be your first dance, my dear.'

'Perhaps,' Claire said.

'Oh, to be young again!' Francesca said before sailing to the counter for her purchase. Then, with the painting wrapped in brown paper and string beneath her arm, she waved on her way out the shop's door.

Rather than be relieved at the woman's exit, Lena felt a pang of worry. Trouble was coming.

The following weeks passed pleasantly. Much to Lena's surprise, nothing further had come of her run-in with Lady Powell. A routine was established at the estate. Ravenwood would meet with his stewards during the day and spend one evening a week with Lord Kent.

Meanwhile, Lena had been spending more time with

Claire. When Claire wasn't taking art lessons, Lena prepared the girl as best she could for her debut, including dancing lessons, proper table etiquette and use of the fan, reinforcing everything she'd mastered at the girls' school.

The nights were entirely different. Brent would spend hours making love to her. He was a skilled lover, and she was eager to learn and to please. Each time they were together, she lost more of her heart to him. The only way to hold on to the last fragments of herself was to shield her growing feelings.

As for Ravenwood, while his actions seemed to speak volumes, he never proclaimed his love in words. Even after initially speaking of his past, he hadn't shared anything more. She'd hoped he would open up further, but instead she'd felt him pulling away. He never spoke of that night at the tavern. She never knew what he was thinking, and that troubled her the most.

One night, after he slipped from her body and she rested a hand on his chest to feel his strong heartbeat, he tenderly pushed back a lock of her hair and looked in her eyes. 'I have a surprise for you.'

Her heart skipped a beat. Would he finally share his thoughts? 'What is it?'

'I'm taking you and Claire somewhere special tomorrow. You'll have to wait and see.' He brushed his lips against hers, and she quickly forgot her disappointment.

Chapter Twenty-Four

The carriage rolled to a stop in front of Somerset House at the south end of the Strand. Lena looked outside the window to see the Neoclassical complex and impressive building that housed the Royal Academy.

Claire bounced in her seat. 'I'm so excited!'

Brent sat forward on the leather bench. 'I thought you would like to see the summer exhibition.'

This was the surprise he'd mentioned yesterday evening. Lena was struck by his thoughtfulness for his niece.

Claire bounced on the bench across from him. 'Yes, you thought right, Uncle.'

Lena cleared her throat. 'I've never been inside the Royal Academy.'

'Then we shouldn't wait a minute longer.' Ravenwood hopped out, and, without waiting for the driver, he lowered the step himself and helped Lena and Claire alight.

He escorted them inside the impressive vestibule, but it wasn't until they stepped into a large hall that Lena gasped. Claire must have been just as distracted, and she nearly walked into Lena from behind.

Claire pressed a hand to her heart. 'I fear I'll faint from happiness.'

The girl's delight pleased her, and once again her appreciation for Ravenwood's kindness grew.

The hall was decorated from floor to ceiling with magnificent gilt-framed artwork. Splashes of colour were a feast for the eyes. Country landscapes, portraits, prints, and drawings were displayed in splendor. Marble and bronze sculptures on pedestals were arranged around the room.

'I see a Rowlandson and a Gainsborough.' Claire pointed, her mouth agape, at each painting. 'I don't know where to look first.'

'Start at the beginning. We have all afternoon,' Ravenwood said.

This side of the duke—carefree and considerate—was just as attractive to her as his appearance. He'd taken time out of his day to escort them, not because he expected anything in return but simply to please Claire.

She watched him from beneath lowered lashes. His powerful frame appeared relaxed, yet, at the same time, his military bearing was evident in the clean line of his shoulders, his sharp profile, and his relaxed air of command.

A middle-aged man approached. A flash crossed his face at the sight of the duke's scar but he quickly recovered. 'It's an honor to have you visit, Your Grace. My name is Horatio Curtis, one of the curators.'

If Ravenwood noticed the man's slip, he paid little heed. He shook the curator's hand. 'May I introduce my wife,

Her Grace, and my niece Lady Claire, who is an aspiring artist herself.'

'A young artist?' Mr Curtis glanced at Claire. 'Have you seen paintings by Mary Moser and Angelica Kauffman, miss? Both women were founding members of the Royal Academy.'

'I'd love to see their work,' Claire said.

'Follow me.' The curator led them away.

As they strolled the academy and viewed artwork by the two founding female artists as well as dozens of other artists, Lena was keenly aware of Claire's joy and Ravenwood's pleasant mood.

While Claire was engaged in conversation with another aspiring artist, Ravenwood took Lena's hand and tugged her away.

'Where are we going?' she asked.

They ended up in an alcove of marble sculptures of Roman Gods and Goddesses. A marble sculpture of a nymph caught her eye. The nymph's hand was pressed to her one bared breast, her eyes wide, lips parted. It looked like she was waiting for her lover.

Brent tugged her into his arms. 'I craved a private moment with my wife.'

She found herself pressed against the wall. His chest was warm, and a scrape of stubble rasped against her cheek. She immediately went soft, and need unfurled in her belly.

'We could be found,' she said.

'Do you care?'

No, not one bit. This obsession with him was frightening. It was also exhilarating. She stood on tiptoe and kissed him.

His growl of approval nearly melted her bones. His hand rested against the wall by her head, caging her in as he ravaged her mouth. She buried her fingers in his soft hair as his hardness pressed against the apex of her thighs. She squirmed closer, her body aching for what only he could make her feel. His lips travelled down her neck to the tops of her breasts above her bodice. Her nipples pebbled beneath the silk, and she threw her head back, giving him better access.

Her eyelids slid open to focus on the statue. She understood the nymph's passion, the desperate aching need as she waited for her lover. Lena felt that same need in her blood.

Madness.

Too soon, Brent lifted his head, his eyes dark with desire. 'I knew better than to touch you and not want you. We'll continue later.' There was a regretful gleam in his eye as he pulled away from her and led her back out to the gallery.

Later, as they sat in the carriage on the way back to the mansion on Berkeley Square, Lena's skirts brushed his thigh. 'Thank you for today.'

'Do not thank me. I enjoyed spending time with my wife and niece.'

She had too…when the three of them were together, it felt like true family. Maybe one day, Ravenwood would come to love her. Lena bit her tongue, afraid to speak, afraid she'd expose her heart.

They returned home and Claire headed to her room. Not wanting to waste a lovely afternoon, Lena gathered the morning post and headed for the terrace for a glass of lemonade. She'd go through the pile of newly arrived invitations and decide which she could convince Ravenwood to attend. She was aware of him trailing behind.

'Are you leaving so quickly?' he asked.

'It's a beautiful day. Come join me.'

A footman stepped outside, carrying a pitcher and glasses on a silver tray. Just as he stepped down the stairs, the footman tripped. The silver tray, along with the pitcher and glasses, landed against the terracotta terrace with a thunderous bang.

It happened so swiftly she would have thought it a shaft of light from an overhead cloud. A strange, faraway look flitted across the duke's face. His expression hardened a split-second before he launched himself at her, toppling her down. At the last moment, he turned to cushion her fall.

Umph! The jolt of the fall took the breath from her lungs. Her heart jumped in her chest, and she cried out.

'Stay down!' he shouted, a strange hysteria in his voice. Turning, he was on top of her, his face fierce, unfamiliar.

'Raven... Ravenwood.'

'Down, I said! Another is coming!'

He didn't seem to comprehend. His breath against her ear was the only proof he was living flesh, not stone. His taut expression spoke of another time, another place. A war that had never fully left him. This was different than his other episode—even more frightening. Panic welled in her chest. He was a solid mass of hardened muscle over her.

She took his face in her hands and willed his blank eyes to meet hers. 'Brent!'

He jerked, blinked, and blessedly, his gaze focused. 'My God! Are you hurt?'

Her breath shuddered. Her nerves loosed, her body seemed to release clenched muscles she didn't know existed. She gave him a wobbly smile. 'I'm not hurt. Just shaken.'

He must not have believed her. His eyes were full of fear. He shifted his weight off her, his large hands running up and down her arms, her torso, then her legs. His hands slipped beneath her skirts to skim her stockings. It was shocking, but he had no intimacy in his touch, only a desperate need to make sure she had no broken bones or abrasions. The servant had fled inside, most likely to get help.

'Are you certain you're uninjured?' A note of desperation tinged his voice. His breath continued to come hard.

She was shaking, the blood in her body still pounding in her veins. 'Yes, yes. I'm certain.'

He rose, then helped her to her feet. That's when he saw it. A scrape on her right palm from the terrace. Blood began to ooze from the wound. She hadn't even felt it until now. She curled her fingers to hide the wound, but it was too late.

He turned pale, his brow tense. 'My God! Please forgive me.'

She shook her head. 'It's nothing.'

A flash of vulnerability lit his eyes that had nothing to do with the fall. 'It's *everything*. It's much worse than the thunderstorm during the ball. You could have hit your head. You could have—'

She was desperate to reach for him. So she did, but he caught her hand. 'Stop. You didn't.'

His expression was haunted as he let her go. 'But I could have. I thought, just for a moment, that I had a chance with us.'

Icy dread settled in her gut. 'What are you talking about?'

His tormented eyes held hers. 'You deserve more than a broken man.'

She fought the urge to launch herself in his arms. To rest her head on his chest. 'It was nothing. A simple loud noise.'

'No. It was more, and we both know it. And what about next time? Or the time after that?' His jaw clenched. 'I cannot be trusted.'

A different angst squeezed her chest. One she'd fought with her head but could not control with her heart. She'd tried so hard to resist this feeling, to stay strong. Standing before the strongest man she knew, a man who was tormented by his own demons, her heart could not be waylaid.

She grasped his hand, willing him to look at her. 'I love you.' The words slipped from her lips. She was as powerless to prevent them as he had been to prevent his episode.

He visibly recoiled. The shocked horror had left him, replaced with something else entirely—longing and fear. More fear than she'd ever seen in the depths of his eyes, more than she thought could be caused from a tray rattling loudly against paving stones. 'No! You cannot. Love was never part of our bargain.'

Their bargain. Her stomach fell. She hadn't thought of their relationship as a bargain in a long, long while. Not when she'd shared his bed and had allowed him to touch her body and her heart as intimately as he had each night.

He pulled his hand away. The slight distance between them seemed cavernous. He stood straight, seeming to gather himself. 'Don't be foolish.'

If she'd thought he could say nothing more hurtful, she was wrong.

Then he turned and walked back into the house.

Lena gaped at the doorway, the birds chirping and the sun shining, oblivious to the fact that she was unravelling inside. She'd been tinglingly aware of his hands on her body to check for injury, too full of the memory of his haunted eyes. He was wrong. He needed her as much as she loved him.

But he was also stubborn and distrusting. And that could lead to more doom than his recurring war episodes—whether awake or nightmares. For the first time she acknowledged the compelling problem was trust. Not *her* ability to trust, but *his*.

His sense of worth had eroded. He believed he was unworthy and therefore could never trust another enough to let them love him. So where did that leave her?

She loved him.

She didn't know what she was saying. She couldn't. No woman would love him after what he'd done, what she'd witnessed.

Ravenwood locked his bedchamber door, then gripped

his bedpost, forcing air in his chest. He was going to be sick. Sweat beaded on his brow and trickled down his back. He tore off his coat and waistcoat. Bile rose in his throat. His cravat cut off his breath and he clawed the silk and tossed it to the ground. The crack of the tray crashing on the terracotta terrace had brought back the boom of a cannon shot. In a flash, he was back on the battlefield, ducking for cover.

Gasping, he counted to one hundred and twenty before his pulse slowed. The trigger was unexpected and came from nowhere and everywhere. The simple slip of a tray from a servant's fingers and he was sweaty, emotional carnage. Worse, because of him, Lena had been hurt. A simple abrasion was too much.

She loved him.

He'd never hated himself more.

God! He could have seriously hurt her...killed her. He was not in his right mind when the episode took over. Nightmares were one thing. Even the breakdown from the thunderstorm could not compare. He'd suffered on his own then. But this episode was something else entirely. He hadn't been gentle when he tackled her. Instinct took over, and he'd feared they'd be blasted into smithereens. Thank goodness, he'd had the foresight at least to cushion her fall.

She was wrong. She could not love him, not truly. Not when he was crazed. Dangerously unpredictable. A beast.

Self-disgust roiled in his gut. The war was long over but his torture continued. In his mind, he deserved every nightmare. He was alive when so many had died. It would have been easier if he'd died on that battlefield alongside his men. An enemy soldier had carved his face *and* his soul.

A slight knock on the door startled him. 'Your Grace?'

'Do *not* enter.' His head snapped up, and his scarred lip curled in a snarl. He recognized Barnes's voice.

A long minute later, the footsteps faded.

He reached for a bottle of whisky on a sideboard.

Later that afternoon, Lena's nerves were wound tight as clock springs as she looked both ways to make sure the hall was empty before slipping out the servants' entrance. She hurried down the street and hailed a hack. It wasn't until she was seated on the bench and the carriage began moving that she let out a slow breath. She moved the curtain to glimpse outside the window at the bustling London street.

Less than fifteen minutes later, she'd arrived at her destination and knocked on the wooden door. She shifted her feet from side to side as she waited.

The door swung open, and Ivan stood in the doorway.

'Lena! I wasn't expecting you.' His dark eyes travelled over her from head to toe. 'Is all well?'

'Is Vartan here?' She hoped to speak with him.

Brent needed more help. She understood there was no cure, no quick remedy or tonic that would ease his torment. But surely, there had to be a way to convince the duke not to give up on himself.

Not to give up on her.

'Vartan may not wish to speak,' Ivan said.

'I can be persuasive.'

Ivan's lips twitched. 'I have no doubt. Follow me.'

Vartan's hair appeared even longer today and brushed his shoulders. His beard was still unkempt, and he sat by his hookah, although he wasn't smoking this morning.

As soon as he saw Lena, he waved her over. 'I take it your man isn't doing well.'

'How do you know?'

'You otherwise wouldn't be here.'

She saw no reason for formalities. 'Ravenwood believes his war sickness is a reason to push me away.'

'Did he meet with the soldiers in the tavern?' Vartan asked.

'Once.' That was a problem as well. She wanted Brent to return, but he expressed no interest.

Vartan let out a huff and said what she'd been thinking. 'It will take more than once.'

'How will I convince him?'

'You cannot. He has to convince himself he is worth saving.'

It was a bleak assessment. There must be *something* she could do. But what? She loved him and he'd rejected her.

On the way out, Lena ran into Ivan's aunties. 'Lena! We have *sarma*!' Aunt Norma said.

Sarma was a savoury dish of grape leaves stuffed with meat and rice. She'd adored the meal and had fond memories of picking grape leaves with her mother and grandmother. It was a special grapevine which produced tender leaves but sour grapes.

Today, her mind was melancholy, and her thoughts were

with the duke. Still, it was rude to refuse food in her culture. Lena's smile felt stiff as she said, 'I'd love some.'

When one of the aunts carried out a plate and the scent wafted to her, a sudden nausea rose in Lena's throat. Horrified that she'd be sick, she covered her mouth with a hand and ran into the back gardens to retch in a corner.

Anoush came out with a cup of water. 'How long?'

Norma trailed behind her and offered her a handkerchief.

Lena wiped her mouth with the handkerchief and rinsed her mouth. 'I apologize. I must be ill.'

'No. How long have you known you were carrying the duke's babe,' Anoush asked.

Lena straightened and her eyes widened. She shook her head. 'You're both mistaken!'

Norma shook her head. 'No, we are old and wise. Have you bled lately?'

Lena's head spun as she thought back. She hadn't had her menses in well over a month. She hadn't paid it much thought since the nights had been filled with breathless lovemaking. Could she be pregnant?

She pressed a hand to her abdomen. She wasn't showing signs, but it was early.

'You are with child, dear. Are you happy?' Anoush asked.

Was she happy? She'd wanted a child of her own for as long as she could remember. She'd wanted two or three. She'd initially thought herself clever to have devised an arrangement that would get her what she wanted. Now things were different. She had fallen in love. But with her love unreciprocated, and her husband suffering from his own demons…where did that leave her?

Lena grew aware of both women watching her. She rested a protective hand on her abdomen. 'Yes,' she said. 'It's a blessing.'

Ravenwood sat in a hackney across the street and watched the strange house.

He knew, before the door of the home opened, and the dark-haired Ivan embraced Lena and kissed her cheek, that his wife had sought solace from another and was distancing herself from him. What woman would stay with a scarred, broken man who had night terrors and pushed her away after intimacy? Even worse, after she'd confessed her love, he'd reminded her of their businesslike arrangement. Why would she stay with him?

He watched as Ivan escorted her to her own waiting hackney. Ravenwood understood the spark of jealousy that tightened his chest was unwarranted. The two were friends, but still she'd been keeping secrets from him and had sneaked out to come here. As for Ivan, he was a rival for her affections, and Ravenwood could never compete. He knew she'd never love Ivan the way she'd love a husband. But Ravenwood could never have as close a bond as Lena did with her best friend.

After their disastrous evening, Ravenwood had not expected her in the breakfast room. And when he'd spotted her tiptoeing down the hall towards the servants' entrance, he'd followed her.

The hackney had travelled out of Mayfair and into a

part of the city he'd never visited. It headed away from the wealthy, aristocratic homes in Berkeley Square and skirted the rookeries without crossing the line. The homes appeared closer together, smaller structures with even smaller gardens. The passersby wore a colourful mix of familiar English dress and foreign clothing. Some men abandoned coats for brightly coloured waistcoats embroidered with silver thread and intricate designs, loose-fitting trousers, and long sashes tied around their waists. If he was not in torment, he'd be fascinated with the scene and would want to ask Lena more about it. Instead, he watched, jaw clenched, stomach tight, miserable.

Rather than rush across the street, open the hackney door, and take his wife home, he banged on the roof of his own cab and instructed the driver to leave.

Chapter Twenty-Five

'You have a visitor, Your Grace.'

Ravenwood had just returned when Barnes made the announcement.

He inwardly cursed. He'd sought isolation in his study to douse his anguish in whisky and erase the image of Lena in Ivan's arms. She was pulling away from him.

Could he blame her?

He became aware of the butler waiting in the doorway.

'Well, who is it, man?' Ravenwood asked.

'Lady Powell.'

Bloody hell. Of all the people he expected or wanted to see, Francesca was last on his list.

'Tell her I'm not receiving.'

'The lady is insistent. She says she has something to tell you, something of importance.'

Whatever Francesca believed was of importance to him, she was wrong. He also knew she could be demanding. He ran a hand through his hair and let out a slow breath. Best if he dealt with her swiftly and sent her on her way.

'See her here.' He'd be damned if he'd receive her in

the drawing room like a proper guest. He'd give her precisely ten minutes.

Francesca swept into his study with the force of a summer storm, her skirts swirling around her legs. She was dressed in a red gown that, in the past, he would have found attractive. Ravenwood was unmoved. How long before Lena returned?

'Your Grace.' Francesca curtsied, revealing the tops of her breasts in the low-cut gown.

His mouth was a thin line. 'Tell me what is of such great importance.' It was rude, but he was not in the mood to be polite.

She pouted. 'Now, Brent. Is that any way to treat a former lover?'

The use of his Christian name irked him. 'It was a long time ago, my lady.'

'We can rekindle our feelings.' Her fair hair was loose around her shoulders and her blue eyes were lined with kohl. She sidled up to him and placed her palm on his chest.

Her attempt at seduction served to further agitate his already frayed temper. God, what had he ever seen in her?

He lifted her hand from his chest and dropped it by her side. 'You should go. Do not waste your time.'

She arched a golden eyebrow. 'Don't tell me you're faithful to your wife. Her mixed blood is beneath you.'

Anger sparked in his chest. 'Don't speak about the duchess that way. You need to leave, my lady. Now.' His voice was harsh.

She drew back, her eyes narrowed, her lips pulled back

from her teeth. 'Did you know your wife is keeping secrets about your niece?'

His head snapped up. 'What would you know about Claire?'

'More than you think. I know the girl has been sneaking out of your home to meet the neighbour's son.'

He stiffened. She had his attention now. 'How do you know this?'

Her painted lips curved in a calculating smile. 'I'm friendly with the young man's mother. She recently caught her son tiptoeing back into the house after a midnight rendezvous. The young man was a blubbering fool when confronted by the marchioness. Apparently, the duchess, your wife, has known of the young lovers' secret outings for some time.'

This gossip was impossible to ignore. He knew Francesca's motives were self-serving. But if this was the truth, why would Lena keep it from him? What would she gain?

If Francesca knew, then others may as well. Claire's reputation would be ruined before she'd even had her debut.

A swish of silk skirts sounded, and Francesca sidled closer to touch him once again, this time on his sleeve. 'I only have your niece's best interest at heart.'

He wasn't fooled. 'The information is intriguing. Your visit is not. It's best if you leave.'

The hackney stopped at the end of the street, and Lena walked the remaining distance to the Berkeley Square mansion. Her steps slowed when she spotted a carriage parked in the circular drive.

Barnes greeted her at the door. 'Who is our visitor?' she asked.

'Lady Powell is in the duke's study, Your Grace.'

Her stomach clenched. Francesca was in her home? In the duke's study? Why not receive the woman in the drawing room? Unless… Lena didn't wait for a response but sailed through the hallway and pushed open the door to the duke's study.

Startled, both Francesca and the duke turned to see her standing in the doorway. Francesca's hand rested on Ravenwood's arm. The tableau took her completely off guard, and she halted. Then her heart quickened, and she came alive to sweep inside.

'What is she doing here?' Lena asked. Her tone was biting but she didn't care.

'Goodness,' Francesca addressed the duke rather than her. 'Is the duchess always this rude?'

'Lady Powell's visit was a surprise.' The duke raised a hand. 'She has delivered some surprising information.'

Lena tipped her chin. 'I'm not interested in hearing gossip.' She narrowed her eyes. 'And it's been my understanding since I've known you that you haven't given a fig about society.'

Ravenwood stood tall. 'You haven't known me that long.'

The barb hurt, especially in front of Francesca. She wanted to cry out but would not give either the satisfaction. Lena faced the pair. Her fingers itched to slap the smug expression from Francesca's face. Whatever she was here for, it was self-serving.

She wouldn't tolerate it, not in *her* home with *her* husband. 'It's time for you to leave, my lady.'

Francesca's eyes flashed in victory, before she lowered her lashes. When she looked at the duke, all traces of maliciousness had vanished.

'Fine. I know when I am unwelcome.' Francesca picked up her reticule and departed.

Lena waited until the front door closed before facing Ravenwood. Why had she come? Why had she found them standing so close together. 'Why was she here?'

'You have no right to ask me. I saw you walk into Ivan's home just this afternoon. Pray tell me, is there another man in that house?'

'You followed me?' Her heart squeezed in her chest. Other than the surprise of finding Francesca in her home, what was more upsetting was Ravenwood's rejection of her love. The pain was still sharp, and she swallowed the despair in her throat. Why shouldn't she visit her friend when she was upset?

At his silence, she spoke out. 'There is no other. How could you even think so?' She heard the hurt in her voice.

'But you have been lying all along, haven't you. What about Claire?'

Her head spun at the change of topic. 'What about her?'

'When were you going to tell me the truth? That my niece has been slipping out of the house to meet the neighbour's son? Peter, is it? The same man whom you arranged to have Claire escort around our gardens the afternoon of the Billingham's visit.'

Oh, God. Things were going from bad to worse in a

heartbeat. She'd made a dreadful mistake. She should have told him about Claire and Peter long ago. Would he ever believe her now? Mistrust radiated from him.

'I... I... It's not that simple and—'

'No more lies, Lena.' His voice held anguish. 'If Francesca knew, who else? Will the girl be ruined before her debut?'

'No! That was not my intent. I insisted she cease meeting Peter at night. You must believe me. I love Claire.'

'But you kept it from me. As well as your visit to Ivan's home.'

'I only sought Ivan's help to meet a man who could help *you*—the same soldier who told me about the group that meets in the tavern.'

His gaze hardened. 'You promised never to tell another about my troubles.'

'I only did to help you!'

How had things come to this? She'd intended to tell him everything. Not for him to learn about Claire through Francesca or for him to learn about Vartan this way. 'You do not trust me.'

'I trust you less now.'

She felt a nauseating sinking despair. She recognized what he was doing. He was using Claire and Ivan and everything else to push her away. After the terrace episode, the tentative feelings that had grown between them had been broken. He feared trusting himself around her. How could a man who didn't trust himself trust another enough to love him?

His mistrust had seeped into their marriage. It was like

a pestilence that grew more and more deadly over time. And all during that time, she had sabotaged her own rules of protecting her heart and fallen helplessly in love with him.

Foolish Lena.

'What else are you keeping from me?' he asked.

She released a held-in breath and faced him with every ounce of bravery in her body. She would not keep another secret from him. She'd wanted a child for so long. It was their bargain, wasn't it? But then she'd lost her head and her heart, and she'd imagined, for a brief, blissful moment, that they could raise the child together as a real family. She bit her lip until it throbbed like her pulse. 'I'm with child.'

He stiffened as if she'd stuck him. 'What did you say?' It was his turn to look stunned.

'I will not keep the child from you,' she said, 'but with the heir taken care of, I will spend my nights in my own chambers.' She needn't say he wasn't welcome in her bed or her life. Her tone was crystal clear. 'Now, if you will excuse me, I am retiring for the night.'

Head held high, she swept from the room.

Ravenwood scowled at Barnes. 'I said no visitors.'

Lord Kent pushed his way inside to find Ravenwood sitting in a leather armchair before an empty fireplace in his study.

'You look like hell,' Kent said.

It had been a full week since Lena had told him about the babe. A full week since Lena had made herself scarce around the mansion. Other than outings with Claire, he rarely saw her. She took all her meals in her room. He'd felt a strange emotion, something he'd never experienced before.

Loneliness.

Claire spoke to him, but she knew something was wrong between them, and she spent her days with her art instructor or with Lena.

Before his wife had entered his life, he'd wanted to be left alone. Now he dreaded the silence. He longed for her smile, her charm. He missed their conversations and their time together. And of course, he missed the nights. He lay awake in his bed thinking about his wife, wanting to hold her.

Only the cat, Bella, would sit in the same room with him. It was ironic that the feline he'd resisted having in his home was the only one to stay by his side now.

Ravenwood reached for his whisky and shot Kent a sideways glare. 'If the only reason you are here is to insult me, then don't bother.'

Kent ignored him and sat in a leather chair beside him. He gave his friend a pointed look, as if demanding Brent explain. 'You told the duchess to leave?'

'She avoids me like the plague.'

'And you let her?'

Ravenwood glared at his friend. 'What would you have me do? Kick down her door?'

'I'd rather you knock and tell her you love her.'

Her confession of love haunted him day and night. If only he was a man who could offer her more, offer her a future. 'It will change nothing. She's pregnant.'

'She's with child? That's wonderful, man. Get off your arse and fetch your wife.'

'She kept things from me.'

'The pregnancy?'

'No, not that.' He didn't think she had long known about the babe. 'I told her never to speak about my war sickness to another, and she did. And then there's Claire. She should have told me right away the girl was meeting a neighbour's son in the middle of the night in our gardens.'

'As far as I know, the girl's reputation is secure. As for the other excuse, she was trying to help you by sharing your war sickness. She did you a favor.' Kent eyed him. 'What else happened?'

Ravenwood took a deep drink before lowering his glass. 'I don't trust myself around her. I tackled her to the ground, man, just from the sound of a servant dropping a tray. You should have seen it. Then you would understand. I could have hurt her.'

'Did you?'

'She scraped a palm. It is enough.'

Kent watched him. 'Did she screech at you. Accuse you? Tell you to stay away from her?'

'No.' She told him she loved him.

Kent continued to assess him. 'I've never known you to surrender.'

Ravenwood scowled. 'What the hell does that mean?'

'You survived a war and God only knows what all happened to you on the continent. You fought for your country. Now it's time to fight for yourself and for whom you love.'

* * *

Fight for whom you love.

As his friend's words sifted through his muddled mind later that day, there was another knock on his study door.

Once again, Barnes made the announcement. 'You have a visitor in the drawing room, Your Grace.'

'Can't a man have peace in his own home? Just send Kent back here.'

'It's not Lord Kent, Your Grace.'

He stormed out of his study, fully intent on sending any unwanted visitor away when he came face to face with a strange, one-armed man in the drawing room. His jet hair reached his shoulders, his beard needed trimming, and he wore a coarse corduroy jacket and trousers. He was a soldier. Even without the missing limb, Ravenwood recognized the haunted look in his black eyes.

It matched his own.

'Who are you?' Ravenwood said.

'My name is Vartan. Your duchess came to see me. I'm the one who told her about the tavern group.'

So, this was the veteran. 'I never told her to seek help.'

Vartan shrugged. 'Does it matter? If she didn't care for you, she wouldn't have bothered. I have family, too much family, and they're always meddling and seeking to aid me. The only relief I found was the group.'

Brent had found camaraderie with the men as well. Hearing their stories was raw, like reliving a bloody battle, but at the same time, it was necessary to hear...and to share. 'What is it you've come to tell me?'

'Lena is your duchess, but she is of our blood. My family's blood. We take care of our own.'

Ravenwood's head snapped up. 'Speak plainly.'

'She has been coming to visit Ivan, myself, and our two aunts. She is sad, and our aunties are driving Ivan and myself mad. So, I'm here on her behalf. Ivan was going to come, but I told him I would do so. We have more in common, you and I.'

Ravenwood grudgingly acknowledged the truth. He could see it in the man's eyes and bearing. A haunted look. A battle-worn soldier's eyes.

'I don't often leave the house. I suspect you are the same. But I heard from Ivan that Lena is upset because of you,' Vartan said.

His words struck a different nerve. She didn't deserve to be unhappy. Or to suffer. He was to blame. She was carrying his babe. *Their* babe.

Standing here, staring at the strange man, he was struck with a pulse-pounding realization. He loved his wife. Truly loved her. He'd been entranced from the first day he'd caught Lena beneath the tree. And when she proposed to him, and each day thereafter, he'd lost a piece of his heart. Love—not memories of a burnt battlefield—was the most fearful emotion of all. He had been a scarred man who'd viewed marriage as a business arrangement, and she'd changed his life forever. While the intensity of his feelings was unnerving, the thought of losing her was unbearable. He trusted her, not only with Claire, but with his life.

'I have nothing more to say,' Vartan said.

'Thank you. You have said much,' Brent said. After the

man departed, he marched out of the drawing room. He had his duchess to find.

For the first time since returning home, he was ready to fight for what he wanted. For whom he *loved*.

Chapter Twenty-Six

Lena sat on a stone bench in the gardens. The scent of wild roses and peonies scented the air with a sweet perfume. Birds chirped in large oak trees. It was a splendid afternoon with only a few clouds in the sky. She dragged fresh air into her lungs, placing a hand on her abdomen. She loved the baby with all her heart. If it were a boy, a male heir to the dukedom, she'd teach him all about her culture and he would have the best of both worlds. Her heart ached, being parted from Ravenwood, but the mansion was big enough for the two of them. She would devote herself to her children and carve her own path forward.

She released a long sigh. Just as she rose, her husband's tall figure stepped into the gardens. Her heart leapt at the sight of him.

Ravenwood's voice was low, earnest. 'I've been searching for you.'

Her stomach flipped. 'Why?'

'Will you come with me?' he asked. 'I want to show you something.' He offered his arm.

'Your Grace, I—'

'It's Brent. Please call me Brent.'

She hadn't called him that since before their argument. She wasn't ready to call him his Christian name. Not when there was so much more at stake. Her fragile existence depended upon keeping herself distant.

His eyes held hers. 'Please.'

Looking into the blue depth of his gaze, she was lost. Placing the tips of her fingers on his sleeve, she let him lead her inside. She was conscious of the heat and strength of him. They wound their way through the corridors. She slowed as she realized where he was taking her, and her slipper missed a step. He immediately caught her arm to steady her.

'You're taking me to the west wing?' she asked.

'Yes. I want to show it to you.'

A mixture of rapt curiosity and anxiety sparked in her veins. He'd forbidden her to come here on her first day and had never invited her thereafter. She knew it was where the fire took place where he had lost his family.

'I come here when I can't sleep,' he murmured. 'I walk through the halls and enter the rooms and think of my brother and his wife. And my father.'

Her already strained nerves tightened at his words. The corridor had an eerie feel. As they walked along, she scanned the wing. The wall coverings were new, a bamboo pattern. The rest of the walls freshly painted a neutral palette. The Aubusson carpet runners replaced. Some of the rooms were furnished, others bare. She envisioned each room occupied.

He halted outside the largest room and what must have

been the master chambers. 'I loved my brother, and we were close when we were young. My father, not so much. He was a hard man, a disciplinarian. My brother and I would often sneak outside and play in the woods. I think of all of them when I come here.'

She stayed quiet, trying to throttle the dizzy current racing through her. He was sharing an important part of himself. He dragged a hand through his dark hair.

'The west wing is a private place,' he said, 'but no longer. I brought you here to show you, to tell what it means to me now.'

She knew it was an intimate place for him and that by bringing her here, he was sharing a part of his soul. Her voice was soft. 'Thank you for inviting me in.'

The smoldering flame she saw in his eyes made her pulse quicken. 'Lena, I have been a fool. Vartan paid me a visit.'

Her chest squeezed. 'He did?' She was surprised Vartan would leave his home and his hookah.

'He explained how you reached out to him to help me. I realize now that I'm undeserving of everything you have done. As for Claire, I should have trusted you then, too.' The tensing of his jaw told her how much he was struggling. 'Despite all of that, my deepest fear is that I cannot keep you safe if I have another episode. I fear I'll hurt you.'

She reached up and placed a hand on his cheek. 'That is for me to decide. You didn't hurt me then. And you won't. Even when you were first rattled, you twisted to protect me.'

'I promise to go back to the meetings to work through my past. But I cannot do it alone. Will you stay with me?'

Hope rose in her heart. 'I haven't left.'

He shook his head, his eyes bright. 'It's not good enough. I thought I wanted a businesslike marriage. But you have changed my world for the better and I cannot live without you. I miss you. I miss your smile. Your company. Your love.' His breath shuddered. 'I love you, Lena.'

She dropped her hand, and a single tear ran down her cheek. 'What did you say?'

He reached out to capture the tear with his thumb. 'I said I love you. With all my heart.'

How she'd longed to hear those words from his lips. Still, she needed to ask. 'Is it because of the child?'

'No. Although I'm thrilled about the babe, my love is for *you*. I cannot promise I'll be cured or that I will never have a nightmare again, but I will keep trying. I plan to go back to the tavern and keep talking about the war... I think it will help.''

Tears formed in her eyes and joy swelled within her. 'I never expected you to be cured. I only wanted your trust. And your love.'

'Then you shall have it. All of it. I will love you forever.'

'I love you, too.'

He picked her up. 'You are everything to me. My life was dark, and you showed up as a ray of brilliant sunlight. Will you have me back?'

Oh, how she loved this man. There was one true way to show him. She threw her arms around him and kissed him.

* * * * *

MILLS & BOON®

Coming next month

COURTING SCANDAL WITH THE DUKE
Ann Lethbridge

His ire rose once more. 'Listen to me, you little fool, you are one whisper away from ruin. Do you not understand this?'

She backed up until the trunk halted her progress, clearly surprised by his anger.

She frowned at him. 'What does it matter to you?'

What indeed? It shouldn't matter at all, but for some reason it did. 'You asked me for advice. Now I am giving it.'

'Then what are you suggesting?'

'It all depends on whether or not you were recognised.' He removed his hat and ran a hand through his hair. 'Why the devil would anyone think going to a gentleman's club would not be a problem?'

Defiance filled her gaze. A dare. A challenge. 'In Paris a lady is welcome everywhere.'

He stepped closer, forcing her to raise her gaze to his face, reminding her that for all that she was tall, he was taller. Larger.

Her soft lips parted on a breath. Her eyelids dropped a fraction. Her chest rose and fell with short sharp breaths.

His heart pounded in his chest. His blood, a moment before warm with anger, now ran like fire through his veins. Desire.

Only by ironclad will did he restrain from unbearable temptation.

'I—'

She raised her palm, face out as if holding him at bay.

He took a breath.

Her hand pressed against his chest, then slid upwards, around his nape, and she went up on tiptoes and pressed her mouth to his.

Luscious, soft lips moving slowly.

He pulled her close, responding to her touch in a blinding instant, ravishing her mouth, stroking her back, pulling her close and hard against his body.

For a moment his mind was blank, but his body was alive as it had never been before. Out of control.

Continue reading

COURTING SCANDAL WITH THE DUKE
Ann Lethbridge

Available next month
millsandboon.co.uk

COMING SOON!

We really hope you enjoyed reading this book.
If you're looking for more romance
be sure to head to the shops when
new books are available on

Thursday 25th September

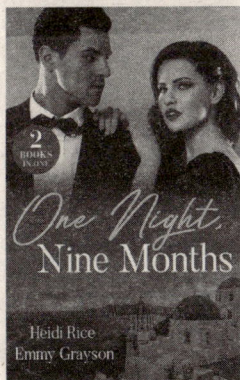

LET'S TALK

Romance

For exclusive extracts, competitions and special offers, find us online:

f MillsandBoon

X @MillsandBoon

⊙ @MillsandBoonUK

♪ @MillsandBoonUK

Get in touch on 01413 063 232